The
Ticket Girl

ALSO BY JAN M. WALTON

River Avenue
The Bookkeeper

The
Ticket Girl

A NOVEL

JAN M. WALTON

Printed in the United States of America
ISBN 978-1-7370022-4-6 (paperback)
ISBN 978-1-7370022-5-3 (ebook)
Library of Congress Control Number: 2025922175

Edited by Carlene Cobb

Cover design by Roy Marshall

Theater interior photograph by Helmut Ziewers
for Historic Detroit, used with permission
Lights: iStock.com/andreonegin
Comedy Tragedy Stage Curtain: iStock.com/CSA-Printstock

Author website: www.janmwalton.com

Windcove Publishing, Clearwater, Florida

In memory of my friend, Sandra Haji-Ahmed,
who lived with grace.

CHAPTER 1

Detroit, August 1946

Mabel choked back a belly spasm to keep from retching on the bank's polished marble floor. Clammy half-moons of sweat seeped through the underarm edges of her sleeveless dress. The valise she carried slipped from her left hand, and she winced as it landed with a thump at her feet. *I can't wait long. Breathe, breathe.* She sucked air through her nose and let it out slowly through her pursed lips. Again. Mabel closed her eyes, willing her heart to stop racing.

Drying out is harder this time. Behind her, a throat cleared. Mabel opened her eyes to see a teller waving her to a window. Clutching her handbag strap and the check in one hand, she picked up her valise with the other and made careful steps toward the teller. Setting the valise on the floor, Mabel shoved the check under the grille, blurting her request over the teller's greeting.

"Cash. Please." Another churn in her stomach pushed her hand over her mouth.

"Good afternoon," the teller repeated, scanning the check and glancing at her. Mabel read the judgment in the woman's eyes. *She's my age. Good-looking as I used to be.*

"The full amount in cash?" asked the teller. Mabel nodded. "May I see your identification?" Mabel swallowed, and with shaky hands, opened her purse. Her unpainted, rough nails met the reach of the teller's perfectly manicured pink fingertips accepting her driver's license. "One moment, please, while I check with the manager."

Mabel rested her elbows on the counter and cradled her head in her palms. She watched the teller's shiny black heels clicking on the tile, going beyond the row of tellers to a sizable mahogany desk where a gray-haired man in a brown suit sat signing papers. The teller handed him the check. The manager put on a pair of spectacles, peered at the check, then took Mabel's license from the teller's hand. *If I don't get the cash ...* She squeezed her eyes shut against tears welling and took another deep breath.

The manager said something to the teller and handed back the check and the license. She nodded and high-heeled her way back to Mabel at the window. "Mr. Kealy left instructions. The full amount in cash." Mabel grasped the edge of the counter and exhaled. He had kept his promise. *Thank you, Al.* The teller pointed a pink nail. "Sign here."

Mabel squiggled her name with the counter pen. The teller used a key worn on a gold chain around her neck to unlock a drawer under the counter. She opened it and began counting out the amount, slapping crisp bills from hand to counter.

Gentle Al had not made Mabel beg. He asked her what she needed and wrote the check. She had cringed at the pity in his eyes as he took in her stringy blond hair, her pale, unmade face, and ragged nails clawing her skin. Seeing her this way must have blurred his memory of the Mabel who wore that green satin gown the night they met, her arms draped around him during the orchestra's final slow dance. He used to whisper in her ear that she took his breath away, and she quivered just thinking about his touch. Relief had edged out her shame as she took his check and stuttered her thanks.

"You'll bounce back," Al had said. "I know you will." Bounce back to what? Her life had been with him. *At least I didn't wreck his life along with mine.*

The teller counted the bills twice, bundled the money into a neat pile, tucked it inside an envelope, and slid it under the grille. Mabel mumbled thanks, not meeting the woman's eyes. She placed the envelope in her handbag, picked up her valise, pushed her shoulders back and made deliberate steps across the floor and through the revolving door. In the vestibule, she leaned against the wall for a moment, her gut uneasy, then began her walk of a few blocks to a downtown rooming house.

Mabel knew where she was, but nothing felt familiar. She hadn't planned to come back to the city, but then she hadn't planned much of anything for more than a year, except staying drunk. Her eyes squinted against the glare behind the smog. The noise from screeching tires, horns, and sirens on the street vibrated under her skin. Crossing the intersections clogged with traffic scared her into scurrying, the weight of the valise bumping her thigh. At the entrance to the rooming house, she gripped the banister to steady her wobbly climb up the steps. Inside, she straightened up and smoothed her dress in an effort to appear respectable enough to be granted a rented room.

During the war, the place had been open to single women only; now single men were allowed to lodge on the first floor. The proprietress narrowed her beady eyes as Mabel approached the desk. The woman's short, gray-streaked hair was combed across her skull in sculpted waves, exposing her plump neck glistening with sweat, despite the table fan blowing directly on her. "You been here before?"

"No, ma'am. I would like to stay for three nights, if you please. What is the charge?"

The woman grunted, opened a ledger book, and quoted the price. Mabel didn't know if it was fair, or the same as other places, but she didn't care. She had to take a room. She rummaged in the bank envelope inside her purse to free the bills to pay. After the proprietress counted the money handed over, she held up a key and stabbed the air with it as she intoned the rules. "No men upstairs. No smoking in the room. I lock the door at ten whether you're here or not. Third floor."

Mabel nodded, and the woman slapped the key into her hand. With a muttered thanks, she aimed for the public telephone booth on the far wall. She crammed her valise into the space below the seat and pulled the folding door closed. From her purse, she took a scrap of paper with a scribbled number and a nickel, dropped the coin into the slot, and dialed. As she listened to the ring, she made a face at the men in the reception area who were staring at her.

A click on the other end. "Hello."

"It's me. I'm at the rooming house."

"Oh, Mabel, what are you doing there? I talked George into letting you stay with us." Her old friend Peggy had gone to bat for her. Mabel imagined that conversation. George had been happy at his and Peggy's wedding to see his best friend, Al, fall for Mabel. After a whirlwind month, when Al got his orders to go overseas, they eloped. But Al had a different wife now.

"Peg, George doesn't want me around. I bet he said not more than a week, right?"

"Well, a week with us would be a good start," Peggy said. A week of George's scrutiny served with breakfast and dinner—no, thank you.

Mabel rested her forehead against the cool glass of the phone booth. She wanted to believe Peggy had the best intentions, but it was her meddling that goaded Mabel into drying out. "I know you mean well, but I'm doing this on my own."

"You're all set with the money?" Peggy's way of asking about her meeting with Al.

"Al kept his word, and I will keep my promise never to contact him again."

She could hear Peggy's baby cooing in the background. Her fragile rule over alcohol would crumble if she held a baby. Peggy had tried to understand, but how could she? She had climbed into the bed where Mabel lay for weeks, cocooned and sobbing after the miscarriage. "Mabel, you've got to get over it. You've put yourself through the wringer and this wasn't your fault." Mabel's grief inhabited her, clear and present, as if she were lying in the street being struck again and again by the trolley, unable to crawl off the tracks. It *was* her fault.

The telephone operator broke the silence between them by asking for another coin to continue the call. There was nothing more to say.

"I've got to find work. I'll call you." Mabel hung the receiver on the hook and pulled back the booth door. A newsboy came into the lobby peddling papers, and Mabel bought a copy of the *Detroit Free Press* before trudging up the stairs to the third floor.

Her nose twitched at the musty smell when she opened the door to the room. Weak sunlight from the lone window shone on the worn linoleum floor. Against one wall was a single bed made up with a threadbare chenille spread and two pillows. Next to it, a night table with a lamp. A shabby armchair sat in the corner, and a bureau with three drawers stood under the window. Two towels and a facecloth sat on the dusty surface. Mabel dropped her valise on the floor, set the newspaper and handbag on the dresser, and plopped into the chair to kick off her sandals. She breathed a sigh of relief at making it this far.

With her foot, she pulled the valise closer, undid the clasps, and reached inside for the bundle shoved in the bottom. She shook the wrinkles from the two other dresses she owned as best she could. Opening the closet door for hangers, Mabel grimaced at her reflection in the mirror tacked on the inside. Emptying the valise onto the bed, she folded her one pair of trousers and two blouses into a drawer and put her few under-garments and nightgown into another. She placed her good shoes next to the chair and her old hairbrush on the bureau, then shoved the bag into the closet. The meager wardrobe and the money in her purse were all she had.

Mabel leaned on the bureau and fought a dizzy spell. She didn't know if her lightheadedness was from not eating or because she craved a drink. The need clutched at her. Drinking had pushed the grief under, lurking like the massive sturgeon that rippled along the river bottom, feeding on waste. She could float on the river, the monsters none the wiser.

She grabbed a towel and a facecloth and took the few steps to the bathroom. Mabel ran the water until it was as hot as she could stand it and bathed her face. The heat eased her.

Back in her room, she sprawled on the bed with the newspaper. She had to find work. Poring over the Help Wanted pages, Mabel ran her finger down the columns of ads.

Her work experience was limited to a few months in an auto factory converted during wartime for making bombs. Now, the factory jobs were listed under *Help Wanted Men,* the women who had carried the war effort no longer needed to churn out cars and machinery. She finally came to *Help Wanted Women* in the bottom corner. Not much to choose from. The Sanders company needed "fountain salesladies" for its confectionery stores, meals and uniforms supplied. Mabel used to love sitting at the counter in the downtown Sanders, lingering over an ice cream float, and taking home a small box of their candy. She tried to picture herself in the uniform, greeting people and serving with the smile and patience of a Sanders lady. But they would ask about her experience, and barmaid wouldn't qualify her. Most of the other ads were for secretarial and clerk positions. Mabel had no typing or shorthand. If she spent the money to enroll in a typing course, how long would it take for her to become proficient at sixty words per minute? Besides, she could reference no prior office positions.

The telephone company's ad seeking women to *train* as switchboard operators caught her attention. Michigan Bell accepted applications from women ages twenty-one to thirty on weekday mornings. In the movies, busy operators sat before panels of wires, having brief and faceless interactions with people on the line. It meant working shoulder to shoulder with other women, but she wouldn't be talking to them. She had no interest in making friends. *I have to start somewhere.* She tore through the newsprint with her nail to cut the ad from the paper.

Mabel padded from the bed to the closet and examined her wrinkled dresses. The old blue day dress with the fitted waistband above the V-neck lace-trimmed bodice was the most suitable. Slipping into her sandals, Mabel pocketed the key and stepped out into the hallway to look for an iron. A cart loaded with mops and cleaning supplies was parked next to the open bathroom door. An older colored woman stooped over the bathtub scrubbing it with a long-handled brush. Her hair was covered with a scarf looped around her head several times, and her blue-checked housedress was splotched with bleach stains. She noticed Mabel and stopped scrubbing. "Be a few minutes to finish in here."

Mabel nodded. "Is there an iron I can use?"

The woman leaned the brush on the tub and shook her head. "Every one of you ask me that. Why don't she just tell you when she give you the key? Closet, end of the hall." She slapped the brush against the tub and restarted the scrubbing. Mabel thanked her, but the woman didn't seem to hear.

After working a hot iron on the dress, Mabel realized she could not apply for a job with bare legs. Stockings used to be cheapest at Kresge's. Kresge's would also have powder and rouge to brighten her complexion. She ran fingers over the top and sides of her hair, and tucked it behind her ears, adding bobby pins to her mental shopping list. And something to eat. Mabel squinted to check the time on her wristwatch. She had forgotten the gift from Al's mother until she found the watch tucked into the pocket of her handbag. The old lady had stood by her until she went so far wrong, she broke her heart. Another thing Mabel could never make right.

She rehearsed the path to the store, close enough to walk. Her queasy gut couldn't be trusted to ride the streetcar. She hooked her handbag over her arm, hoisted the pressing board under it, and grasped the iron. Mabel made sure the door locked, then replaced the iron and board in the hall closet. She resolved to act like a trip to Kresge's was her habit, though she hadn't shopped in a city store for over two years.

On the sidewalk, Mabel concentrated on the route and on blocking out the grating street noise. Sounds that once had excited her now throbbed in her head. Her eyes flicked at the people passing by, fearing someone might speak to her. Sweat was trickling along her neck, and the back of her dress was damp by the time she reached the store at the corner of Woodward and State. A man coming out held the Kresge's door for her to enter.

Inside, Mabel blinked at the brightly lit interior. To her right, a cluster of young boys milled around the racks of comic books. A short line of shoppers waited near the cashiers' counter. Ahead, aisles ran from the front to the rear of the store. Along each one, shelves, racks, and bins displayed the wares. At the back, a lunch counter offered drinks, sodas, ice cream, and sandwiches. Her stomach balked and her hand pressed over her nose to block the smell of hamburgers on the grill.

Signs hanging overhead and posted on tall poles directed shoppers to clothing, housewares, rugs, curtains, sewing supplies, music, toys, and more. She aimed for the *Ladies* aisle, remembering what she used to like about shopping in Kresge's. The merchandise sat on open counters, no need to ask a saleswoman for help. Mabel spotted a poster for stockings—*Sleek and sheer in fashion shades*—and went for those first. When she found her size, she thumbed through the cellophane packets for a light shade and pulled out two pairs. The pin-up girl featured on the package smiled coyly and stuck a shapely leg in the air like a dancer. A memory of her wedding night appeared in Mabel's mind: Al unhooking her stockings and sliding the nylon down her thighs. *Jesus.*

Mabel leaned against the counter and took a breath. When her older brothers would lock her in the closet for hours, she had learned to let her mind go empty in the dark. She had to put Al into that dark. It was the bitter cost of ruining the happiest time of her life.

Clutching the stockings, she chose a garter belt, white and unadorned, nothing fancy in Kresge's. Shoppers' handbaskets nested in a pile on the floor. Mabel tossed the belt and stockings into the top basket and picked it up, then moved along the aisle toward the cosmetics.

The lighted mirror over the counter told the story of her decline. A harsh display of her sallow skin, sunken cheeks, and the dark circles around her eyes. Her lank hair hung in the uneven strands she had chopped with scissors. She hadn't cared about her looks, or cared for her body, in a long time. She had to present herself as best she could tomorrow.

Choosing shades of powder and rouge to color her face, she put those into the basket along with a sleeve of hairpins and a bottle of Halo shampoo. She walked along, grabbing a tube of Pepsodent toothpaste and a new toothbrush. A poster proclaiming, *Keep confident and carefree with Kotex,* made her stop and stare.

In the drawing, a woman in an elegant gown with a serene smile danced with a tuxedoed man. *What if ...* Her monthly hadn't ever been monthly, and it hadn't come since ... she wasn't sure of her dates. The painful scene in the factory lavatory replayed. She had gone to work that morning pretending the red smear on the toilet paper was not a worry. The nurse pulling away her bloody trousers, the ambulance siren colliding with the screams in her head. Her breasts had swelled and her belly rounded with the promise of Al's baby. She didn't care if her monthly never happened again.

But what if ... Her hand fumbled for a package of pads and a sanitary belt. Then she hurried to the front of the store.

At the checkout counter, the cashier placed the items in a shopping bag as she rang them up. Mabel paid, took her bag and receipt, and outside the store, took a moment to get her bearings. The sidewalks were crowded with people leaving the office buildings, stopping in the shops, and running for the trolleys. Mabel began retracing her steps along Woodward. She was half a block from the rooming house when her shaky stomach grumbled. Too late to go all the way back for an egg sandwich at Kresge's lunch counter. She'd have to find something else.

At the corner, waiting for the light to change, Mabel looked across the street and gasped. Jack leaned against the brick rooming house. Hands in his pants' pockets, one leg crooked over the other, the way she had seen him slouch against the wall in school the many times he was called to the principal's office. She thought of turning away, but as the traffic stopped, he caught sight of her and waved. Mabel's surprise at seeing him mixed with embarrassment. Peggy must have told him her sorry story. Jack straightened up and smiled as she approached him.

Mabel shifted her bag to her hip. "Peggy called you?"

He chuckled. "Hello, Mabel. Nice to see you, too." He kept a calm expression, but she saw him take quick stock of how she'd changed in the years since they'd seen each other.

Mabel gave him a weak smile. "Hello. Why are you here?"

Jack shrugged. "Okay, yes. Peggy asked me to check on you. And I wanted to."

Mabel drew back. "I'm not a charity case. I'm fine."

"I am not judging you."

She wanted to believe that, but she had to look away from his gaze. "It's a shock to see you, that's all." Mabel had last seen him at Peggy's wedding, where she had been so enthralled with meeting Al she had barely talked with Jack.

Jack glanced over his shoulder at the rooming house. "There's no dinner here."

"I can manage." She moved away from him. "I have to go."

He touched her arm. "Come out with me."

"I can't." Mabel looked at him. "Are you even allowed to do that?"

Jack shrugged. "I'm in the seminary, not prison. I'd like to take you for a meal."

Mabel sighed. She could try to find a market for something to take to her room, but she'd rather not eat than roam the streets with taverns on every block. "Where would we go?"

Jack smiled. "I know a small place. It's not far." He read the distress on her face. "No bar. Don't worry." He knew. But he had come. Going with Jack might get her through an hour.

Mabel lifted the shopping bag. "I must take this to my room."

"I'll be waiting right here."

Mabel turned and went up the steps. Inside, she nodded at the woman at the desk, who raised a brow in acknowledgement.

Taking the stairs quickly, Mabel was out of breath when she unlocked her room. He had seen her rough condition, but she could improve it a little. She pulled the brush through her hair and left it loose. She patted the new powder and a bit of rouge on her face.

Mabel went back down the stairs at a slower pace, thinking about what she should say to explain herself to Jack. She hadn't considered Peggy telling her brother what had happened to her. What she had done. It might be better if she asked Jack to leave, or if he had tired of waiting and gone. But he was still there.

He offered Mabel the crook of his arm. "C'mon." Mabel nodded and slipped her arm through. He tucked it against his side, and she felt a safeness, letting him lead her. He smiled at her as they began to walk.

She didn't make conversation, and he didn't seem bothered by the silence. As they strolled, she glanced at his profile. Jack had grown a full beard, and his thick, dark hair waved on top. He was two years older than Peggy but had always been close to his sister. Mabel had spent so much time at their house, he was as familiar to her as her own brothers. But Jack was nothing like the brutes in her house. In school, he had been a good student and a rascal, pulling all kinds of pranks, shrugging off the demerits with his nothing-bothers-me attitude. She had envied that ease. His height and coordination, combined with his grit, made him a star on the baseball team. At home, he challenged Mabel and Peggy at cards and board games and kickball, but he would never do anything to hurt them.

Holding his sturdy arm reminded Mabel of the night of his senior prom. Jack had declared to Peggy that he wouldn't go. He hadn't dated much and didn't have his eye on anybody in his class. Peggy was adamant; as baseball team captain, he must go, begging, "Take me," knowing he wouldn't let himself be ridiculed walking in with his sister. Peggy grabbed Mabel and stood her next to Jack. "Then you'll take Mabel." Mabel had laughed out loud, and so did Jack. But then he asked, "Would you?" and she heard herself say yes. She had a crush on one of his teammates and figured she'd make that guy notice her with Jack. On prom night, rain spotted her dress and made her hair frizzy; Jack was a terrible dancer, and after two numbers, they gave up; and her crush announced his engagement to another senior during the dance. She reported to Peggy that the evening had been a disaster.

Jack had left Detroit for college in a town near Ann Arbor. Summers, he volunteered with the Civilian Conservation Corps, living in remote forest camps in northern Michigan, where the corpsmen carved out the roads and buildings for new state parks. No one was surprised when after college he began preparing for the priesthood.

His mother believed her son dedicating his life to God was the highest honor she could achieve. She had let Jack know every day since he began as an altar boy that God had called her son. As Peggy told it, their mother rejoiced over his acceptance into the seminary as though her own entrance into heaven was guaranteed. Mabel had lost track of his progress, but he must be close to his ordination.

At the next corner, Jack gestured for her to turn. "It's just here. Italian." He pointed at a storefront with a picture window covered on the inside by a filmy white curtain, the name *Luna* stenciled in green lettering on the window. Jack reached for the handle on the wooden door, pulled it open, and stepped back to allow Mabel to enter first. The dining room was large enough for only eight tables. Colorful murals painted on the walls of tiny houses nestled on hillsides by the sea made it cheerful, and milk-glass fixtures overhead brightened the space. In the open kitchen at the back, an aproned woman bustled around the stove, and two young men were serving diners. One man saw Jack. "Ah, Father, please, take the window."

Jack steered Mabel to the table and pulled out her chair. The woman approached Jack with her arms outstretched. "Welcome, welcome, you like my cooking, eh?" Jack grasped her wrists and let her buss him on both cheeks. "This is your sister?" Jack looked at Mabel, who shook her head. "Like my sister, yes." Mabel locked eyes with Jack as the woman took her hand. "I cook spaghetti tonight. Please, be comfortable." A crashing sound caused the woman to yell something in Italian. She patted Jack on the arm and hurried back to the pots.

Jack sat in the chair across from Mabel. "How do you like the place?"

Mabel glanced around. "It's homey, like we're in her kitchen. And the walls are pretty." She looked at him. "How do you know it?"

He nodded toward the stove. "Mrs. Marini cooks at the seminary on days the regular cook is off. She's just opened here."

"The waiter called you Father."

"Officially, that's after I'm ordained. But people use it anyway."

A waiter brought a tray with a pitcher of cold water, two glasses, and a basket of bread. He set the bread in the center, then filled their glasses. When he walked away, Mabel asked, "When will you be ordained?"

"Six months or so. Depends …" He shrugged. "You know, seminary students couldn't be drafted. I wanted to quit and enlist in '42. All hell broke loose with that idea."

"Your mother."

He smirked. "My mother, yes. Anyway, I made a deal to do volunteer homeland service and part-time studies. So, I have ground to make up for ordination."

The waiter came with two steaming bowls of spaghetti and set one before Mabel with a slight bow. He placed the other bowl in front of Jack. The aroma of meat simmered in tomato sauce enticed Mabel to grab her fork and take a mouthful. She glanced at Jack, who had yet to pick up his fork. His eyes were closed and his hands were clasped in his lap. Mabel had forgotten about saying grace before meals. It was a regular practice in her friends' house growing up, and she had taken part. She had been baptized Catholic and taken to church as a tiny girl by her mother before she died. Her father had taken her brothers out of the Catholic school to go to work. He brought Mabel to the nuns for Saturday Catechism lessons because they fed her and kept her until one of her brothers remembered to fetch her. But she had stopped praying; she had experienced God's betrayal and lost trust in him.

Jack crossed himself, then opened his eyes and took up his fork.

Mabel placed her fork on her dish. "Sorry."

"Don't worry about it."

"I haven't been thankful for a long time." *Why did I say that?* She felt the tears well again.

"Mabel." He said her name in a soft tone. She looked at him and flashed back to the carefree afternoons she had spent with him and Peggy on the sandlot where he taught them to play softball. Her sorrow for the loss of that Mabel dripped down her cheeks. Jack reached across the table for her hand. He had been kind to find her and bring her here, and she was ruining it. She pulled her hand away and pushed her chair back. "I should go."

"Please stay." He pushed her water glass closer to her. Mabel wiped at her eyes and turned her face toward the window. She didn't want to embarrass him in front of Mrs. Marini. But being with him was tugging on her emotions, and that scared her. Drinking used to help her go silent, pull the hard feelings under like a tortoise into its shell. She had only her will now. Mabel reached for the water glass and took a drink.

She nudged her chair closer to the table and grasped her fork. Jack nodded and picked up his fork, not forcing conversation. They ate their spaghetti in silence. Concentrating on chewing and swallowing, Mabel fortified her resolve. After dinner, she would bid goodbye to Jack and ask him not to seek her out again. He could only pity her, and she could not abide that.

The waiter cleared their plates and brought a dish with a wedge of lemon cake and two forks. Jack speared a bite, swallowed, and smiled. "You should try this." Mabel forked a piece of the cake, aware he watched her. The sweetness choked her, and she clamped her napkin over her mouth as she swallowed, then gulped water. He looked away and motioned to the waiter for the bill. Mabel sat back to calm her stomach. After he paid, she stood and gathered her purse. He motioned her ahead of him and called out goodbye to Mrs. Marini, who waved a spoon, saying he should bring Mabel again for dinner.

Outside the restaurant, Jack again offered his arm, but Mabel clasped her purse to her side and began walking. He smiled and walked alongside her. They made their way in the evening's fading light. The streetlamps had come on. A patchwork of lighted windows in the surrounding buildings made bright spots amidst the dark offices. When they reached the rooming house, Mabel put on what he used to call her game face, the look that gave nothing away. "Thank you for dinner. Thank you for coming to see about me. I'm fine. No need to check again."

Jack stuck his hands into his pockets and studied her. She expected him to protest, but he said, "How long will you stay here?"

"A few days." She stared at him and he didn't ask about after that.

"Will you stay in touch with Peggy?"

Mabel nodded. "I will."

Jack kept her gaze. "If you need anything …" She held her chin up so he would not press her further. He leaned closer. "I pray for you." He turned and walked away.

He had cornered her, like the times her brothers would run their dogs into the yard while she perched on a branch in the maple tree. They knew she feared the mutts jumping on her with their sharp teeth and claws. If she cried for them to take the dogs away, they laughed. They would leave her trapped in the tree, scared of the barking dogs, for hours.

Mabel watched him until he reached the end of the block and hopped on a streetcar. She let out the breath she had held in her chest and went inside the rooming house. Seeing Jack left her uneasy. She wasn't the girl Jack used to know, and she regretted he had seen the wreck she had become.

CHAPTER 2

Thrashing against something holding her down, she couldn't tell where she was. Her hands tore at a sheet wrapped tight across her midsection. Seeing a man's undershirt covering her chest, she felt for her panties. Had he undressed her? Rawness in her throat dammed up the scream she tried to make.

Mabel jolted awake, panting for breath. Visions from the harrowing days and nights in the cabin, the worst of the dry-out, menaced her when she slept. Too faint to stand, she had leaned on Tom to make the slow walk from the car, wincing at the sun's glare glinting off a lake. The next thing she remembered was waking up in the dark, Tom's face hovering in the firelight. She had swung between fighting him with fists and curses and going limp after brutal bouts of vomiting. Hissing at him, "*Why can't you let me go?*"

She sat up in the lumpy rooming house bed and pushed her feet to the floor, tugging her damp nightdress away from her clammy skin. The room was stifling. A beam from a spotlight on the building across the street sneaked around the curled sides of the roller shade on the window, making it seem as though Mabel hadn't clicked off the lamp. She had been away long enough to forget the twenty-four-hour light in the city. She stood and tugged the window open halfway, letting in the nighttime bugs and voices from the street below.

The traffic noise hovered at a droning hum. Hardworking people were home in bed, but she could sense the drinkers roaming the night spots. Afraid to go back to sleep, she wished for the whiskey that had glided her into dreamless nights. She plopped into the chair, her fingers pulling at the worn threads on the armrest.

Drinkers always found their places, like she had the day she stumbled inside the tavern the locals dubbed "the farmhouse." Mabel sighed and rubbed her fingers across her forehead. She had gotten comfortable there, sure she was forgotten. The three-story house had been the center of a family potato farm until twin brothers John and Joseph, hearty men and heavy drinkers, made the first floor a tavern. Beer sales supported the property and the twins' fondness for spirits.

Never had she expected Tom to show up, a week ago, out of the blue. He told her, "It wasn't hard to find someone who had seen you. Miss Front End graces the walls in many taverns. Birmingham is my beer guy's last stop."

After the miscarriage, Mabel lied that she had gone back to work. She used Al's key to let herself into the tavern he owned with Tom, his cousin. Al had gone overseas, but Tom's bad knee had forced him to serve homeland duty.

Al's main job was in advertising. Two weeks into their romance, he had set her up with a modeling job. Her chesty figure, long legs in a bathing suit, posed on the hood of a roadster, was the inspiration for a roomful of Detroit designers imagining hood ornaments. Pencils poised, hungry eyes on her body, they dubbed her *Miss Front End* for the publicity. In the newspaper photo, Al was in the background. She cringed at remembering the heartbreaking love on his face, and the exhilaration on hers.

Hiding in the closed bar, toasting Miss Front End's photograph on the wall, Mabel drank. The arty guy who had done her makeup for the shoot called her hair "dirty blond," which at first offended her. But as he worked on her face, he admired her cheekbones and the tone of her skin, showing her how to use the cosmetics to play up her eyes. Mabel remembered his compliments, and his soft touch, the gentle pull of his fingers twisting her hair into an updo, how he turned her to the mirror to approve his work with a cry of "Voila!" Her delight at the transformation boosted her natural feistiness. Mabel had strutted to the front of the sedan and looked the director in the eye as he grasped her midriff to help her step up onto the fender and strike a pose. The photographers captured angles highlighting the pointy cups of her bra top and the curve of her legs arched on the hood. Giddy with the attention, Mabel didn't notice the leers. Miss Front End had bared herself with the naivete of the inexperienced girl she was.

Tom found her in his tavern, passed out. Sobbing in his arms, she had played on her sense that he had a crush on her lingering in the shadows, though she was married to Al. She swore she would quit drinking, and Tom kept her secret.

But Mabel didn't stop. When Al came home, he had tried to save her. A year in a hospital paid for with borrowed money. Without the numbing alcohol, she curled up and went silent, like a wounded animal that burrows as it's dying. She didn't care about recovering. Al's visits were no comfort. His slow amble, the familiar way he tipped off his hat and moved to slip an arm around her. Mabel would not let him touch her. Declaring that she was not in love with him anymore, she demanded a divorce. He had cried, but she gave him no choice.

Mabel had thought no farther than the drink she wanted. A pilfered nurse's cap and glib talk got her into the passenger seat of the laundry truck leaving the hospital grounds. At a bus stop on Woodward Avenue, she paid to go to Birmingham, the end of the line. When she stepped off the bus, she saw—was craving for—the weather-beaten *Beer* sign swinging from the farmhouse porch.

The tipsy rush of downing two beers thrilled her after the long drought in the hospital. Mabel knew she had found her place when the twins didn't look up from the hand of cards they played with some patrons as she stepped behind the bar. Refilling her glass, she announced she would fix their sloppy setup. Half-gone with whiskey, the brothers joked with the other drinkers about her, but they had stayed in their chairs and she stayed behind the bar for the evening. Keeping her own glass filled, Mabel chatted up their customers, making a show of dropping coins in the till. At closing, the twins had taken the cashbox and lurched upstairs. Mabel had wandered into the kitchen at the back of the house. She found an old camping cot on the porch and hauled it inside. When the brothers stumbled downstairs in the morning, she was standing behind the bar with a pot of coffee and the whiskey bottle. They accepted their spiked mugs and asked if she was staying.

She'd been good for their business, charming the old guy customers into drinking more and more often than they used to. Nipping beer all day and evening, keeping a hum in her brain while mixing drinks and managing the till. At closing each night, Mabel locked herself in the kitchen with whiskey to bring on sleep.

Mabel had played her last card when Tom appeared at the farmhouse, betting that he still had feelings for her. "If you care about me, and I know you do, forget me. Don't come back."

Tom said, "Ma got talking to Peggy about you, and they called me. I *will* tell Ma I found you. *She'll* come here. Leave with me tomorrow."

A vision of Ma walking into the farmhouse stewed in Mabel's brain, more vivid with each beer and shot she gulped. Ma knew how to get what she wanted. If Tom went back without Mabel, Ma would have another plan. She had to be quicker than Ma.

Mabel felt no duty to the twins. The arrangement had been a convenience on both sides. They had not paid her, but she had saved her tips. After Mabel closed for the night, she set the money box on the back bar. She cleaned the glasses, swept the floor, and wiped down the tables. With a last look, she flicked off the lights and went into the kitchen.

Her valise had been under the cot for a year. Inside were dresses she hadn't worn, her handbag, and her good shoes. Her daily uniform had been trousers and shirts she had scrounged from donated clothes in the basement of a church in town, with the twins' mother's old sweaters and jackets found in the kitchen pantry. Mabel crammed her few belongings into the valise. She counted the money she had stashed in a coffee can on the shelf above the stove and put it into the handbag.

Mabel had another shot of whiskey and sat on the cot, thinking about the walk to the train station and the cost of tickets to towns north, until dawn streaked the sky outside the kitchen window. The August night had cooled, and she wrapped a sweater over her shirt. Mabel picked up the valise and her handbag, opened the kitchen door and stepped onto the back porch, making no sound.

Birds waking each other in the orchard trees chirped a chorus she heard as *Where are you going?* She cleared the yard and at the side street, turned and headed toward the avenue. The headlights of a car behind her lit the walkway. It pulled alongside her. Al's sedan. Mabel stopped short, and the car braked. Tom leaned from the driver's seat to speak through the open passenger window. "Get in, Mabel."

She shook her head. "Go away."

He placed his hand above the horn button in the middle of the steering wheel. "Get in, or I will wake up the neighborhood."

Mabel raised her voice. "Don't you dare!" A light flicked on in a house across the street. She flung open the passenger door, threw her valise inside, slid onto the seat, and slammed the door shut. She rotated the handle to roll up her window and pointed at Tom to do the same on his side. He rolled it up.

"You have some nerve! I told you I am not going with you."

"It looks like you're going somewhere."

"None of your business."

"The divorce came through. Al met someone. He's married."

Mabel gripped the seat cushion, dizzy from the bugs swirling in the beam of the car's headlights. Her last shot of whiskey backed up and burned her throat. She breathed in the car's scent—Al's aftershave.

She pounded the seat with her fist. "*Why* are you doing this to me? You used to like me. Now you threaten me and throw Al in my face. Just go and leave me alone!"

"You're a *drunk*." The look on his face as he spat out the word stung as if he had slapped her. He had ripped away her mask. She panicked like she had inside the hall of mirrors at the county fair, where no matter which way she turned, her reflection terrified her. Mabel grasped the door handle, desperate to get out of the car.

Tom grabbed her hand and held it. "I won't leave you like this. I could never forgive myself."

"Not forgiving myself is my punishment." Tears rolled down Mabel's cheeks and her shoulders shook. Tom pulled her closer, got his arm around her. Mabel fell against his chest and sobbed. He held her, running his hand over her hair. She moaned and cried, letting her snot wet his shirt.

Tom murmured, "Let me help you for a few days. Then if you want me to bring you back here, I will."

"You know I can't come back." She was as defenseless as a pawn on a chessboard. Humiliated by his seeing through her, and not knowing what else to do, she waved her arm at him. "Drive."

Peggy, Ma, Tom, and Al believed they had "fixed" her. Mabel was supposed to find her way now, but it was like being trapped in the tree by the snarling dogs. The money wouldn't make her whole. Nothing would.

Why didn't they just let me go?

CHAPTER 3

The humidity leached the crispness from her dress as Mabel walked to the streetcar stop. She had twisted the front sections of her hair and pinned them off her face. She had no hat to shade her eyes, heavy with lack of sleep, against the sun's glare. No gloves, just as well in the heat. With every lurch of the trolley through the busy streets, she pressed her lips tight against the lingering nausea.

Mabel checked and rechecked the time on her wristwatch. The closest bus stop left her with a short walk to the Michigan Bell building on Cass Avenue. On the curb, merging into the throng of hurrying people made her pick up her pace. At the building's entrance, she angled her way into the bunch stepping through the fast-revolving door. Sprung into the lobby, Mabel moved away from the stream of people. She scanned left and right, looking for a clue about where to go, and spotted a pedestal bearing a sign: *Applications*. Mabel pushed her hair off her neck, straightened her shoulders, and strode into the hallway beyond the sign. *Hiring Office* was stenciled on a set of double glass doors, and another pedestal sign at the right directed: *Form a Line Here*. Six women, all wearing summer hats and gloves, stood along the wall. Mabel bit her lip and joined the line, turning sideways to avoid the eye of the woman in front of her.

The shakiness started at her knees and crept up her spine, milder but still unnerving. Mabel's hands tightened around her bag. She pressed against the wall, concentrating on slowing her breathing. The lobby clock chimed nine, and the glass door opened.

A middle-aged woman with short gray curls framing a round face, wearing a white blouse with a parade of black buttons tucked into a black pencil skirt, stepped into the hallway. She leaned to get a view of the entire line, a pair of glasses dangling from a gold chain around her neck, and said, "Good morning. Please enter." She stood sentry at the door, eyebrows raised, as the line of women passed her. Mabel kept her lips tight and eyes forward as she moved into the room. There were no windows, only the garish light shining from overhead fixtures. A table sat in the center, chairs along the sides, with a paper and a pen at each place. The woman closed the door and directed the applicants to take seats. Mabel slid into a chair.

"Thank you for your interest in working at Michigan Bell. I am Mrs. Miller." Standing at the end of the table, she put on her glasses and pointed at the papers. "Please fill out the application, answering all the questions. After my review, some of you may advance to the interview. You may begin."

Mabel picked up the pen, glanced sideways at the others bent over their papers, and wrote *Mabel H. Kealy* on the first line of the form. Who was that person? One who had to forget Al but hold his name. Could she change it back to *Hunt*?

She hesitated at answering the next question: *Single, Married, Widowed, or Divorced?* With a sigh, she underlined *Divorced. Children?* No. She scribbled the details for *Address* (temporary), *Age* (24), *Nationality* (her Canadian mother had given birth in a Detroit hospital, so she was both), *High School Graduate?* (Yes), *Present Employment* (none), *Typing WPM* (none), and paused at the line for *Reference.* Mabel hadn't considered that a reference would be needed. She wrote in Ma's name and the address of the diner. She had not asked Ma for this favor, but there was no one else. Mabel capped the pen, stood and handed the form over to Mrs. Miller, then sat waiting for the others to finish. When all the women had handed their forms to her, Mrs. Miller tapped the edges of the bundle against the table to neaten the pile. "Please step into the hallway. I will be with you shortly." She held the door open while the group filed out, then closed it.

Several women took out cigarettes and clustered around the standing ashtray against the wall. Mabel paced across the main lobby and back. She had done this three times when the glass door opened, and Mrs. Miller propped it ajar with her foot. She called out two names, and those women stepped forward. "Everyone else, thank you for your interest."

Heart racing, Mabel dashed for the water fountain at the end of the corridor. She gulped a mouthful, then splashed some on her neck and let it dribble down her skin under the dress. Wrinkles didn't matter now. Mabel made for the lobby, shoved into the revolving door, and stepped out onto the sidewalk.

The morning air had become sultry, gray clouds streaking the blue sky. She turned south on Cass Avenue, staying within the meager shade close to the buildings. She watched her feet move along the pavement while her mind shouted at her. *Divorced and no experience—it was stupid to try.* When Mabel reached Lafayette, she realized she was going in the opposite direction from the streetcar line heading to the rooming house. She turned left to circle back, but the thought of returning to that room to stew in her failure stopped her.

Drinking Mabel's voice whispered, *One cold one on a hot day won't hurt.*

Her eyes scanned the block ahead on both sides of the street. The neighborhood had not been one of her haunts, but she knew how to spot a joint open early. After the ordeal at Michigan Bell, she deserved the relief of sliding onto a bar stool, grasping a sweaty beer glass, and savoring the sensation of the liquid going down her throat, easing her worries. Mabel fished in her bag for her handkerchief and wiped the sweat from her neck. Having just one beer was the verdict.

The boom of a thunderclap jolted her. Pelts of rain splattered her bare arms. People scurried to find shelter as the downpour hit. Looking for cover, Mabel splashed half a block and ducked under the overhang of the Lafayette Theater marquee. She flattened against the entry doors, but the wind blew rain in her face. She grabbed at a handle, and the door opened. Mabel lurched into the vestibule and pulled the door closed against the sheeting rain. Her relief was tempered by the feeling of water squishing inside her shoes. Her dress was soaked. Mabel pulled her wet skirt away from her legs, shaking off the drips.

"You're late." A man's voice came from a half-open door leading into the theater.

"Sorry, I only came inside because …"

The voice cut her off. "Come along. Let's get started."

Mabel went closer to see who was speaking. A tall young man pushed the door open wider. His eyes scanned from Mabel's dripping hair to her wet shoes. She took in his long arm in an elegant suit jacket, his creased trousers, and polished brogues. He called to someone behind him, "Have you got a towel there?"

Mabel shook her head. "You don't understand. I ..."

"I understand you're dripping."

She looked into his pale, clean-shaven face framed with curly blond hair. She figured him to be about thirty, though his starched white shirt collar covering a satiny tie, and the suit, gave him a mature distinction.

A stout older woman about half his height, wearing a dingy apron and a kerchief covering her hair, waddled around the door frame holding out a towel. "Ruined them shoes, didja?" Mabel stared at the two of them.

The man nodded for Mabel to take the towel. "Dry off a bit."

She glanced through the street doors at the pouring rain. She was stuck here. With a shrug, she took the towel and mumbled thanks. The man watched as she wiped the wet from her arms and scrunched the towel around the ends of her hair. She caught his eye. "There's been a mistake. I'm not who you were waiting for. I only came inside to get out of the storm."

"Ah, I see."

Mabel jerked the towel off her hair. "Thank you for the towel." She handed it to the old woman, who shuffled back from where she had come. "I'll be on my way as soon as the rain lets up."

"I mistook you for the girl I was about to hire for the ticket office."

Mabel clutched her wet skirt. She had run out of the rain into this moment. She believed in signs. "The ticket office? Could I apply?"

The man raised his brows. "I thought you were only getting out of the rain."

"I'm looking for a job."

"Your experience?"

Mabel cringed at the question. "I've never worked in a theater."

"Where have you worked?"

Something told her not to lie. "A factory during the war. Then barmaid. I can manage cash."

He hadn't asked her name. Which occurred to him because he said, "Your name?"

"Mabel Hunt Kealy." If she had to carry Kealy, she'd take Hunt, too.

"Married?"

She looked him in the eye. "Divorced."

"The other girl just got engaged." He shrugged and extended his hand. Initials embroidered on the shirt cuff peeked from his jacket sleeve. "Michael Macready, House Manager. You're hired. On a trial basis."

She had put herself in dicey situations in the haze of alcohol, but sober, she didn't trust what she was hearing. Desperation overcame her reluctance to believe this was real. She accepted his firm handshake. When he let go of her hand, he opened the door wider and gestured for Mabel to step through.

Outside, the building was a four-story brick box. Inside, the height of the lobby, rising two floors, startled Mabel. Glittering chandeliers hung high above. Ornate plasterwork designs on the walls framed painted murals of idyllic landscapes. Staircases on both sides rose to the second-floor balcony. Mabel longed to go up, but Mr. Macready had crossed the lobby and waited near a paneled door next to three ticket windows. She held her wet skirt away from her legs and wished she could ditch the shoes to sink bare feet into the plush carpet. He held the door open and ushered her inside the ticket office.

The space was as cheerless and cramped as the lobby was splendid and expansive. Mabel squinted at the glaring fluorescent light from fixtures running along the ceiling. In the center of the room, four desks sat shoved together, papers and binders piled atop, typewriters perched on rolling stands. Built-in racks beneath the ticket windows sprouted a mish-mosh of envelopes, ticket rolls, and handbills. Filing cabinets and a long table holding some kind of machine, a paper cutter, and boxes crowded the side of the room. A telephone began ringing.

A silver-haired woman sitting at one of the desks answered it. She furrowed her brow at Mr. Macready as she spoke into the receiver. "Good afternoon, Lafayette Theater Box Office. Mrs. Butler speaking."

Mr. Macready turned to Mabel with a finger to his lips. Mabel nodded and studied the woman taking the call. Mrs. Butler wore her hair in a style Mabel hadn't seen since her factory days, the hair over her ears swept above her forehead and twisted into a knot. The rest of her hair formed a knot at the nape of her neck. Mabel recognized the white plastic frames of her round eyeglasses from a display of sunglasses she had seen in Kresge's. Only these were not sunglasses, and Mrs. Butler's eyes filled the circles. She wore a bright red pleated skirt below a short-sleeved white knit sweater and a scarf patterned with blues and greens tied around her neck. As she listened to the caller, she raised the telephone receiver from her right ear and, with her left hand, pulled off the red hoop earring clipped on her lobe. She flipped the earring onto the desk and picked up a pen as she continued the conversation.

Mrs. Butler took down the caller's name and telephone number. Ending the call, she replaced the receiver in the telephone cradle and wagged a finger at Mr. Macready. "I can't keep telling people we'll call them back about the new subscription rates. They'll lose interest."

He nodded. "We'll get to that. First, meet our new ticket girl, Mabel."

Mrs. Butler lit a cigarette and inhaled as she eyed Mabel. "You're the one used to work at the Avenue Theater?"

Mr. Macready shook his head. "That girl never showed. A stroke of luck—or thunder, as it were—brought Mabel to us."

Mabel stepped forward. "Happy to meet you, Mrs. Butler."

"Which theater did you work for?"

Mr. Macready waved an arm at the desks. "We're going to train Mabel. She'll take a typing desk."

Mrs. Butler puffed. "Easy for you to say."

Mr. Macready started to say something but stopped when a door at the far end of the office opened. A short, wiry young man strode in. He wore suit pants but no jacket and had rolled up the sleeves of his shirt to his elbows. His collar sopped up the drips falling from his dark curly hair. "Morning. Had to meet my father and got caught in the storm. Who's this?"

Mr. Macready smiled. "Jimmy, good day. This is our new ticket girl, Mabel."

Jimmy came forward a few steps and pointed at Mabel. "She's not the one I talked to you about." Mabel froze, conscious of her dress dripping on the floor.

Mrs. Butler blew smoke from her mouth and pointed the cigarette at him. "Jimmy, it was news to me, too, that Michael hired this girl from nowhere."

Jimmy put his hands in his pants pockets and rocked on his heels. "What theater does she come from?" Mrs. Butler smashed her cigarette in an ashtray, raising her eyebrows at Mr. Macready as if to say, *Hah!*

He turned to Mabel with a tight smile. "Would you wait in the lobby for a few minutes?" He opened the door. "I will be right with you." Mabel nodded and stepped out. After the door closed behind her, their muffled raised voices filtered through the closed ticket windows.

Jimmy talked in quick, urgent bursts. Mr. Macready answered in a determined tone. Back and forth, like a tennis match, with Mrs. Butler chiming in on Jimmy's side. Whoever Jimmy was, he wasn't backing down. Mabel flashed back to her brothers yelling over her head about who was supposed to walk her to school, not noticing she'd left the house. Mabel's stomach gurgled with the unsettled feeling. She shivered in the wet dress despite the stuffy air in the lobby.

Jimmy's voice came louder from the other side of the window. Mabel backed against the wall, staring at the mocking faces of the people painted in the murals. She scolded herself for getting her hopes up. *I should go before they tell me to go.*

The door flew open, and Mabel jumped. She had lingered too long. Mr. Macready leaned out looking for her. He had to know she had heard the quarrel. Bracing to excuse herself with some dignity, she opened her mouth to speak, but he said, "Mabel, thanks for waiting."

"It sounded like there was a misunderstanding."

Mr. Macready shook his head. "I apologize. We need a ticket girl, and I hope you'll give it a try."

These people were unlike any she'd ever met. She had made her way among drunks. How could this be worse? She was desperate for work and didn't know what else to do. "Thank you. I'd like to try."

Mr. Macready pointed at the staircase. "Come see the theater, and I will explain a few things." Mabel walked alongside him to the staircase curving up to the first balcony. He gestured at the murals as they climbed the steps. "This is a performance theater, not a movie palace. We're losing money, and our owner expects me to change that."

At the landing, he led Mabel to a set of double doors, which he pulled open. Mabel stepped through to a railing running along the rear of the balcony seats. She had been to opulent movie palaces with every surface gilded or mirrored, but in the Lafayette, less fancy surroundings drew attention to the stage. The chandeliers on the ceiling were dark. Spotlights directed beams at the stage. The curtain was raised, and several men worked on assembling three walls of a room, like a dollhouse made life-size.

Mr. Macready spoke as they watched. "We've got twenty-five hundred seats to sell. James—or Jimmy, as he likes to be called—is the son of our owner. He's out to convince his father the Lafayette can be the leading house in Detroit. He's got a lot of ideas. We'll see how far his father lets him go."

Mabel thought back to her early days with the twins, trying to work out their moods and where she fit into their habits. She risked a direct question. "Am I working for him or for you?"

"For me. I'll manage Jimmy."

She nodded. "And Mrs. Butler?"

"Mrs. Butler's been here for over twenty years. She'll teach you the ropes." Mr. Macready faced Mabel. "Your day starts at ten and ends when the box office is settled for the night. Six days a week."

Leaving only Sunday at loose ends. "That's fine."

He turned and opened the door. Going down the staircase, Mabel kept a tight grip along the banister. She hadn't eaten, and a lightheaded feeling hobbled her balance. When they reached the last step, she asked if she could use the ladies' room. He pointed to a side hall behind the staircase. "It's just there. I'll see you in the office tomorrow morning." She thanked him, and he went through the ticket office door.

Mabel found the ladies' lounge and pushed the door open, surprised to see Mrs. Butler half-reclining on a settee, the red skirt splayed around her, reading the newspaper and having a smoke. She brought the cigarette to her lips and tilted her head at Mabel. "You look white as a ghost."

The smoke heightened her lightheadedness. Mabel plopped into a chair across from the settee. "I'm all right."

"So, Michael hired a girl with no experience. Against my judgment. You'd better learn quick."

Mabel nodded, wary of the underlying message. "I'll do my best."

"He would've paid the other girl twenty-five a week, so you'll get that, not that you deserve it." Mabel had forgotten to ask about the pay. Again, she nodded. Mrs. Butler had more to say.

She pointed her cigarette at Mabel. "But don't think for a minute that *he's* in charge. Jimmy's gonna be steering things, and he listens to me." She rose from the settee and wiggled a finger at Mabel. "Girls like you think you're the whole package. But look at you. I know you haven't come from anywhere respectable." Mrs. Butler ground out her cigarette in the standing ashtray. "Don't be late tomorrow." She spun on her heel and swept out of the lounge.

Mrs. Butler's directness took Mabel aback. The remark about respectability rankled, as though she knew her past. Worse, Mrs. Butler was warning her. What had she stumbled into? Mr. Macready said he was her boss, but Mrs. Butler believed she and Jimmy had the upper hand. Mabel wanted only to keep busy with no time to think. She'd had plenty of experience dodging her brothers' schemes by watchful evasion. She'd have to outfox Mrs. Butler.

Mabel caught her reflection in the full-length triple mirror on the wall. Her body had withered to a skeleton of the full-bodied Miss Front End. The make-up had done little to mask her pasty skin, sapped from the drink and sagging around her eyes and at her chin. The out-of-style dress hung a size too large on her scrawny frame. Her "good" shoes were an old lady's cast-offs from the church rummage. Clear-eyed about what she'd lost, she felt profoundly sad.

She noticed the newspaper on the settee, open to a dress ad from Winkelman's. Miss Front End would have looked stunning wearing the chic outfits. How was the worn-down version of that girl supposed to look?

Wiggling inside the soggy dress, she adjusted the damp wrinkles as best she could. Wisps of hair had loosened from the pins and frizzed around her face. She finger-combed her hair, adjusting the pins. Winkelman's would be open until seven o'clock. Handbag over her arm, she struck a pose with straightened shoulders and fingers on her hip. She'd pull herself together before tomorrow.

Peeking out from the lounge door, Mabel scanned the empty hallway, then made for the lobby. Seeing no one, she trotted through the door into the vestibule and out to the sidewalk. The storm had passed, leaving an afternoon hazy blue sky. Mabel judged the distance to Woodward Avenue and concentrated on steadying her gait.

Before she stumbled into the theater, Mabel had teetered on the edge of giving up and having a drink. The nuns would say that the grace of God or a guardian angel had saved her. Mabel didn't expect to be saved, but if she didn't mess it up, she had a chance.

CHAPTER 4

Mrs. Butler scowled at Mabel plunking the typewriter keys with two fingers. "Did you fail the commercial classes in high school?"

Bad luck that Mrs. Butler had given Mabel a typing task first thing. She had racked her brain for the rules about placing her fingers on certain keys but had fallen back on using only two fingers. Flicking her eyes from the sheet of handwritten scribbles to the keys, with Mrs. Butler watching, tensed her fingers into claws. Mrs. Butler hadn't bothered to explain what the list of names was for.

Mabel glossed over her clumsy attempt. "I'll get the hang of this machine."

Mrs. Butler rolled her eyes and reached over to jerk the sheet of paper from the Remington. She made a show of crunching it into a ball. "Start over."

Mabel gritted her teeth. She longed for coffee, but didn't dare ask. She wiped her sweaty fingertips along her arms and tucked a blank sheet behind the roller. Turning the knob to position the paper, she shoved back the paper lock and pushed the carriage to the right. She memorized the first name and telephone number. Mabel concentrated on pressing the correct keys to peck out the name and flicked the return lever to the next line. Out of the corner of her eye, she saw Mrs. Butler staring through her cigarette smoke.

Neither Jimmy nor Mr. Macready had been in the office when she arrived a few minutes before ten. Mrs. Butler had been watching for her from one of the ticket windows and opened the door with a terse, "Good morning." Mabel returned the greeting, enjoying a smug moment as Mrs. Butler took in the difference in her appearance.

On her way to Winkelman's the day before, Mabel had noticed a sign, *Walk-ins welcome,* outside a hair salon. Peering through the glass door, she saw no customers and stepped inside. A man and a woman behind the reception counter greeted her, introducing themselves as the husband-and-wife owners with the French-Canadian accent Mabel remembered of her grandmother.

The woman led her to a swivel chair set before an oversized mirror studded with lightbulbs. "If I may," the man said as he touched her hair and, at her nod, removed the pins. He ran a brush through her locks. "What style are you looking for?"

Mabel shook her head. "I don't know." She had not been in a salon since before she married Al.

"Perhaps we take up this length to allow your natural wave to frame your face." He raised Mabel's hair above her shoulders and furled it around her ears. Their kind faces reflected in the mirror convinced her to agree.

At the shampoo sink, the wife gently glided the spray nozzle over her scalp. Mabel closed her eyes and breathed in the aroma of lilacs as fingers massaged the lather from her nape to her forehead. After rinsing and wrapping Mabel's dripping hair in a fluffy white towel, she led her to the chair facing the mirror. Tying a pink plastic cape around her shoulders, the woman stepped aside for the husband.

Soft orchestral music played from the radio on the counter. With a comb, he parted and clipped strands into sections. Mabel kept still, watching him manipulate the scissors, feeling renewed with each clump of hair that fell away as he combed and snipped around her face. Strand by strand, he rolled and pinned curlers in a pattern around her head.

"Would you like a manicure while you are drying?" Mabel held out her hands. The woman lowered the hood over the curlers and turned the machine on. Hot air lulled Mabel as the woman massaged her hands, then filed and polished her nails.

She was half asleep when the dryer clicked off. At the mirror, the man unwound the rollers, then turned Mabel away from the reflection while he styled her hair. When he spun the chair to face the mirror, her hands flew to her cheeks. Soft curls touched her shoulders and waved around her face. The spirit of Miss Front End winked at her.

Making her way along the avenue toward Winkelman's, Mabel sensed the admiring eyes of those passing by. The nuns had slapped her on the wrist for defying their rules for modesty ("Such boldness!"). Bold Mabel had outsmarted her brother's ruses to gang up on her. That girl had eloped with Al three weeks after they met. Now, she held her head high and soaked in the glances, tapping the courage that still lingered somewhere inside her.

At Winkelman's, mannequins with painted-on expressions taunted her with chic outfits. She and Peggy used to love window shopping downtown, imagining going to parties dressed in elegant gowns, while in their purses they only had money for grilled cheese sandwiches and Cokes at the Kresge's counter. Mabel flipped her hair at the models and went inside.

Plush gold carpet cushioned the main aisle. Tall mirrors along the walls reflected the light from the milk-glass chandeliers hanging above. Garment racks sprouted into side aisles from the center, interspersed with low settees covered in water-blue velvet. Saleswomen neatened the displays. Mabel walked toward the section with skirts arrayed on revolving racks. An hour later, she left the store with a skirt and two blouses to see her through until she could budget for more clothes.

This morning, Mabel pranced into the theater with her shorter hair and wearing a crisp white blouse tucked into the navy skirt. Mrs. Butler looked her up and down with a smirk, then grumbled about wasting her time on the extra paperwork to add Mabel to the payroll. "You'll be paid every other Friday. Your $25 a week won't stretch for fancy hairdos." She sniffed. "Not my business, of course, how you waste your money."

Jimmy burst into the office from the inside door while Mabel was hunched over the typing. Mrs. Butler gave him a cheery greeting, which he did not return as he was already speaking. "Come upstairs. We've got the new prices figured out."

Mrs. Butler glanced at Mabel. "I can't leave her here for the walk-ins." Jimmy marched over to the window and pulled a sign from the ledge below: *Open in 30 minutes.* He stood it against the glass and then rolled down the blind. "Both of you come up." He wiggled his fingers at them and rushed out the door.

Mrs. Butler picked up her cigarette pack and lighter and groaned as she pushed up from her chair. "I don't know why they want *you*, but come on." She waddled to the doorway and turned into a narrow hallway.

Mabel came alongside her. "Where are we going?"

"Michael's office on the second floor."

The windowless corridor allowed passage from the office to backstage without going into the public areas. A stairway went up, and ahead were doors marked *Lobby* and *Backstage*. Mrs. Butler gestured for Mabel to start up the stairs, huffing and moaning behind. On the landing, Mr. Macready's voice came from an open door. Mabel tapped a knock.

When he saw her, Mr. Macready rose from the chair behind his desk. "Good morning, Mabel. Help yourself to coffee."

"Good morning. I would love some coffee."

Jimmy nodded from the end of a long table, shuffling through a stack of papers. She went to the windowsill where a carafe and mugs sat ready. As she poured a cup, she noticed a caravan of trucks had pulled along the curb on the side street bordering the theater. She carried her cup and settled into the nearest empty chair. Red-faced Mrs. Butler came in, refused the coffee, and fell into the chair opposite Mabel. She grabbed an ashtray from the center of the table and lit a cigarette.

Mr. Macready came from his desk carrying papers and a pen and took the chair at the head of the table. "We'll keep this short so you can get back to the office. Jimmy?"

Jimmy tossed a stapled set of papers at Mrs. Butler and flicked another in front of Mabel as though he were dealing cards. "We have new pricing for all sections, and different pricing depending on the show."

Mrs. Butler tapped a finger on her smoke. "Depending on the show?"

"The bigger shows have higher costs. Our advertising is increasing. Tickets must bring in a larger percentage of our nut." He pointed at the seating chart. "Each section has a base price, and we'll raise it depending on the show."

Mabel looked over the seating chart printed on the paper. In a tavern, pours of top-shelf liquor had a premium price. Jimmy was using a similar scheme.

Mr. Macready tapped his pen. "We've got two runs selling at the old pricing—one loading in now, one in two weeks—and we'll advertise the new prices for the next shows coming in."

Mrs. Butler made a face. "Jimmy, how far out are we selling?"

"Six months. At the Cass …"

"At the Cass, they hire proper girls." Mrs. Butler turned to Mr. Macready. "We're to keep the bookings for six months of shows, and you hired a girl who can't type."

Jimmy raised his eyebrows but said nothing. Mabel fingered the corner of her papers and felt her face get hot.

Mr. Macready kept his eyes on Mrs. Butler's frown. "You take care of the typing." Mrs. Butler froze. "Mabel's going to man the window. You'll both be working the telephones and organizing the ticket orders."

Mrs. Butler stubbed out her smoke with a force that spilled the ashes over the edge of the ashtray. "*I* should do the typing?" She looked at Jimmy as though she expected him to say something, but he busied himself with jotting on his papers. "I've been here twenty years."

"Yes, in the ticket office, which has become disorganized."

"I'll thank you not to question my methods."

Mr. Macready leaned toward her and spoke in a firm voice. "Changes are ahead, Mrs. Butler." He checked the clock. "I'll let you get back to the office now." She sniffed, gathered her papers and smokes, and pushed back her chair. Mabel stood, figuring she should follow Mrs. Butler.

Mr. Macready capped his pen. "I'll be down after lunch. Have you let Mabel know about lunch?" Mrs. Butler ignored him and left the room. "I guess not."

Jimmy got to his feet, exchanged a glance with Mr. Macready, and left. Mr. Macready spoke to Mabel. "When we have a load-in, lunch is delivered from the deli for the crew, including the ticket office. One of the boys will bring sandwiches up front."

Mabel considered telling him about Mrs. Butler's icy manner. The old bitty had ratcheted things up during the meeting, and Mabel didn't know what battles lay ahead. In the factory, women would never tell a higher-up about a supervisor's shabby treatment, and Mabel had stood on her own against the groping and refused breaks. She didn't have a read on Mr. Macready yet, though he seemed to be in her corner. But she held back. "Thanks. I'll learn this chart." She picked up her papers and headed for the door.

"Wait a second." Mr. Macready went to his desk and picked up a folder. "You need this." Mabel took the folder and inside found copies of the floor plans of the theater. "Lots of nooks and crannies in this place. Get familiar with the layout." Mabel nodded. His telephone rang. Before he lifted the receiver, he said, "I'll see you after lunch." Mabel left the office as he took the call.

She went down the stairs and heard men shouting over rumbling and thumps from the other side of the backstage door.

Curious, Mabel turned the handle and pulled it ajar. A gust of hot air swooshed into her face. Crates and rolling carts covered with canvas bunched together in a cavernous space. Men hauled pieces of scenery and stacked them against the wall. Something heavy fell amid oaths loud and furious. Mabel pushed the door shut. She jumped at seeing Jimmy just behind her.

"Dangerous to go back there right now."

Mabel adjusted the papers she carried and nodded. "Just taking a peek." He stood looking at her long enough to make her wary. Then he stepped away and bounded up the stairs. She hurried along the corridor to the ticket office, taking a deep breath to steady herself for Mrs. Butler's criticism. *Be bold.* Mabel entered the office and looked around. Mrs. Butler wasn't there.

The telephone on Mrs. Butler's desk was ringing. Mabel stepped around to her own desk and grabbed the receiver, stretching the cord to reach her ear. "Good morning, Lafayette Theater box office, Mabel speaking." She smiled at the ease of saying the greeting. Hearing the inquiry, she tensed. Mabel could only take the name and telephone number with a promise to call the customer back. The caller's impatience came through, and Mabel hung up with a sigh. Mrs. Butler had wasted time with the typing when Mabel lacked information about selling tickets for the shows.

Stacks of handbills stuffed the cubbies beneath the ticket windows. Rifling through, checking the dates, Mabel discovered programs from old shows not cleared out. But she found sealed boxes from a print shop. With scissors, she cut a box open, finding the programs for a vaudeville show with an opening date the next week. She took a copy to her desk. The caller had asked about the balcony tickets. The back of the program showed the ticket prices. How was Mabel to know which seats were still available?

Where was Mrs. Butler? Mabel's frustration propelled her out of the office and into the lobby. She marched toward the ladies' lounge, rehearsing choice words to let Mrs. Butler know she would not take the brunt of the old woman's upset with Mr. Macready. Approaching the door, Mabel smelled cigarette smoke.

She flung the lounge door open and began to cough. A full ashtray of butts smoldered. Mabel waved the smoke out of her eyes with her hands. Then she saw Mrs. Butler sprawled face down on the carpet. Mabel got down on the floor next to her and jiggled her arm, calling her name. Mrs. Butler didn't move. Mabel grabbed under her with both hands and pushed until she flopped onto her back. Mabel gasped at Mrs. Butler's ashen face and bulging eyes. She jumped up and ran into the lobby, yelling for help.

CHAPTER 5

Mr. Macready walked behind the men pushing the gurney to the ambulance. Mabel, hunched over on a step of the grand staircase, drew in her breath at the sight of the shrouded figure. Mrs. Butler's gray face loomed in her vision. Mr. Macready glanced back at her as they went through the vestibule doors to the street.

The cleaning woman was already busy inside the ladies' lounge. She had propped the door open, letting a lingering smell of smoke waft into the lobby. Mabel shivered. She needed to use the toilet but couldn't bear to go in there.

Footsteps thudded down the stairs, and Jimmy landed next to her. "Tough luck, you finding her like that." Mabel nudged away from him, leaning into the banister. He reached inside his suit coat. "Got something from the boys in the back." He unscrewed the top of a flask and pushed it against her arm. "Take a big swig."

She stared at the flask, inches from her grasp, the open spout singing to her. Mabel wanted it, and one swig would not be enough.

Mr. Macready was back. "Jimmy, don't."

"No?" He shrugged and put the flask to his lips, took a long pull, then grimaced.

Mr. Macready reached out to Mabel. "Let's get you back to the office." She wanted to take his offered hand, but her arms gripped her legs and wouldn't let go. She put her head on her knees. Mabel heard him talking to the cleaning woman, and then he offered her water. She raised her head and clenched her fingers around the paper cone, and took a sip, then a mouthful.

Mr. Macready spoke to Jimmy. "I've got to work out a problem backstage. Walk Mabel into the office. I'll be there as soon as I can." Jimmy screwed the top onto the flask and tucked it inside his jacket. He moved off the steps and offered Mabel his hand. With the help of his firm grip, she got to her feet. Mr. Macready steadied her with a hand under her elbow. When she had taken a step, Mr. Macready nodded and left them.

Jimmy guided Mabel's slow steps toward the office. "Hell of a day. Tomorrow's gonna be worse."

Mabel grimaced. Mrs. Butler had died of a heart attack in the ladies' lounge. "Worse?"

"Yeah. We have to make sense of the mess in the office and sell thousands of tickets." He shook his head. "And neither of us is a good bet."

Mabel looked at him. "What do you mean?"

Jimmy shrugged. "My father is waiting for me to fail at this and go back to law school." He opened the office door and ushered her in. "And you have no experience."

Mabel lowered onto her desk chair and gazed at the overflowing ashtray on Mrs. Butler's desk. Jimmy came around and sat in Mrs. Butler's chair. He pulled the wastebasket from under the desk and scooped the ashtray into it. He looked over the array of papers and folders covering the desktop. "She had some kind of system, but who knows what it was?"

In taverns, barkeeps had their own particular set-ups. The taps were fixed, but they arranged the bar front and back to suit themselves and the place. Mabel had set up the farmhouse bar in her own way. "Can we make our own system?" Jimmy shot her a look. She waved her hand over the piles. "Sort this out, then …"

He rolled his eyes. "Then magically sell thousands of tickets? Sure, we can."

Mabel shrugged. "I don't know. I only discovered which show is loading in just before I found Mrs. Butler."

He shook his head. "Oh, boy."

Both telephones began ringing. Jimmy looked at Mabel. She reached for the receiver on her desk, nodding toward the one in front of him. "Answer that." She spoke to the caller. Jimmy waited, listening to her greeting. She waved her arm at him, and he picked up the ringing call. Mabel took the pad where she had written the earlier message and added the caller's information to the page. She apologized. "We've had an emergency here today."

Jimmy reached across and grabbed the pad. He scribbled a name and telephone number and ended his call. He pushed the pad back to her. They looked at each other. How could this ever work?

Mr. Macready strode in from the corridor and pulled a chair over to the desks. "Are you doing okay, Mabel?" She lifted a shoulder and nodded. He looked at Jimmy. "Your father will have the last word on the staffing when he hears about Mrs. Butler."

Jimmy pursed his lips. "Understood." Mabel lowered her eyes and waited. There was no reason for Mr. Macready to keep her on. She didn't blame him.

"But I intend to convince him we can carry on. The head of the office at the Cass is willing to show us their set-up. I arranged for the two of you to go there tomorrow morning. I'll deal with this office while you're out."

Not fired. Mabel looked up in surprise. Jimmy drummed his fingers on the desk. It occurred to her he might have been waiting for her firing, too.

Mr. Macready stood. "Mabel, you've had a shock, and you haven't eaten. Come with me backstage and get a sandwich."

"I must go to the lounge first." She couldn't avoid it.

Mr. Macready nodded. "Take your time. I'll wait here."

Mabel half ran to the restroom. Seeing Mrs. Butler's ghost scared her as much as the moment she almost took Jimmy's flask. The cleaning cart still sat outside the lounge. Mabel took a gulp of air and pushed inside. The cleaner stood on a stepstool, swiping a cloth across the top of the vanity mirror. "Geez, you comin' back in here?"

Mabel rushed through the archway to the toilet stalls. Relieving her bladder relaxed her body. She sat there for a few moments. The flask was a warning. If Mr. Macready had not appeared, she would have taken a drink. Her craving was strong. She was her own ghost, never mind Mrs. Butler.

At the sink, she washed and dried her hands and straightened her skirt and blouse. She crept around the wall to view the settees. No presence of Mrs. Butler, only the cleaner rubbing at the mirror. The woman caught her eye. "You okay, hon?"

"I'm better."

"She was no prize, that one. May she rest in peace." Rag in hand, she crossed herself.

Mabel almost laughed. "I'm Mabel. What's your name?"

"Tilda, pleased to meet 'cha." She folded her rag over the cart. "How 'bout you use the restroom on the first balcony from now on?"

"Thanks, I will." Mabel held the door for Tilda to push the cart through to the hallway. She parked it and took the rag to the fixtures along the wall.

When Mabel reentered the ticket office, Jimmy was on the telephone. Mr. Macready stood and looked at her with concern. Mabel reassured him, "I'm feeling better."

"Good. Some food will help. I'll show you the pantry." He led her along the corridor and through the door to backstage, and she followed his path weaving amidst carts and trunks and packing cases. The wooden-plank floor creaked and dipped in spots. Overhead, rope pulleys moved pieces of scenery and, way up, men on a metal bridge worked on the lights. Mabel glimpsed the stage set and the immense curtain before he turned into a side hallway lined with doorways. "Dressing rooms and wardrobe, both sides of the stage, and upstairs. The pantry is here."

He opened a door into a windowless room with three scuffed-up tables and folding chairs, a counter holding a coffee urn, a hot plate, and a tiny sink, and in the corner, an old Frigidaire. Mr. Macready opened the icebox and pulled out a tray covered with a dishtowel with one hand and grabbed a jug of iced tea in the other. Setting them on a table, he invited

Mabel to take a chair. She sat as he rummaged on the shelves above the counter. He held two glasses up to the light. Satisfied that they were clean, he set a glass before Mabel and poured the tea. "Help yourself to a sandwich."

Mabel's appetite came alive with a stomach gurgle. She lifted the towel and chose a half of a ham and cheese sandwich and paused. Mr. Macready lifted the towel on his side with a nod. "Don't wait for me. Eat, please." She took a bite and made herself chew slowly, though she wanted to wolf it down. When Mr. Macready had had a few bites, he sat back. "While you eat—and eat as much as you want—let me tell you about the Cass." Mabel chewed as she listened.

"You've heard of the Shuberts? No? They've got the best theaters in town, helped by the deep pockets of the owner of the *Detroit Free Press*. They took over the Cass before the war. Jimmy's old man doesn't have the cash to buy the Lafayette, so he made a deal with them. He runs the operation, and their name is going on the marquee. The Shubert-Lafayette."

Mabel reached for another half of a sandwich. She took a paper napkin from a pile on the table and wiped her mouth. "Is that why the Cass is helping us?"

Mr. Macready shrugged. "Yes, but we're competing with them, too. Broadway road shows going west come to Detroit for their first performances. The Cass is the most successful theater in the city. Jimmy intends *this* to be the best theater in the city. We've got more seats. But we'd have to sign Broadway road shows before they do and sell them out."

"Do you think that's possible?"

"Depends on Jimmy. I came to Detroit from New York five years ago to be house manager at the Cass. When Jimmy's father offered me this house, I figured it would be a tough haul. Mrs. Butler knew sales, though she was hard to get along with, but we needed more. Jimmy persuaded me he'll fight tooth and nail for the Lafayette, and he quit school to take over the business."

"Jimmy told me his father is trying to scare him into going back to school."

"The old man says that, but he's betting on him as the future."

Mabel thought for a moment. She figured she might as well be direct. "Why are you betting on me?"

He smiled. "Part of it was serendipity. You walked in at the right moment. Should I have looked into your skills a bit further? Probably. The girl I was waiting for trained at the Cass. She didn't show, and I'm guessing it's because word is going around the theaters that we won't cut it. My instinct was to go with someone who has no loyalty to our competition."

Mabel appreciated his honesty. She sensed he wanted to ask her more about herself and steered away. "Tomorrow at the Cass, where do we start?"

Mr. Macready reached into his suit pocket and pulled out a folded paper. Spreading it open on the table, he referred to a list of terms Mabel had not heard of.

Mabel threw up her hands to stop the overload of information. "I need to make notes."

Mr. Macready chuckled. "Of course you do. Let's go back to the office."

They tidied the pantry, then made their way through the backstage jumble. Mr. Macready reminded Mabel about the floor plans he had given her. "Once the show is up, things will settle down back here. Walk around and get your bearings."

The show would open in two days. How many tickets had been sold? Mabel held back the question.

When they entered the office, Jimmy jumped up from Mrs. Butler's chair. Mabel guessed it would be his chair now. "I've been selling tickets!" An auto dealer had telephoned to buy one hundred seats to lure customers to his showroom. "He'll do radio advertising, so we're bound to get more sales from that."

He pulled a notebook from the desk. "I found Mrs. Butler's book on the sales for this run." He handed it to Mr. Macready. "Did she show you the bank on this?" Mr. Macready opened the notebook and started to answer as the telephone rang. Mabel answered the call. She asked the customer to wait for a moment and put the call on hold.

"Can you tell me how to take a telephone order?" The two men looked at her. "We've been saying we'll call back, but the customer is on the line now."

Mr. Macready reached for the receiver. "Okay, listen to me handle it."

They spent the rest of the afternoon taking calls and going over details about procedures to study at the Cass. Mabel took notes. Jimmy said he had it all in his head. At six o'clock, Mr. Macready went backstage, telling Mabel and Jimmy to go home.

Outside, Jimmy asked if she needed him to see her home. Mabel wasn't sure how to take the offer, and she didn't want Jimmy to know where she stayed. He sensed her hesitation. "Just so you're steady to get there."

"I'm fine, thanks."

"Then I'll meet you at the Cass at nine tomorrow." From where they stood, the lights of the Cass marquee were visible down the boulevard.

"I'll be there. Good night, Jimmy."

"Night, Mabel." A green sedan pulled to the curb and beeped its horn. A young woman with a head of curls was driving. Jimmy ran around the rear of the car and jumped into the front passenger seat. He waved to Mabel as the sedan merged into the traffic.

Mabel began making her way to Woodward Avenue. The evening air was cooler, and she walked toward Luna. It was the only place she felt comfortable eating as long as she was lodging at the boarding house.

After dinner, before she went up to her room, she asked about staying week to week. The landlady shrugged. "A monthly rate is gonna be cheaper."

Mabel shook her head. "I'm looking for a place." She hadn't looked, but with a paycheck, she could move somewhere closer to the theater.

"It's your money." The proprietress took Mabel's cash for another week. She reached behind her for an envelope and held it out. "This came for you."

Mabel recognized the handwriting. In her room, she opened the envelope to read a note from Jack. An invitation to come to the ten o'clock Mass at St. Aloysius on Sunday and have breakfast afterwards with the seminarians. Mabel tossed the note onto the dresser. He meant well, but she had been clear that he didn't need to check on her. He'd get the idea when she didn't show up.

The next morning, Jimmy stood under the marquee of the Cass Theater, on the corner of Lafayette and Washington Boulevard, when Mabel arrived just before nine. "Morning, Mabel. You okay?"

"Good morning. I'm fine." She had tossed and turned until dawn and hoped the cup of coffee she'd gulped would keep her tired eyes open. She held out the pad with her notes. "Ready for school."

He laughed. "You're like my fiancé. Esther writes everything down. That was her driving the car last night." He lowered his voice. "Before we go in, I should tell you they know me here."

"Mr. Macready gave me some background on your father's business."

Jimmy rocked on his heels. "I'm the thorn in his side at the moment. I intend to make us a big fish in the theater business. He doesn't see what I see since the war." He motioned toward the entrance. "While we're inside, though, I'd like to keep the focus on the ticket office."

"Of course." Mabel waved an arm at the six stories of windows towering above the Cass marquee. "This looks like an office building."

Jimmy opened one of the brass doors and held it for Mabel. "The theater was built *behind* these offices." An entry foyer opened onto a wide lobby, and the passage led away from the street to the theater doors at the far end. "The theater sits sideways, stage on the left, main aisle behind the orchestra. Not as many seats as we have."

Jimmy led her to the ticket windows along the side wall and tapped a knock on a door labeled *Box Office*. The middle-aged woman who opened it wore a dark blue business suit Mabel recognized from a window display at J.L. Hudson's, *For the Girl with a Job*. Fitted straight skirt and matching jacket with a peplum waist, buttoned up to the rounded collar, topped with a double strand of pearls. Coiffed brown waves with a hint of gray at the temples swirled and touched her neckline. With a cool glance at Mabel, she arranged her lips to suggest a smile and removed her glasses. "Jimmy, nice to see you."

"Miss Barnes, good of you to see us. This is Mabel …"

Mabel chimed in with, "Hunt. Good morning."

Jimmy gave her a quizzical look. "Right, Mabel Hunt—new in our office."

"Yes, so Michael said." Miss Barnes motioned them inside. "Please follow me to my office."

Mabel's eyes widened at the sight of eight desks with clerks typing or speaking on the telephone. Miss Barnes waved a manicured hand. "Sales are good for the little play we've been running this summer. As you know, we're gearing up for *Carousel*. We've locked in an extension. *Everyone* in the city will see the show *here*." She added over her shoulder, "No comps for that run."

Jimmy muttered to Mabel, "I wouldn't take 'em, anyway."

They trailed her to the far end of the room into an inner office enclosed by glass windows. Miss Barnes swept behind an oak desk larger than Mr. Macready's and gestured for them to sit in the two chairs at the side. "So sad about Lea Butler." She picked up a black three-ring binder sitting on her blotter pad and held it out to Mabel. "I had the girls put together a copy of our office manual for you."

Mabel took the binder onto her lap and opened it to the first page. The manual's contents almost matched Mr. Macready's list. Of course, he had worked here. Miss Barnes perched on her chair and clasped her hands on the desk. "Basic ticketing. Nothing there gives away our secrets." She smiled at Jimmy with a shrug of one shoulder. "We aren't worried you'll catch up with us."

Jimmy's jaw tightened, but he returned Miss Barnes's smug smile. "We have more seats."

She shook her head. "We have the shows that command the highest prices."

"For now." Jimmy glanced at Mabel with a wily glint in his eye. "Mabel may have a few questions."

Miss Barnes had another card to play. "As a matter of fact, I have no more time, as I must attend a meeting upstairs."

Jimmy had had enough. "Very good, Lucy, thank you. We'll take it from here." He stood, and she rose, neither one offering a hand to the other. Mabel clutched the binder to her middle and rose from her chair, expecting Jimmy to storm out of the office. But Miss Barnes made the first move by striding around her desk and out of the office to speak to the nearest clerk.

Jimmy whispered, "We're getting out of here." He had let Miss Barnes rile him up. Mabel worried he was blowing the opportunity Mr. Macready had given them to learn about the operation at the Cass.

Miss Barnes wagged fingers at them. Mabel and Jimmy joined her next to a dark-haired young woman seated at the desk. "This is my head girl, Greta. She'll answer questions." She eyed Mabel. "If you aren't in over your head, Miss Hunt. Jimmy, give my best to your dear mother." With that, Miss Barnes strode away.

Greta offered them a tight-lipped smile. "How can I help you?"

Jimmy did not hold back. "I bet you've been instructed not to help us at all." Mabel shot him a stricken look, and Greta tilted her head as if confused.

"On the contrary, Miss Barnes asked me to attend to questions you have about our procedures."

Jimmy shook his head in disbelief. "C'mon, Mabel." She frowned at him. They couldn't go back to the Lafayette without getting the information. Mabel had an idea.

"Jimmy, why don't you go back to our office and I'll work with Greta for the rest of the morning? Let Mr. Macready know that the staff at the Cass is most gracious and helpful." She flashed a broad smile at Greta. Jimmy blanched, but he took her cue.

"Gotcha, Mabel. Greta, thanks. I'll be going." He raised a brow at Mabel, which she took as a warning to be careful in enemy territory. She nodded, and he made his way out of the office.

Greta offered Mabel the chair at the side of her desk. "Miss Barnes will be out until lunch, so we have time." They both sat down, and Mabel opened the binder, not meeting Greta's glance, trying to get her thoughts in order. Mabel *was* in over her head. Greta was about her age, and Mabel guessed she had spent her recent years in the Cass, not in taverns. Yet Mabel sensed she had a kinder streak than Miss Barnes. "Where would you begin if you were me?"

"I was you five years ago." Greta shrugged. "Mrs. Butler was my lifesaver."

Mabel stared at her. "Mrs. Butler?"

Greta nodded. "I was drowning my first week here. At lunchtime, I would go outside and cry. Mrs. Butler walked by and saw me. She gave me a cigarette, and we talked. After that, she would meet me, give me pointers." The story stunned

Mabel. She wished she had seen that side of Mrs. Butler. "It's too bad she died before she could teach you. So, it's up to me."

The old biddy's reputation with Greta would work in Mabel's favor. She played along. "Thank you, Greta, on Mrs. Butler's behalf." She opened her pad to the notes she had made.

Greta tapped her pencil on the open binder page. "The manual will guide you through the procedures. Start with the ticket chart for the particular show." She pointed to the far wall of the office. An oversized map of the theater space designated the sections and seat numbers. "Mrs. Butler would have done it the same way, so look for her files on the show opening now. The treasury differs for every show."

"Treasury?"

"The expected cash total for each performance when all seats are accounted for."

Mabel understood running tabs and cashing out, and soon she and Greta were deep in conversation about the practices followed at the Cass. Mabel made notes of the tips Greta gave her as they went through the binder.

Over two hours had gone by when Mabel checked the wall clock. "I've kept you from your coffee break, and it's almost lunchtime."

Greta shrugged. "It's the least I can do for Mrs. B."

Mabel gathered her notes and closed the binder. "Thank you, Greta. Will it be all right for me to call you if I get stuck?"

"I have a direct line." Greta scribbled a telephone number on a notepad, tore the sheet off, and handed it to Mabel. Mabel put the note in her handbag and stood, hefting the binder on her hip. She wanted to leave before Miss Barnes returned. They said their goodbyes, and Mabel saw herself out of the office. She scanned the Cass lobby before making her way to the door and out to the sidewalk. Mabel was surprised to see Jimmy crossing the street to meet her. "What are you doing here?"

"I came back to make sure you made it out of there alive."

Mabel laughed. "Greta's all right." She kept the part about Mrs. Butler to herself.

"I told Michael I will beat the Cass no matter what it takes."

Mabel shifted the binder to her other hip. "You could start by carrying this the rest of the way."

Jimmy took the binder under his arm. "Let's go for lunch, my treat."

Mabel demurred. "I'd like to get back to the office."

"C'mon, the place is just down the alley here. A joint with good sandwiches. Mostly theater people at lunchtime." Jimmy started walking, expecting her to follow.

Mabel eyed the neon sign pointing to a tavern tucked between buildings. Her craving was instant. She had to get away. Mabel caught up with him and tugged at the binder. "I'm not going with you. I'll take this."

He tightened his grip on the binder. "Look, I apologize for not standing up for you with Mrs. Butler. And I owe you for keeping me from punching Lucy Barnes. Let's go in."

"It's got nothing to do with you." Mabel walked away from him, droplets of sweat running down her chest inside her blouse. At the corner, Mabel tapped her foot, waiting for the traffic to clear. Jimmy came next to her.

"You got a problem going into taverns? My fiancé was like that until we'd been to a few."

Mabel scoffed. "I've been in plenty of taverns." Why did she let him goad her into saying that?

"Then what's the big deal? We sit in the back at lunch, not at the bar."

"No!" Mabel knew her voice was too loud and forceful. She grabbed at the binder and he let it go. Whirling away from him, she stomped across the street. She felt his eyes on her, but he didn't follow. She kept walking to the Lafayette, trying to shake off a vision of the cool, dark tavern and an icy mug of beer waiting there.

Desperate for water, Mabel marched across the lobby and flung open the door to the ticket office. She gaped at two strange girls at the desks, fingers flying on the typewriters, and a smiling Mr. Macready sipping a cup of coffee.

CHAPTER 6

Tolling church bells awakened Mabel. A chilly breeze from the half-open window blew over her bare arms. She pulled the thin bedspread up to her neck and wished Sunday away.

During the days at the theater, steeling her control, wary of embarrassing herself in front of Mr. Macready, she had side-stepped her cravings for a drink. She'd not considered how she would manage the long empty hours of Sunday and the Labor Day holiday.

At the farmhouse, Sunday had been the best day of the week. The closed barroom freed Mabel and the brothers to drink. The twins would gulp coffee and disappear upstairs with bottles. In winter, Mabel camped in front of the fireplace, refilling her mug whenever she came around from her daze. In summer, she moved her cot to the back porch with beers in the ice chest.

Last Sunday, she had been with Ma in the apartment above the diner. Shaky and dry heaving, worrying it might be the last time she'd see her. She didn't blame Ma for relying on Al's salesmanship to grow the pie business, and she would not make trouble for them. That last night, Ma had cuddled Mabel to sleep, soothing her shivering and sweating with cold cloths. As they said their goodbyes, Ma had wagged her finger in her Ma way. "Girly, you're gonna be okay on your own." Mabel had walked away from Ma with tears running down her cheeks, not looking back.

She had made it through one week, thanks to Mr. Macready.

He had solved the typing problem by hiring girls from the Kelly Office, a temporary agency. "Mr. Kelly guarantees their skills, and we can get more help if we need it." When Mabel walked into the office after the meeting at the Cass, typists were busy labeling names on two hundred envelopes for blocks of tickets Mrs. Butler had sold to businesses.

Envelopes also had to be prepared for the subscribers, patrons who paid ahead and claimed particular seats for every show during the year. Mabel kept the Cass procedure book handy, and Mr. Macready explained details as they worked. She strained to keep up with his fast-talking directions for filling the envelopes with the correct tickets.

Jimmy returned to the office while Mabel and two of the girls, Cora and Bridget, were taking a short break. Introducing him to the typists, Mabel kept her voice even and waited for what he might say about their exchange on the street. But Jimmy teased the girls, then took off his jacket and got busy counting cash into the drawers beneath the counter at the ticket windows, avoiding contact with her.

Mr. Macready checked as Mabel loaded the will call envelopes into the alphabetical slots in a cubby at the window. About eight hundred ticket sales were accounted for in the two sets of envelopes—a long way from selling twenty-five hundred seats.

The unsold tickets for the Friday opening sat ready in the slots between the cash windows. The bet was that the advertising would bring a walk-in crowd that night and on Saturday.

Jimmy shoved a cash drawer closed and turned to Mr. Macready. "You with me on the windows tonight?"

"Mabel's on will call, we're on cash. Mabel will help with cash sales when we have a line. *If* we have a line." Mabel nodded, unsure of how it would work, but aware that Mr. Macready relied on her to step up to the plate. She stared at the seating chart taped to the counter at her window. Jimmy came beside her. "Offer people the rear orchestra or the first balcony. Try to fill the seats the actors can see." He lowered his voice. "You okay?"

Mabel took that as an olive branch. "Fine. Ready for a crowd." Jimmy gave her a thumbs-up.

Before they opened the ticket windows, Mabel made a quick trip to the restroom, applied fresh lipstick, and neatened her hair. When Mr. Macready gave the signal, they rolled up the blinds and raised their windows.

The mass of people lined up propelled Mabel into action. "Good evening. Name, please."

Bridget had gone home, but Cora stayed at Mabel's side to reorganize the alphabetical order as her frantic fingers pulled envelopes from the slots. Mabel had the fleeting thought that selling tickets was less messy than sloshing beer. The rush at her window dwindled, giving her a pause to view the steady stream of patrons at the cash windows. Jimmy and Mr. Macready pulled tickets and made change in a smooth rhythm that kept the line moving. Cora grabbed the seating chart Jimmy waved at her and handed it to Mabel. The main floor was sold and the first balcony half-gone.

Mabel motioned waiting customers to her window and offered the balcony. Mr. Macready had one ear on her line while his hands worked his own. She slapped money on the counter with an order, and he had the tickets and change ready in seconds. Fifteen minutes before the show began, Mr. Macready closed his window and went to check backstage. Just before the lights went down, a patron rushed in for the last envelope. Mabel handed it over and closed her window. Jimmy still had balcony tickets and was keeping his window open until the first intermission. "It's not a play. Latecomers can still enjoy the laughs."

Mabel dropped into her desk chair, drained and elated. The rush had fully occupied her brain. She would take that diversion. Cora grinned at her. "This place is more fun than the other offices I'm sent to."

Mabel had to smile. "You were a great help."

Cora shrugged. "Sure thing. No date tonight anyway." She lowered her voice. "Do we get to watch the show?"

Mabel looked over her shoulder at Jimmy. "Jimmy, would you excuse us for a few minutes?"

He waved his arm as a patron approached his window. Mabel motioned to Cora and led her into the inner corridor. Cora giggled as they came to the backstage door. Mabel put a finger to her lips. She opened the door for them to squeeze through and nudged it closed. She had explored the wings and watched snippets of the rehearsal from a niche in the shadows where the set was visible. Grasping Cora's arm, she tip-toed to the spot. The music and costumes for the full-on show, and the audience's laughter, mesmerized her. When the stage darkened for a set change, Mabel shook herself, unsure how long they had stood there. She pinched Cora, and they moved toward the door.

Stepping into the corridor, they came face-to-face with Mr. Macready. He tilted his head, and Mabel saw the furrow in his brow. She braced for his scolding about sneaking backstage, but he simply waved them ahead to the office and followed them. Mabel scolded herself. She should have been at her post in the office for whatever he needed.

Cora collected her things and said goodnight. Mr. Macready had booked her for Saturday and both typists for the next week. Mabel kept her eyes down and tidied her desk. Jimmy handed the night's treasury report to Mr. Macready. Sales had fallen short of a full house, but the ticket blocks sold to businesses had boosted the total. "Minus the comp tickets we spread around for Saturday night, the opening weekend has a shot at breaking even."

Mr. Macready handed the report back to Jimmy. "A long shot." He bid them good night and left the office.

Mabel pulled her purse from the desk drawer and counted change for the streetcar. "I'll be going."

Jimmy sighed his exhaustion and plopped into a chair. "You kept up at the window. Where'd you work before?"

Mabel looked him in the eye and decided to tell him. "Taverns." She folded her arms. "I was a barmaid." She watched for his reaction.

Jimmy raised his brows. "I see. Okay." She had bet her past wouldn't matter to him, and she was right. "Tomorrow night, you take a cash window for the rush, and we'll manage the will call with Cora's help." He shrugged and tapped a finger on the desk. "I used to be in law school. You used to work in taverns. Neither of us is going back." Their eyes met.

A clamor in the lobby ended the moment. The show was over, and the crowd poured through the lobby to the street doors. Jimmy listened with a smile. "I hear buzz." Mabel didn't get his meaning at first but then understood. Excited talk on the way out was a good sign. He pushed back from the desk. "I'm going home."

Mabel accepted his offer to walk her to the streetcar. The cooler night air revitalized her. They strolled in contented silence past clusters of people outside the restaurants serving a late supper. Mabel spied the streetcar coming down the block. "Thanks, Jimmy. Good night." Jimmy tipped his hat. "See you tomorrow, Mabel Hunt." He strode to the corner and crossed with the light.

Jimmy and Mabel worked side-by-side during the rush before Saturday's show. Mr. Macready stuck his head in to ask if they needed help, and they waved him off. He took Cora to the pantry, and she came back with Cokes and leftover sandwiches from the cast meal. After they closed the windows, the three of them munched on the food. Jimmy talked Mabel through reconciling the sales book for the evening. Friday and Saturday together had not broken even. Jimmy put a good face on his disappointment. "I'll spin it to satisfy my father—for now."

She hadn't expected to like the job, but she did. When she left the theater late on Saturday night, Mabel was heartened by having done her part, giving silent credit to Greta's tutoring. She had fallen asleep thinking that if Mr. Macready kept the typists, she could work with Jimmy on the business sales and signing up new subscribers.

If she could get through two empty days away from the theatre. The bells had gone silent. Mabel threw off the covers and reached for her hairbrush on the dresser. Her hand caught the corner of Jack's note. She read it again. Ten o'clock Mass and breakfast. Going to Mass was the last thing she wanted to do, but he had not stopped fussing over her. If she sat through the service, at breakfast she would convince him there was no need for him to act like a big brother.

Mabel talked herself into going to St. Aloysius.

The granite and stone façade on Washington Boulevard looked as if the church had been carved from a rock wedged between the buildings on either side. Above the center wooden doors, a stained-glass window made of panes shaped like flower petals reflected the sunlight. The crowd on the sidewalk was moving inside, women in their Sunday bonnets on the arms of men tipping off their hats as they entered the church. Mabel had fashioned hair ribbons into bows pinned atop her head, the way she and Peggy used to, to pass for a hat.

She made her way into the vestibule. Worshippers dipped their fingers into a marble font holding holy water and crossed themselves. Mabel pressed against the wall until the crowd thinned, then swept past the font into the nave.

St. Aloysius was like no other church she'd been in. Where she stood was the middle tier of three levels, like a theater. The altar sanctuary was an ornate alcove with walls and columns carved from marble. The communion rail circled an opening in the floor. Peering over the rail, Mabel marveled at the pews below, and looking over her shoulder, at the tier above with the organ and choir. An usher approached her. "Miss?" He pointed to a stairwell. "There are seats upstairs. The Mass is about to start."

Mabel climbed to the upper level. She slid into an empty rear pew, tucked away from a cluster of people kneeling at the balustrade. The organ bellowed chords, and the choir launched into the entrance hymn with full-throated voices. The low notes throbbed in her temples. In the center aisle below, the priest and altar boys strode to the altar in pace with the hymn. Mabel tried to picture Jack wearing the priest's embroidered robes. Instead, she remembered him in his baseball uniform, posing for the newspaper when the team won a championship. He had winked at her and Peggy while the flashbulbs crackled.

Mabel looked up, and there was Jack, winking at her now. He stood in a pew on the other side of the choir, among a dozen seminarians singing out the hymn. Mabel blushed and looked down, embarrassed at being caught off guard. She wished she had spotted him first. She didn't want him to take her accepting his invitation as a sign of needing his help. Mabel edged further down the pew, out of his line of sight. She kept her gaze on the altar as the priest began the Mass.

A baby wailed from the pews below. The cries competed with the priest intoning the Latin prayers. Mabel clenched her skirt. The crying persisted. She wrapped her arms across her chest and squeezed her eyelids shut tight. At last, an usher escorted the woman carrying the bawling child out of the nave. Mabel crumpled into the hard corner of the pew. *Breathe, breathe.*

She had calmed when the priest mounted the pulpit and began the sermon, only to feel her pulse quicken as she listened. He proclaimed the power of prayer and faith to transform human frailty into strength. Mabel tightened against his message. It was God who had inflicted frailty on her and left her to eke out the days in regret and loss. She had no faith. Only her own willpower got her up each morning and pushed away the cravings.

It had been silly to think she could sit through the Mass as if she were watching a movie. She would not come to church again. Mabel stayed seated during the communion, head down, clutching her bag, waiting out the final minutes of the Mass.

The organ blared the closing hymn as the priest and altar boys made their way down the aisle. The last notes echoed in the cavernous space. Mabel stood and smoothed her skirt, trying to compose a neutral face before seeing Jack. She shuffled along the pew to the aisle, and he came from the other side, smiling, holding out his hand to her. Relief flooded Mabel. She didn't care what he believed or what he might suppose about her accepting his invitation. Her hand in his was a comfort.

Jack squeezed her fingers. "I'm glad you came."

She smiled and whispered, "I need coffee." He let go of her hand and motioned her to follow him. They made their way in silence down the stairways to the lowest level. Jack led her into a side hallway and into a room set for dining. His fellow seminarians and their guests were gathering around the long table in the center. Mabel had a sudden worry. Were Peggy and George invited? She hadn't called Peggy as she had promised, and her friend would have a million questions. Eyes darting at the faces, Mabel followed Jack to chairs at the far end of the table but didn't see them. She breathed out and managed to smile as Jack pulled a chair out for her.

Jack took the seat on her left. The man on her right stuck out his hand. "Hello, Mabel. I'm Daniel Bern, Jack's roommate. Everyone calls me Dan." Mabel took in his broad smile on a round face, green eyes, a stubbly beard, and a mostly bald head.

She shook his hand. "How do you know my name?"

"Jack talked about you coming this morning."

Mabel sat back, tilting her head towards Jack, who was listening. "Did he? What did he say?"

"That you are his good friend. And friends with his sister." Dan took a coffee carafe from the center of the table and hovered it over her cup. She nodded, and he poured. "And that you were his high school girlfriend." Mabel lifted her cup to her lips to cover her surprise.

Jack leaned in and pointed a finger at Dan. "Steady now, Dan. Enough said."

Dan was enjoying the moment. "Look at the red faces on both of you." He chuckled and turned to pour coffee for the matron on his other side.

Jack grimaced. "Don't pay attention to him." The coffee was settling Mabel's nerves, and she felt no need to protest the remarks. She had listened to plenty of men exaggerate in barrooms. If he let his fellows think she had been his girl, what was the harm?

Mabel placed her cup on the saucer and changed the subject. "I have a job." She told him a shortened story of the events in the theater, as they served themselves from the platters of sausages and scrambled eggs and toasted bread that came around. Jack listened, nodding, then raised his glass of orange juice to her. "Congratulations. That's great news."

She clinked his glass with hers. "You can stop shadowing me, Jack. I'm doing fine on my own." Their eyes met.

He set his glass on the table. "You know why I invited you here today?" Mabel shrugged. He sighed. "I *have* been worried about you, but that's not the reason." He waved a hand at the group around the table. "I am supposed to be the model seminarian. To my mother, her family, I am *Father*. I'm under the pressure of what everyone expects, every minute." He leaned closer to her ear. "I don't have many people from before … all this. I miss being with someone who knows me."

Mabel turned to him. "It's been a long time. And I … I'm different."

Jack nodded. "I know a lot has happened." He looked at her. "But with you, I'm still Jack. To me, you're still Mabel."

He wasn't like Al, who had loved Miss Front End, or Tom, who had pitied her as a drunk. Jack knew the girl he played softball with, who beat him at chess, and who shared cold cream for their sunburned faces. Mabel understood his longing for the simpler times their younger selves had known. Her heart swelled with gratitude for his assumption that, despite the wrong turns she had taken, they were still those friends.

Mabel smiled at him. "Thank you."

He shook a finger at her. "Peggy wants to hear from you."

Mabel nodded. "I should have called her. I will tomorrow."

"Call in the morning. George is marching with his union in the Labor Day parade. Peggy's staying home. The little one has a cold." He understood her keeping a distance from George.

After the dishes had been cleared, Jack and Mabel lingered over coffee and chatted with Dan. The serving girls fidgeted at the side, anxious to finish the cleaning up. Finally, the head girl rang a handbell, and the lingerers around the table stood to leave. Mabel excused herself and asked a server where to find the ladies' room. She made her way down a flight of stairs, wondering how much time Jack had before he must return to the seminary.

When she came up, Jack and Dan were waiting for her. Jack pointed to the exit. "Can you spend time walking with us for a bit?"

"I'd like that." On the sidewalk, both men offered Mabel an arm. She laughed and took both, walking between them. Dan explained that on Sundays, the seminarians were freed from the strict schedule of their studies. "We go to different churches and listen to the sermons. Pretty soon we'll be up there."

Jack kicked at a pebble. "You write a good sermon, and your booming voice will get everyone's attention. No matter what I write, when I see the faces looking at me, I doubt I'll say anything they care about."

Mabel flashed on a scene in the vaudeville show that got raucous laughs from the audience. Jokey one-liners poking fun at human nature made more sense to her than lecturing people about their frailty. But she gave Jack's arm a slight squeeze to show she understood his dilemma.

They strolled around a downtown park, blending in with the many others passing time in the afternoon sun. Jack kept her arm tucked in his. Dan chatted about his fascination with the city, entirely different from the small town in northern Michigan where he grew up. Mabel thought Jack was lucky to have Dan as a roommate.

The men walked Mabel to the boarding house before going to catch a bus returning to the seminary. Jack warned her about the huge crowd expected on the streets for the Labor Day parade. "I heard on the radio this year's parade will have more marchers than ever. Most taverns will be closed, but the drinking goes on. Best if you stay inside." Dan nodded his agreement. "You don't want to get caught among any rough characters."

Mabel took Jack's meaning. "Not to worry. I want no part of the parade."

Dan bid goodbye to Mabel and walked ahead to give Jack a moment alone with her. "Talk to Peggy. I know you don't want me hovering, but you need to keep in touch."

"I will. Thanks for today."

Jack hurried to catch up with Dan, looking back with a wave as they boarded the bus.

Mabel checked her wristwatch. Mrs. Marini was still serving Sunday dinner. At Luna, Mabel ate and counted the hours until going to work on Tuesday. Staying inside her room all the next day would drive her cockeyed. Her tension about doing ordinary things had eased during the afternoon with Jack and Dan. They were right about avoiding the parade, but where could she go?

She overheard the couple at the next table talking about meeting their friends for a picnic on Belle Isle. In her old life, Mabel loved spending time on that island in the river. She and Al had had their secluded spot for a blanket under the trees, hidden from hikers and canoers. Before Al, Mabel rowed boats in the canals and swam at the beach with Peggy and Jack. She remembered her hair blowing free of her ribbons while riding a tandem bike across the bridge with Ma's strong legs pumping fast in front of her.

She had hibernated in the farmhouse with her despair. Like a bear after a long winter, she was shaking off sleep. She *would* go to Belle Isle. An early start would get her away from Woodward Avenue ahead of the parade throngs.

The next morning, Mabel dressed in trousers and tied a scarf around her hair. Overnight, the weather had turned cooler, hinting at fall. Mabel pulled an old sweater from the farmhouse over her blouse. She buttoned her key into her trouser pocket with money for coffee and lunch. Her sandals were comfortable for walking, but when she stepped outside, the nippy morning air on her toes reminded her she must buy winter shoes and warmer clothes.

The bus left her on East Grand Boulevard near the promenade to the Belle Isle Bridge. Walking on the bridge over the Detroit River, Mabel took in the view of the city and realized she had forgotten to call Peggy. Jack would have told her he saw Mabel, and Peggy was probably waiting for the telephone to ring. There was no help for it now.

A stream of visitors to the island in cars, on foot, and on bicycles flowed along the bridge. Mabel quickened her pace and reached the gardens at Central Avenue. She walked further to the skating pavilion's refreshment stand and bought a coffee. She stood in the sun and watched the eddies in the river as she drank the brew. *Coming here was a good idea.* She decided to walk along the center road, then around the canal paths to the picnic grounds. Mabel bought two donuts to munch along the way.

The maples, oaks, and elms lining the roadway were still lush with summer leaves, and the lawns spiked with growth from the recent rain. The temperature was climbing, and soon Mabel stopped to take off the sweater and tie the sleeves around her waist. Couples, families, and people on their own ambled or rode bikes along the paths. She had forgotten how calming simply walking among the island's trees and gardens could be.

Her meandering took her to the baseball fields, and she climbed into the bleachers at one of the diamonds to watch a pick-up game. It didn't matter that she didn't know the players;

she quickly got into the excitement of the scoring by both sides as the innings progressed. Mabel was on her feet cheering with others on the benches when a walk-off homer won the tied game. She got a kick out of watching the winning players jump on each other with joyful cries of victory. A sense that something inside her had revived, or at least wasn't frozen, tugged at her. She brushed away the wetness around her eyes and collected the moment, hoping there would be more. The old geezer who had been sharing the bench with her said, "Missy, don't cry. It's not the World Series." Mabel waved him off with a smile and jumped down from the bleachers.

Her stomach growled for lunch. She bought a sandwich and a Coke at the field house refreshment stand, then walked along the river pathway looking for a picnic table in the shade. Groups with coolers and hampers had claimed the tables nearest the water. The grass looked inviting, and Mabel figured she could spread her sweater under a tree. She made her way past the busy tables and headed for a stand of maples.

Someone called her name. Mabel stopped and turned in the direction of the voice, thinking she had misheard. She tucked the Coke bottle under her arm to free her hand to shade her eyes. "Yoohoo, Mabel!" A woman with a dark bob stood at a table, waving her arm. Mabel froze. Was she from a tavern? She wanted to turn away, but the woman was walking toward her. She wore a peasant blouse embroidered with red and yellow smocking that hugged her shoulders, over a red cotton skirt and sandals. As the woman stepped closer, Mabel recognized Polly Williams, an actress from the show.

During one of the show's rehearsals, Mabel had gone backstage curious to see the skits. To stay out of the way, she had stepped into a fold in the curtain outside the lights and watched the scene in progress. A tap on her shoulder made her jump. Mabel had swirled around and faced a laughing Polly, decked out for the rodeo skit in an oversized cowboy hat that crushed her bob and a buckskin vest and skirt. Polly pointed the end of a rifle at Mabel. "Relax! It's a prop." She had poked Mabel with the barrel before she trotted to the wing for her musical cue. Belting out a comic song, she made the crew crack up. Mabel couldn't take her eyes off Polly in the spotlight, embodying the shoot-'em-up cowgirl of the lyrics. When she ran offstage at the end of her number, she had pulled off the hat and waved it at Mabel.

"You remember me?" Mabel asked. "How do you know my name?"

Polly chuckled. "I asked Michael about the new ticket girl. I heard you were there when Mrs. Butler bought it." Mabel blinked at the reference. "Sorry, forget I said that. You're alone?"

Mabel clutched the sandwich. "I'm going to eat my lunch under those trees."

"Come sit with us." Polly took her by the arm and propelled Mabel across the grass to a picnic table. A woman with hair as dark as Polly's and a little girl sat side-by-side on the bench. "Mabel, this is my sister, Madge."

Madge smiled. "Hello, Mabel, happy to meet you."

"And this is my daughter, Betsy, three years old today." Mabel stared at the child. Betsy's blond hair curled around her neck and ears. Her green eyes matched her mother's. She wore a red and white striped romper with a fabric bear sewn onto the bib. The strap on one side had fallen off her shoulder. Betsy flipped onto her tummy on the bench and dangled her legs until she dropped on the grass, then looped both her arms around Polly's leg.

Polly gestured at the table. "C'mon, sit with us. We have a birthday cake." Polly scooped the girl up and carried wiggling Betsy to the other side of the table. She kissed Betsy's cheek and set her down on the grass, then swung her legs over the bench.

Mabel froze. It should have been she and Al picnicking with *their* three-year-old. Her hand tightened around the Coke bottle. She wanted to smash it against the table until it shattered.

A sharp pain shot up her leg. Mabel yelped and dropped the bottle.

Polly jumped up. Betsy's teeth were clamped on Mabel's shin. She had crawled under the table and crouched at Mabel's foot. Polly fell to her knees next to Betsy and pinched the girl's cheek. Betsy's jaw opened with a wail. Mabel dropped to the grass on her rear and grabbed her leg.

Polly looped her arms around the squirming Betsy, shaking her head at the reddening marks of little teeth. "Oh, God, I am so sorry! Madge, get ice from the cooler pail."

Mabel lay propped on her elbows as Madge slapped an ice cube against her leg. The cold trickle stung the chafed skin, and she flinched. Polly stood Betsy up to face Mabel. "Don't bite! Bad! Say sorry to Mabel."

Betsy stuck her thumb in her mouth and eyed Mabel. She crouched down on her knees to see the mark. She reached out a pudgy hand and patted Mabel's leg. "Sorry. I kiss it." The baby-soft lips touched her skin.

"No!" Mabel scooted backward, her foot kicking up, missing Betsy by inches. She tried to get to her feet, but her sandals got no traction on the grass. Mabel rolled onto her side, sobbing and pounding the earth with her fists.

CHAPTER 7

Mabel lay on the grass, longing for the ground to open and suck her in. When she was young, her brothers would step up their torment if she cried, and she had hardened against shedding tears. After the miscarriage, Peggy said she needed "a good cry." Mabel had stayed drunk to keep the tears back. That defense gone, she had tumbled off the cliff of grief when the little girl kissed the sore spot on her leg.

Her sobs had waned to sniffles. The earth wouldn't swallow her; she had to run away. She swiped at the snot under her nose and turned onto her back. Her legs bumped Polly, sitting cross-legged next to her. Mabel's puffy face flushed hot with embarrassment.

Polly patted her arm. "Here, take this." She held a dish towel. "I dunked it in the ice. For your face." Mabel avoided Polly's eyes but took the cloth. She shivered at the cold as she pressed it to her face. When she lowered the towel and looked around, Polly followed her gaze. "Madge took Betsy for a ride in her wagon."

Mabel breathed in and blew it out, then shifted her legs and pushed up onto her knees. She handed the towel back to Polly. "I'll be going now."

Polly took the wet cloth and put her other hand on Mabel's arm. Mabel pulled away from Polly and braced against the bench to stand. Polly uncrossed her legs and raised up in one motion, coming eye to eye with Mabel. "Madge cares for Betsy while I'm on the road. She sees me only a few times a year when my show plays in Detroit. I made it for her birthday this time." Polly sighed. "I can't fault Madge for the biting, for anything." She shrugged. "I'm not the ideal mother."

Mabel busied herself with brushing the grass and dirt from her trousers, aware of Polly's gaze. "I'm not one to judge." She untied the sweater twisted around her waist. The scarf had tangled in her hair, and she pulled it off. "I have to go."

Before Mabel could pull back, Polly began smoothing her hair. When she had gathered the strands in a bundle, she took the scarf from Mabel, looped it around and tied it in place. "There, that's better. I *am* sorry. Can we be friends?"

Mabel blinked away fresh tears rising. "I don't really have friends." She hadn't meant to say that. Polly had been kind, and Mabel didn't want to offend her. She marveled at Polly's presence on the stage, the magical way she jumped from character to character. They would cross paths at the theater. She didn't want trouble at work.

Polly put her hands in the pockets of her skirt. "I don't either, except for my sister. On the road, it's a lonely life." She toed the grass with her sandal. "Something tells me you know what that's like." Polly persisted. "Whatever you've been through, I'm sorry you've been hurt."

Mabel's throat tightened, and she shuddered against breaking down again. "I lost my baby. Three years ago." What had she done, blurting her deepest secret to a stranger?

Polly grabbed Mabel around the shoulders and clung to her in a tight embrace. "Oh, my god. Oh, oh, I am so sorry."

Mabel stiffened and pulled back. "Please don't tell anyone at the theater." She couldn't bear Mr. Macready to know.

Polly tried to lighten the moment with a salute. "You have my word."

Mabel grimaced. "I must go."

Polly dropped her arms and nodded. "I'll see you tomorrow."

Mabel grabbed her sweater and strode through the maze of tables, not looking back, winding toward Central Avenue. The breeze had cooled, and she tied the sweater around her shoulders. She marched across the bridge to the bus stop and waited, hugging her arms to her chest. When the bus pulled to the curb, Mabel fished coins from her pocket for the fare and curled into a window seat in the back, her stomach growling over missing lunch.

Before the bus reached Woodward Avenue, the driver detoured to avoid the mass of parade-goers. Mabel got off at the stop she figured was closest to the boarding house. Parade vendors were still on the corners, and she bought a pasty from a man from Copper Country making his grandma's recipe. Sitting on the steps of a school, she bit into one end of the warm meat pie, the way Ma had taught her, so the juice wouldn't leak. She used to help Ma with mixing the flour, water, salt, and lard, and stuffing the dough pockets with her mixture of meat, potatoes, onions, rutabagas, and carrots. Mabel licked the pastry flaking on her fingers after she gobbled the last bite. It was as good as Ma's.

The cool air again whispered of fall. Mabel hugged her knees and lingered on the steps. The parade over, a steady stream of weary folks strolled by. She wondered if they looked forward to work tomorrow as much as she did. Mabel had a place at the theater, if she could hold herself together. At the factory she had groaned with the other women punching their timecards at the start of the week. Now, the theater was her oasis. Mr. Macready had given her a chance, and she owed him her best effort. Jimmy had oodles of ambition and had pulled her into the wake of his determination to push the Lafayette ahead of the Cass. He didn't care that she had been a barmaid. Even Polly, whom she had foolishly told her secret, had asked to be her friend.

The pasty vendor packed up and tipped his hat to Mabel. She straightened up to make her way to the boarding house before dark. That night, Mabel dreamed she was standing in a room looking through a window at a stormy sea. The walls of the small space were sky blue, and there were no doors, nothing inside. The angry water churned and hit against the window, but there was no sound. In the morning, as she washed up in the bath, Mabel remembered an old woman from the diner who would read tea leaves. Ma pooh-poohed the practice, but would hand her cup over and listen. Mabel had been fascinated with the messages the woman saw in clumps of soggy tea. Now, she saw her fear of the raging sea breaking through. Worry tugged at her during the bus ride to the theater. Polly swore not to tell Mabel's secret, but could Polly be trusted?

Jimmy was already working the telephone calls when Mabel entered the ticket office. He flapped a hand at her, and from his side of the conversation, she understood he was closing a sale.

Cora and Bridget arrived, and after the call, Jimmy talked with the three of them about the tasks for the day. They got to work. The telephones rang often enough throughout the morning that Mabel had only short breaks to run to the ladies' lounge.

Cora's smart wool plaid jacket on the coatrack reminded Mabel she must shop for warm clothes. She considered the amount of money in her purse and her first paycheck coming at the end of the week and decided to use the lunch hour to buy shoes. Cora and Bridget had bag lunches and could take telephone messages. Jimmy had gone upstairs to use Mr. Macready's office while he was out somewhere. Mabel told the typists she'd be back in an hour and left the office.

The city hummed with traffic and workers spilling out of the buildings in search of food. She strode at a brisk pace toward the shops on Woodward Avenue and realized the city's din no longer crashed inside her head or brought up heaves. At the shoe store window, she perused the styles and prices. A short time later, she left the store carrying a shopping bag with two pairs of the newest pumps, one with a higher heel, and a pair of rain boots. She checked the clock outside Kern's; time enough to pick up a deli sandwich before heading back to the theater. With the wrapped sandwich tucked in the bag atop her shoeboxes, Mabel rounded back toward Lafayette Boulevard.

Ahead of her in the throng of walkers, she thought she saw Mr. Macready's curly hair bobbing along. The changing traffic light stopped her and a cluster of people on the corner, and she moved to the side for a better view. It *was* him, and he had a woman on his arm. Polly. Mabel pressed into a doorway and watched them. He smiled as Polly talked in her animated way, grasping his arm. When the light changed, he steered her across the street. Mabel trotted into the crowd behind them, hurrying to make it across. On the opposite corner, Mabel hung back, keeping the couple in her sight until they turned under an awning. Mabel ducked into the crowd and passed the entrance with her head down. They had gone into a hotel. She hurried to the theater.

Why would Polly and Mr. Macready go into a hotel together? Mabel had observed her backstage talking with Mr. Macready several times, but it was his job to make sure the actors were satisfied with the house arrangements. Could he be interested in Polly in a personal way? Did he know she had a child? Mabel shook her head. It was none of her business. But she couldn't stop thinking about them during the afternoon. She handled the messages Cora had taken and went over the evening's available seats with Jimmy. They didn't expect many walk-ins on a Tuesday night, especially with people getting back into their post-summer routines of work and school. He closed the second balcony and upgraded the few tickets already sold there to the first balcony. Mr. Macready didn't come into the office, and she avoided asking Jimmy about him.

When Jimmy went upstairs, the girls wanted to see her new shoes. Their approving smiles satisfied Mabel that she had purchased the right styles. Then urgency took her to the ladies' lounge. While she was washing her hands, she heard someone come in.

Polly poked her head around the wall. "Cora said you were here."

Mabel dried her hands, not comfortable meeting Polly's eyes. "Here I am."

"Can we sit for a minute?" Polly moved toward a settee.

Mabel made a show of looking at her watch. "I have to get back to the office."

Polly nodded. "And I'm due in the makeup chair. But I want to tell you something." Mabel leaned against the vanity and folded her arms. Polly took a deep breath. "You told me something private yesterday that you want me to keep secret. But you aren't sure you can trust me." Mabel raised her brows, and Polly held out her hands. "You didn't say that, but that's what you're thinking. *I'm* going to tell *you* something private, to show you *can* trust me."

Mabel dropped her arms. "Please don't. It's not that I …" What she wanted to say was, don't give me something of yours to carry on top of my own.

"Michael Macready is Betsy's father."

Mabel stared at Polly. She had seen them go into the hotel together, but the declaration shocked her. What did Polly expect her to say?

Polly held out her hands. "Say something."

Mabel found her voice. "Does Mr. Macready know you're telling me about Betsy?"

"No." Polly bit her lip. "That's the thing. He doesn't *know* he is her father."

"*He* doesn't know, but you told *me*?" Mabel glared at Polly. "I *work for* Mr. Macready."

Polly looked away. "I didn't think about that."

Mabel tapped her foot. "No? You've put me in a terrible spot."

"I mean to tell him. Soon."

"Leave me out of this!" Mabel turned on her heel, yanked the door open, and rushed from the lounge. Damn Polly and her "trust." The last thing Mabel needed was to be caught in a tangle between Polly and Mr. Macready. Was it even true? He *had* looked happy with Polly. But the child was three years old. What was Polly up to? Mabel's instinct was to protect Mr. Macready. But there was nothing she could do except keep quiet and avoid Polly. She would not go backstage. The vaudeville revue closed on Saturday night. On Sunday morning, Polly would be gone.

Mr. Macready was in the ticket office when Mabel came back. He looked up from the papers he was studying and greeted her with a hand wave. Trying to keep a calm face, Mabel waved back and slid onto her chair, relieved to give attention to Cora asking her a question.

Then Mr. Macready made an announcement. "The cast will have a closing party backstage on Saturday before they leave on a night train. All of you are welcome at the party if you want to stay late."

Cora and Bridget giggled their excitement. Jimmy said he would ask his fiancée to accompany him. Mabel managed to thank Mr. Macready for the invitation, though she had no intention of attending the party. Out of the corner of her eye, she watched him talking with Jimmy about the sales for the remainder of the week, wondering what Polly would do next.

The week's shows dragged on. Every night, they kept a window open for latecomers, but sold few tickets. On Saturday, the last night of the run, Jimmy let Cora and Bridget watch the entire show from the balcony. Jimmy had assigned the week's treasury book over to Mabel. She sat with him to review her work, and with a few corrections, he signed off on the ledger. Mabel put the ledger away and began tidying her desk. She intended to leave before the cast party began.

"You're getting the hang of it. It wasn't the best run, but it wasn't a great show." He leaned in and lowered his voice. "If things work out the way I plan, we're getting a very big show." Mabel raised her brows, playing to Jimmy's tendency to boast. He sat back and folded his arms, enjoying her look of surprise.

"What are you up to?"

"Booking is a long game. The show I'm after will come in a year from now. We've got second-tier road shows in the meantime." He slapped his hands on the desk. "You'll be in charge of the treasury and take over the sales I've been working on."

"What do you mean?"

"I'm going to New York. Make myself known among the Broadway men to get in the running for the biggest shows." Jimmy straightened his tie and nodded his head toward the lobby. "I hear the curtain call. The cast party will be starting."

"You're leaving? I've worked here for only two weeks!" Mabel pressed her hand on her knee to calm her shaking leg.

"Seems like you've been here longer." Jimmy stood and put on his jacket.

Mabel squirmed in her seat. This was crazy. Could Mr. Macready have agreed to this? She was about to ask when he burst through the door from the inside corridor.

"Close up and come backstage. I'd like the two of you to be witnesses. Polly and I are getting married."

Jimmy jumped over to shake Mr. Macready's hand. Mabel clutched the edge of her desk. "You and Polly, marrying? Now?"

Mr. Macready glanced at her on his way out the door. "She wants all of us to dress in costumes from the wardrobe room. I'll see you back there." He disappeared in the hallway.

Mabel held her hands out to Jimmy for an explanation. "What is going on?"

"You heard the man. This is a Polly performance. Let's go." He waited for her by the door.

Mabel sighed. "I meant to duck out."

Jimmy chuckled. "You don't want to miss this. I guarantee you the cast and crew are giggling over this impromptu wedding. Those two have been an item for years."

Cora and Bridget were already in the wardrobe room, rifling through the cowgirl garb. Mabel stood in the corner, uninterested in costumes. Esther swept in, and she and Jimmy went for the grandest of the king and queen robes. Cora urged Mabel to try on a hoop skirt. "You have to dress up!" They heard the director call for everyone to assemble on the stage. Mabel grabbed a velvet cape from a rack and threw it around her shoulders. Cora rolled her eyes.

A parson stood with Mr. Macready among the cast and crew members. Mabel stayed back from the spotlight. Polly startled her from behind. "You look too plain for my wedding." She planted a fruited headpiece atop Mabel's head. Mabel grabbed at it, and Polly took her hand down. "Let it be, Mabel."

"What are you doing, Polly?"

"Shhh. I have your secret." Polly skipped away to center stage and took Mr. Macready's hand for the ceremony.

The crew cheered when he kissed the bride. It occurred to Mabel that Mr. Macready might have known about Betsy all along. He was marrying the mother of his child, but did he expect them to be a family? Tilda came next to Mabel and provided the opinion of the backstage crew. "If the boss thinks she's ever settlin' down with him, he's got another think coming."

He was the kind of guy who would take on his obligation to provide for Betsy regardless of Polly's career. That may have been what Polly was after when the couple had gone into the hotel.

Mabel watched Polly kissing Mr. Macready in a close embrace before the cast hurried away to Michigan Central Station. After, he nursed a bottle of champagne. When the party broke up, he went upstairs to his office with another bottle.

CHAPTER 8

March 1947

The wedding photograph of Polly and Mr. Macready hung in a gilded frame on the wall in the ticket office amidst others from bygone productions. The bride, beaming in a feathery gown and tiara, and the groom, in top hat and tails, stood arm-in-arm center stage, surrounded by Polly's fellow vaudevillians, the backstage crew, and the staff from the ticket office.

Polly had not returned to Detroit in the six months since. The typists delighted in reading aloud the snippets in *Variety* about Polly landing roles in different productions and where she was performing. Jimmy, telephoning weekly from New York, had seen Polly several times, but swore to Mabel he had no conversation about her with Michael.

Mabel worried that Mr. Macready was unhappy. With Jimmy gone, he had more of the business to shoulder, but she sensed his downcast manner was personal. His demeanor had become solemn. Gone were the light-hearted moments he used to add to their days in the ticket office. He stayed upstairs most of the time and took his lunch alone. Tilda whispered the crew's grumblings about his lack of attention backstage. When Mabel reviewed the treasury reports with him, he stared at the pages, flicked his pen across items needing correction, and dismissed her. He never mentioned Polly or Betsy, and she would not ask. She stayed alert to his mood and did her best to stay on top of details so she needn't bother him.

Jimmy's going to New York had also put a different, heavier burden on Mabel. Two more typists from the Kelly service joined the office. Mabel trusted Cora to portion out the work she tasked them with, but she had to supervise and correct mistakes. The crew placed a larger desk for Mabel in the farthest back corner of the office, where she could talk on the telephone away from the clacking of the typewriter keys. She had forged her way through selling blocks of tickets to the regular business customers, except for the automobile dealers. Their receptionists confided to Mabel that those men preferred dealing with Jimmy. Mr. Macready had gone after some of them, and Jimmy made long-distance calls to the holdouts.

Mr. Macready surprised Mabel with a pay raise. With that, and the money remaining from Al, she set out to find an apartment. Mabel longed for the tucked-away privacy she'd had at the farmhouse. She hoped her budget would allow for living near the theater district, but she wasn't familiar with the nearby neighborhoods. Mabel was looking over the city street map tacked on the pantry wall when Tilda waddled in. "You're not lost since you're standing here."

Mabel had gotten used to the cleaner's way of starting a conversation. "I'm looking to rent an apartment somewhere around here."

Tilda exclaimed, "I've got the place for you!"

That afternoon, Mabel took a short bus ride along Michigan Avenue and rang the bell at Tilda's sister's two-story home in Corktown. She and her husband were going back to Ireland for a year to care for his aged parents. "Can't leave the house to sit, letting the pipes freeze, or worse. Tilda says you're a steady girl, not one of those flighty actresses. Wipe your feet." In the entry hallway, a polished wooden staircase led up, but the sister opened an oak-paneled door at the side. "The downstairs for you." She busied herself sweeping the hall while Mabel viewed the apartment.

Mabel knew she would live there the moment she stepped inside. A davenport, an armchair, and a bookcase furnished the modest living room. A large window faced the trees running alongside the house. On the right was the bedroom, its curtained window looking onto the front porch, with a double-size iron bedstead and a dresser placed on a rag rug. Down the hall on the left, past the tiny bathroom, was the kitchen with a window over the sink looking at the neighbor's lilac bushes. A table with two chairs sat atop shiny linoleum. A rear door opened into the backyard, where the owners kept a vegetable garden. Muffled street noise from the avenue and a train whistle played in the background. With agreement on the modest rent, she and Tilda's sister, Aileen, shook hands.

She moved in the following Sunday. Aileen had stocked the kitchen with a set of dishes, utensils, and basic cooking pans, and left laundered sheets and towels in the closet with an iron and a pressing board. Mabel bought an alarm clock, a table radio, and coffee for the percolator.

As she came in each evening, she turned on the radio and fell asleep to it. She willed herself out of bed each day when the alarm rang and went to the office where she was happily swamped with the relentless activity of the routine.

Mabel had found the cocoon she needed, but drinking Mabel's urges popped up without warning. One Sunday at Luna, Mrs. Marini's son poured red wine for a diner at the next table, and a forceful urge to grab the glass and gulp it rushed through her. Another night, going for the bus after closing, the impulse to sit at the bar in the tavern she had refused to enter with Jimmy drew her to stop at the entrance for a long moment before she made her feet move and walked away.

Those scares caused Mabel to double-down on her work, hoping more effort would distract her, like pasting wallpaper over a bumpy surface. Cora and the typists did their jobs seriously, but they lightened the mood of the group with friendly chatter during lunchtime. Mabel didn't join in their talk about dates, outings, and clothes. They didn't pry into her private life, though she sensed they were curious. When Cora suggested it would be fun to celebrate each other's birthdays, the girls jumped on the idea with glee. Mabel signed their cards and chipped in for the cakes, but she hedged on revealing her birth date. Cora tried to wheedle it from her, and Mabel was embarrassed by the snappy end she put to Cora's pushing, but she didn't apologize.

She clamped a mask over her shaky resolve and jittered her way through the theater Christmas party, letting others believe she had spiked her Vernor's with vodka, fighting the yen to take the bottle. On New Year's Eve, lying in the dark, dance music on the radio, her mind replaying nights with Al, Mabel half-wished she had bought whiskey to blank her brain.

The sleet coating the city, icing over the apartment windows, kept her huddled inside.

She pulled herself together to hunt the after-Christmas sales, needing a warmer coat and aware she could do better with her wardrobe. Compared to the smart outfits the typists wore, her presence as the boss was lackluster. One trip to Hudson's had overwhelmed her with the choices.

Mabel confided her confusion to Greta. After running into each other at the sandwich shop near the theaters, they had been meeting there on Mondays for quick bites. "I don't know where to start or what looks good on me."

Greta scoffed. "*Everything* will look good on *you*." She pulled the day's paper from her coat pocket. "Look at this Winkelman's ad. Why not try their personal shopper? I happen to know Miss Barnes uses one."

Mabel telephoned the downtown Winkelman's for an appointment.

At the store, mannequins beckoned, clad in the styles pictured in the newspaper. A smiling saleswoman wearing a tailored suit greeted her. "How may I help you?"

"I have an appointment with Mrs. Miller." The woman nodded and led Mabel through the maze of racks to a settee. "Please have a seat. I will let Mrs. Miller know you're here." Mabel perched on the cushion and looked around. Miss Front End would have been excited, not nervous. *Be bold.*

"Miss Hunt, hello." Petite Mrs. Miller wore a plaid wool suit matching one from the window display. She rolled a frame with various dresses swinging from the bar and positioned it in Mabel's view. "Since we talked on the telephone, I've selected garments for a theater office. Modest necklines, dresses, separates, one or two suits." The saleswoman's eyes lit up. "With your proportions, any of these will look lovely, but one in particular …" She lifted a hanger from the rack and swept the fabric of a dress over her arm. "This is the color Vogue calls 'steel gray.' Would you like to try this on?"

A fitted bodice with seven pearl buttons, a demure rounded collar, and three-quarter length sleeves, over a swirling skirt. Mabel fingered the soft wool and nodded her agreement. In the dressing room, Mrs. Miller zipped her into the dress. Turning front and back before the triple mirror, she ran her hands down her hips. She wished Al's last look at her had been this beautiful.

Mrs. Miller caught her eye. "Stunning. If this pleases you, I'll bring in the other pieces I suggest for your wardrobe." Mrs. Miller offered the judgment Mabel needed in a comfortable manner. She left the store with the gray dress and a layaway receipt for several more dresses, skirts, and blouses. The next week she made her payment and brought the new clothes home. Slipping into the outfits and posing in front of her bedroom vanity mirror made her smile. But it was the admiring compliments from Cora and Bridget when she walked into the office that voted in her confidence.

On the next opening night, the gray dress drew an appreciative nod from Mr. Macready, and Mabel blushed at his approval.

She had had lunch with Peggy that day. Mabel had put off meeting her during the holidays, unable to cope with the merriment in the downtown restaurants or Peggy's nosy questions. Weeks passed, and Peggy had taken to calling the theater. "This is the only way I can check on you, since you never call me."

When Mabel at last agreed to the lunch date, Peggy booked a table in one of Hudson's dining rooms. Mabel finished a full

Maurice salad while Peggy chattered about George, the baby, and her longing for a new house. Peggy was nagging George to move to Fordson. She claimed it was for space and air, but Mabel suspected Fordson's restricted zoning appealed to her.

Over the coffee, Peggy focused on Mabel. She was pleased Mabel had her own place but dubious about the location. "Are you safe there? Who are the neighbors?"

Mabel scoffed. "Don't be a snob. It's perfectly fine and close to the theater."

Peggy rolled her eyes. "If you say so." She stirred cream into her coffee. "It seems like the job agrees with you."

Mabel smiled. "It does."

Peggy waited for Mabel to say more. After a moment, Peggy cleared her throat and touched her napkin to her lips. "Jack's ordination date is set."

Mabel swallowed coffee and set her cup on the saucer. "He's ready? When?"

Peggy nodded. "They say he's ready. The last Sunday in April." She tapped the table. "You'll be there, won't you?"

Mabel moved her fork around her dessert. "That's next month. Where will it take place?"

"In the cathedral, of course." She took an engraved white card from her purse and slid it across to Mabel. "My mother had these printed. She's inviting the immediate world."

"Including me?"

"Jack is including you. I promised I would give this to you." Peggy sat back and folded her hands in her lap, watching Mabel.

Mabel fingered the invitation. "He's made it to ordination." She thought back to the day months ago she had spent with Jack and Dan. He had confided that he felt he could be himself with her, and she had grabbed at the comfort of his company at her low point. But she hadn't responded to his Christmas card, still sitting on her dresser. At Luna, Mrs. Marini would mention she'd talked with Father Jack at the seminary, and Mabel guessed she did the same to him about seeing her. He had his studies to finish, and she worked six days a week. They had both been busy. Still, had she hurt his feelings? It pained her to realize she must have. She would write to him.

Peggy leaned in. "Don't tell me you're not coming."

Mabel looked Peggy in the eye. "Why would you say that?" She cringed at Peggy's assumption, though her past behavior had given Peggy reason for it. "Where will Jack go after?"

Peggy shrugged. "I don't know. He expects he'll be somewhere in the city. Most parishes are growing." She reapplied her lipstick. "I'm going to shop today for the ordination. George cannot argue about this occasion requiring a new dress." George had put the brakes on Peggy's tendency to overspend. "You should wear the dress you have on. Give the seminarians a last look at the feminine figure." Mabel rolled her eyes, but secretly enjoyed Peggy's approval. Leaving Hudson's, she hugged Peggy goodbye with a promise to be at the Cathedral.

That evening, Mabel started a letter to Jack three times and threw the pages into the trash. They were old friends. Why was it so hard to apologize for her silence and congratulate him on the ordination? Peggy would report to him that she had given Mabel the invitation. A simple note was called for. But when Mabel wrote *Dear Jack*, she felt the loss of the boy who had taken her to the prom, the cocky baseball player, and the sturdy man who clasped her arm to his. She scolded herself for her selfishness when he had been kind to invite her. Mabel wrote belated New Year's greetings, thanked him for the invitation, said she would see him after the service, and signed her name. In the morning, on her way to the theater, Mabel left the envelope for the postman in the box on the porch.

Jack remained in the back of her mind as the days ticked forward to the ordination. She hoped her note had smoothed things over. Jack had not wavered in his friendship, and she wanted to live up to his faith in her. She would get a moment with him after the ceremony to assure him she had not meant to be distant.

She decided to unravel whatever Peggy's family might think of her by making a striking impression at the ordination. She called Mrs. Miller about a proper hat and shoes to wear with the gray dress. In Winkelman's, Mabel pranced across the dressing area in ankle-strap pumps, surprised and pleased with how they flattered her legs. Mrs. Miller didn't know of Mabel's aversion to fussy hats but chose "a sedate style given the nature of the occasion." She slid a brimless, off-white oval woven with delicate flowers onto Mabel's hair. Perfect. Mabel anticipated the startled look on George's face, and Peggy's husband could be counted on to report to Al.

With Easter approaching, the spring theater season went into full swing. The Lafayette was prospering due in some part to the Cass having the bigger show. The advertising for *Carousel* created a clamor for tickets beyond the weekly number of seats the Cass could offer. Jimmy and Mr. Macready had booked a series of plays, both comedies and dramas. A different show every two weeks created the buzz of something new opening. Patrons unwilling to accept a date a month or more away at the Cass found tickets down the block at the Lafayette. The subscribers had responded heartily to the schedule, and the office hummed with sales activity. Because of the Easter holiday, the theater would go dark after Thursday evening's show until Tuesday.

The typists received a thank you for their hard work on Thursday afternoon when Mr. Macready had Easter flowers delivered for each of the girls. He hadn't come down to the ticket office all day. Mabel collected his mail and went upstairs. She tapped on the open door. Mr. Macready was standing by the window, gazing into the distance. When he turned to her, she saw the worry lines creasing his forehead.

She held out the bundle of envelopes. "Your mail. The flowers were a big hit with the girls."

He motioned her to a chair at the table and pulled one out for himself. She placed the mail on the corner, away from the clutter of newspapers and dirty coffee cups, making a mental note to ask Tilda to tidy his office. The cleaner couldn't help his less-than-crisp appearance. Wrinkled white shirt with dingy cuffs, no jacket, and his tie pulled away from his collar. He was clean-shaven, but razor nicks marked his chin. The dark patches under his eyes had been obvious for days. Mabel hoped he would skip greeting patrons before the show that evening, looking as he did.

Mr. Macready gave her a weak smile. "I'm pleased they liked the flowers. You've come up at the right time. Jimmy's on the way."

"He's in town?"

"For Passover. His parents are strict about the family observance."

Mabel hid her vagueness about the Jewish faith. She knew of Passover, but not when it occurred or how it was observed.

Ma had told her Jews and Catholics didn't like each other, but that hadn't been true in her dealings with Jimmy. Theater people shrugged off different ways, as they had accepted her being divorced.

Stomping up the stairs, Jimmy burst into view, red-faced and glowering. "Michael, I must use your telephone. Our deal is at the finish line, and I *should* be in *Manhattan*." He plopped into the chair behind Mr. Macready's desk, dialed for a long-distance operator, and barked a telephone number.

Mabel and Mr. Macready exchanged a glance. Mabel rose to leave, but Mr. Macready shook his head. "Stay, please. When Jimmy's finished, we have something to discuss with you."

The receiver slammed into the cradle. "Gone for the day. Too much time wasted on that train. I'm flying back. Don't care what it costs." Jimmy threw his hat on the desk and came to pull out an empty chair at the end of the table. He caught Mabel's eye. "Nice to see you, Mabel. Have the girls missed me?"

"Hello, Jimmy. They haven't mentioned it."

He picked up her tease. "You got me." He looked at Mr. Macready. "Have you told Mabel what we're thinking?"

"Why don't you explain?"

Jimmy leaned his arms on the table, fiddled with a pen lying there. "Here's the thing, Mabel. We're leasing a Broadway theater. I've convinced my father to play in the big game. This is the first step. We'll also open an office in Manhattan."

Mabel sat back. Another theater and a New York office. Jimmy's ambition was coming true. She looked at Mr. Macready's approving expression and understood what they intended. He was leaving the Lafayette to return to New York and run the operation. Her leg jiggled under the table. He had given her his confidence, and now he needed her support, no matter the disruption his leaving would cause her.

Mabel pulled up straight and folded her hands on the table. "Mr. Macready, I'm happy for you."

"What do you mean?"

"Going back to New York."

"I'm not going back to New York." He exchanged a glance with Jimmy. "What Jimmy's getting at is we want *you* to open the New York office."

Mabel gasped. Her nails dug into her clenched hands. She shook her head. "I … this is …" She sat back and tried to organize her thoughts.

Mr. Macready looked at Jimmy. "This is a lot for Mabel to take in. Can you get her a glass of water?" Jimmy looked around for the pitcher and saw it empty alongside the dirty glassware. He rose from his seat. "I'll be right back."

Mr. Macready lowered his voice. "Mabel, Jimmy is hitting his stride, better than I expected. He asked for you."

She breathed deeper to curb the flutter in her chest. "Why?"

Jimmy came back and set a glass in front of Mabel. She took a gulp. He leaned against the windowsill, hands in his pockets. "The New York scene is tough. You come from here, and I trust you."

A vision of Fay Wray in the grip of King Kong atop the Empire State Building flashed through Mabel's mind. Her hand trembled around the glass. "I can barely type."

"Plenty of typists in New York. You're gonna be my right arm."

"What does that mean? And what about this office?" She looked at Mr. Macready.

"If you go with Jimmy, I can get Greta to come over here."

Mabel knew Greta chafed under Miss Barnes and *would* leave the Cass for a good offer at the Lafayette. "I don't know." Mabel sipped more water through her dry lips.

Jimmy came back to his chair. "Let us tell you more. Then you decide."

CHAPTER 9

The sun flicked away the last of the early Saturday morning shadows. Mabel hid in a doorway across the street from the diner, watching through the window as Ma loaded pies into the tiered display case. Boxed pies for the Easter orders were piled on the counter. As a girl, it was Mabel's task to fold the boxes for the pie assembly line. Ma placed a pie in a box and scribbled the flavor on the flap. Mabel and the counter girl tucked them closed and tied the twine. When they finished, Ma would wrap warm towels around Mabel's fingers to soothe the chafing from tying box after box.

She had come to ask Ma's advice about going to New York. Jimmy had flooded her with his plans. He was moving quickly to take advantage of older theaters sitting empty. Leasing one of those scruffy playhouses in the heart of the theater district offered a toehold while he grew the operation. She would work in the office he had rented on Broadway, on the fourteenth floor overlooking Times Square. "Center of the universe," Jimmy chortled.

The offer tempted her. In New York, she could invent a wiped-clean version of her past, become Mabel who had never been married, carried no grief for a lost baby, wasn't a drunk. She could bid goodbye to Miss Front End.

But did she have to leave Detroit to be different? Her job had steadied her, and she had kept her embarrassing past hidden. Mr. Macready had shrugged off her divorce and she had worked hard to live up to his faith in her. Jimmy planned for the business to grow with multiple theaters in New York and Detroit. At some point, Mr. Macready would move on, either to a bigger theater or for Polly. Mabel could work her way to becoming the "Miss Barnes" of the Lafayette.

She wanted Ma's take on the choice. Having eyes on Ma soothed Mabel's heart. Staying away had been hard. Peggy had likely passed the news about Mabel's job to Ma. She longed to hear Ma say, "Girly, I'm proud of ya."

The first time Al had driven her to see his tavern, Mabel was thrilled at the coincidence—Al's place was on the same block as Ma's diner. Those days she spent drinking there, Mabel had snuck in and out from the back alley to avoid Ma catching her, knowing there was no explanation Ma would believe.

Mabel's father (who Ma called "your sonofabitch so-called father") and Ma's husband ("my deadbeat old man") had been day laborers together. He never had a steady job and always talked about going back Up North. Ma's pies made their living. Pie money had bought the diner with the baking kitchen and the apartment above.

Eight-year-old Mabel's mother had passed, and on days when all of her brothers were working, her father kept her back from school and brought her along to sit in the truck. One morning, Ma discovered Mabel in the cab and learned what had been going on. Ma cussed out her father and commanded Mabel to get inside the diner. Mabel had spent many happy hours sitting at the counter eating grilled cheese sandwiches and pie.

Ma, clad in faded housedresses and men's slippers, stockings rolled to her ankles, commanded her kitchen like a drill sergeant. Her short hair slicked with pomade, and arms muscled from kneading dough. Ma's tough-as-nails, no-nonsense manner had compelled young Mabel to fall into line. Mabel was careful not to let Ma see the bruises her brothers put on her. She half-feared Ma would come to her house and kill them, and she half-wished for that. She had grown taller than Ma but being on the wrong side of her strong will still scared her.

After the dry-out in the cabin, Tom had delivered Mabel to Ma. When Mabel shuffled into the diner, Ma threw her arms around Mabel. Then she shooed her upstairs. "Get yourself into the bathroom for a wash." During a long soak, Mabel rehearsed her apologies. When she came out, Tom was gone, and Ma wouldn't hear it. "It don't matter now, girly. This is a fresh start. Don't look back."

Ma concocted the plan to ask Al for money. He was doing well as her pie salesman, and he didn't refuse her asking him to meet Mabel at the diner. Al's handsomeness gave Mabel shivers when she peeked from the kitchen as he entered. But he had treated her as if it were a business transaction, and she had had no choice but to accept the deal.

Mabel checked her wristwatch. There was time before the diner opened. As she took a step toward the curb, a motion on the block caught her eye. A young woman riding a bicycle approached the diner. Mabel stepped back into the doorway to wait for the bike to pass. But the rider stopped the bike at the diner window and parked it against the brick. Mabel recognized

Ma's bookkeeper; they had talked in the diner that day she waited for Al. Ma bustled over to unlock the door for her. They moved away from the window, and Mabel lost sight of Ma.

Mabel held her scarf across her face and scurried down the block to the bus stop.

She hated to miss the chance to talk to Ma, but the glimpses through the window had fortified her. Her bond with Ma was like breathing. Leaving Detroit would mean leaving Ma behind. She had promised to stay away from Al, but she would not cut her connection to Ma. One day, she would again sit at the counter eating pie and laughing with Ma.

At Woodward, instead of transferring to the bus taking her home, Mabel walked to the theater. To pass the morning hours, she'd take care of things needing her attention. Closed for the holiday weekend, only the crew chief, who lived in the basement, would be there. He let her in the backstage door and she went through the dim hallway to the front. To her surprise, the ticket office lights were on, and Mr. Macready sat typing at a desk. He looked up, then continued hitting the keys. "I made coffee, if you want a cup."

Mabel hung her coat on a peg and went for the coffee. She sat at Cora's desk, sipping and watching him. Shirt open at the neck, sleeves rolled up, he pounded the keys and swiped the return at a pace to rival Cora's. The shadow of whiskers on his face made her suspect he'd slept in a dressing room, which he had often done in the months since Polly left. He stopped typing and yanked the sheet from the roller.

Mabel judged his mood from his thrashing of the keys and tread lightly. "Is there anything you need from me this morning?"

He folded the page to fit inside an envelope he had hand addressed. "Neither of us should be spending our free Saturday here, so no, thank you."

She chalked up the annoyance in his tone to whatever he had been typing. Still, it was not the moment to tell him she'd decided against the job in New York. "I won't stay long. Tidy up a few things I didn't finish."

Mr. Macready slapped the envelope face down on the desk. He drank his coffee gone cold and grimaced. "Since we find ourselves here, I'd like to ask a personal favor of you." His face flushed, and he cleared his throat. "Would you accompany me to Jimmy's wedding reception?"

Jimmy's summer wedding date had been scrapped. His fiancée was more intent on living in New York than on having a lavish wedding. The couple had threatened to elope unless their parents agreed to a small ceremony while Jimmy was in Detroit. They were to marry on the last Tuesday in April.

"His wedding reception? I thought it was for only the family."

"The ceremony is family only. My invitation is for the gathering afterwards."

"I wasn't invited."

"His parents invited me and my wife." Mabel's brows shot up. "I am not suggesting you go as my wife. Please. Jimmy told them she's away, and he asked me to escort you." Mabel had never seen Mr. Macready this flustered. His mind was on Polly, and Mabel sensed he pulled back from saying more about her. "If you're willing, we will represent the theater staff."

Mabel smiled and attempted to lessen his discomfort. "In that case, you are asking a business favor, not a personal one."

Mr. Macready sat back and nodded. "Just so. Business." He ran the hand bearing his wedding ring through his shaggy curls.

"I will go with you." Mabel pushed back the chair and stood to move to her own desk.

Mr. Macready also stood. "Thank you."

Mabel smiled. "I look forward to it."

He tucked the envelope into his pants pocket and moved to the door. "I'll be upstairs."

Mabel watched him go, thinking, *Polly, you rascal, look what you've done to him*. Mr. Macready's distraction was another reason to stay at the Lafayette. Of course, he could function without her. But it pleased her to manage details and head off problems that never had to reach his desk. She owed him that and more. She'd find the right moment to announce her decision to stay in Detroit, and she guessed he'd be relieved. But she hoped he'd find a way to smooth out the rough spots Polly scratched on him, for his own sake.

Easter Sunday dawned brisk and sunny. Mabel put on her wool coat over trousers and took a walk to work her legs and see more of the neighborhood. She passed front yards where children clutching baskets hunted under bushes for hidden colored eggs while their parents looked on. A little girl pulling off her white bonnet and throwing it on the ground made Mabel chuckle, though the mother was not happy. Families in their Easter finery gathered outside Holy Trinity church greeting others before the bell announced the service.

Tilda and Aileen spoke fondly of their Corktown neighborhood, and they bemoaned the changes since the war that demolished blocks to build factories and a new highway. Walking along, Mabel realized she had never been attached to a place. She had escaped her unhappy family home to marry Al, and they had lived their brief marriage in his mother's house. If they had stayed together, they would have put down roots somewhere. She had drifted far from that dream.

Mabel had walked over a mile and came to the park outside Michigan Central Station. She headed inside to warm her face and hands. Cradling a hot chocolate at the lunch counter, Mabel eyed the departures listed on the board. Travelers bustled to the gate when the announcer called for passengers taking the *Empire State Express*. The arrivals board listed several more trains expected from New York. If she *did* go with Jimmy, it would be easy to come back. But she was not going. Mabel left coins on the counter with her cup and made her way outside.

On Tuesday, Mabel set her mind to talk with Mr. Macready and Jimmy first thing. When she arrived, Jimmy was sitting at her desk, making telephone calls. Mabel chatted with the typists waiting for him to finish. When he ended the call, Mabel asked, "Can I meet you upstairs, please?"

Jimmy gathered his briefcase and stood up. "Yes. I'm holding the fort. Michael's not here." Seeing Mabel's puzzled look, he said, "Taking care of a personal matter."

"I'll come up in a few minutes." She'd rather talk to them together, but wanted to get her decision out in the open.

Mabel took her time organizing the day's work, then plodded up the staircase, worrying how Jimmy would react to her decision. Her heart thudded and she breathed deep before entering.

He sat at Mr. Macready's desk, talking on the telephone. "Yes, honey, we have the cash. I will get the paperwork. Don't worry." He waved at Mabel. "I'll talk to you tonight. Bye now." He tossed the receiver into the cradle and rose from the desk.

"The parents came through with the money saved on the wedding. We're getting an apartment on the Upper West Side." Mabel smiled as though she knew where that was. "Things are working out better than I'd hoped."

He came around to the table. "You won't have any trouble finding a place in the city. Esther has friends you can share with."

Mabel grasped the back of a chair. She looked out the window, then faced him. "The thing is, Jimmy, … I want to stay here."

After ten minutes of cajoling ("You'll have easier hours, no nights."), arguing ("How can you leave me in the lurch after what I did for you?"), pacing ("Do you know how hard I've worked for this?"), and offers ("We can give you a raise."), Jimmy threw up his hands.

"Fine. Stay here. Pass up this chance. I'll find a girl in Manhattan." He breathed out a sigh. "Michael might be relieved you've turned me down."

"I think so, too. He's … at loose ends."

Jimmy rolled his eyes. "He called. He's taking the rest of the week off. I'll cover backstage for him. Good thing I'm here." Thrusting his arms into his jacket, he muttered, "Damn Polly." He thudded down the stairs.

Relieved, Mabel slumped into a chair. Jimmy's temper had flared, but he'd accepted her decision. She expected he'd tell Mr. Macready before she could. It was unlike Mr. Macready to take a week off. Mabel would give him the courtesy of speaking with him herself when he returned. And try to find out what was going on.

The following week, on the morning Mr. Macready was to return, Mabel arrived first and had the coffee ready when he came in. He accepted a cup. The dark circles under his eyes had disappeared, but his manner was abrupt. "You've decided. Very well." He waved away her attempt to explain. "You need say no more. I'll be upstairs."

The pace of sales had slowed, and the office crew shouldered his tension. Every morning, he stood with folded arms while Mabel presented a review of the previous night's ticket sales. The girls kept their heads down and fingers busy on the keys while he was there. Both balconies were closed, and Jimmy reset the pricing for the main floor. He and Mr. Macready worked the telephones. By the last Tuesday in April, the day of Jimmy's wedding, they had sold two-thirds of the tickets for the remainder of the spring season. Jimmy spilled his frustration to Mabel. "If Michael was on top of his game, we wouldn't have had to work this hard."

The wedding reception was set for seven o'clock that evening. Mr. Macready had said nothing more about Mabel going with him until he passed her in the corridor that morning. "I will pick you up at your house at 6:30." She hurried through the day's tasks, leaving at five to go home and change her clothes. She hoped Mr. Macready would be as crisply groomed for the occasion as he used to be.

The bus ride took longer than usual, and when she got inside her apartment, Mabel hurried. She clicked on the radio and pulled off her work skirt and blouse, wrapping her robe over her slip. The gray wool dress lay ready on her bed alongside stockings and the new pumps. The evening clutch she had borrowed from Cora waited on the dresser with the new hat. She had washed her face and was in the bathroom combing out her hair when the front door buzzer rang. Mr. Macready could not be this early. In bare feet, she dashed to the bedroom window to peek around the shade for a view of the front porch.

Jack stood there, his finger on the buzzer.

Shock and worry froze her. He could only have come because something terrible had happened. She buttoned her robe to her throat and went to the door in the front hall. He saw her through the glass.

Mabel unlocked the door and held the frame ajar. "Jack, what's wrong? Why are you here?"

He shook his head. "Sorry to surprise you. But I must talk with you."

"What's happened? I'm dressing to go out. My ride will be here soon."

"I *must* talk to you." He ran his hand through his hair and sighed. "Please let me in for a few minutes." Jack met her eyes with a pleading look. Something was eating at him.

"Just for a few minutes." She stepped back and opened the door for him. Her landlady had returned from Ireland earlier than expected, and Mabel wanted to avoid her coming down the stairs and seeing them. She ushered Jack into her apartment and closed the door.

She took a closer look at him. The beard was gone, replaced by a shadow of whiskers. He wore an old sports shirt and a college pullover with dungarees. His face was flushed, and he leaned against the door with hands in his pockets.

The radio blared a dance number, and he smiled. "Do you remember dancing on prom night?"

Mabel folded her arms and studied his face. "Jack, what is going on?"

"I'm bunking in my old room at home this week. We seminarians stay with our families for the last time before ordination." She pictured his mother's house, his room next to Peggy's, the arguments in the upstairs hallway when she stayed over about the girls taking too long in the bathroom. "I've been thinking about … you."

What was he saying? Mabel shook her head. "Jack, why …?"

Jack held up his hands. "Let me say what I came here for." His words rushed out. "On prom night, I was a clod. You hated dancing with me. But it was the best night I'd ever had. When you agreed to go with me, my head spun. I had a whopping crush on you, but there was no way I could tell you. Peggy would have tormented us for fun. And I had no reason to think you cared for me. You had your heart set on that other guy. I kicked myself for not kissing you, anyway."

Mabel gulped for air. She stepped back and sank into the armchair. Images from their days together played in her mind like a silent movie. She had wished her brothers were like him, but she had never wished for him to be her brother. His teasing had excited her, and she enjoyed his attention. Peggy was the buffer, keeping Mabel's girlish daydreams about Jack in check. But he had seen her.

He came to the chair and knelt in front of her. His eyes searched her face. "I never got over you. At Peggy's wedding. I watched you fall for Al, and I knew I had missed my chance. I had to act like I didn't care."

She struggled to speak. "Oh, Jack, Jack."

He took her hand in his. "You are all I have been able to think about this week. I have one wish before I take the vows on

Sunday." He gazed into her eyes with a tenderness that clutched at her heart. "May I please kiss you?"

She answered by moving her face closer to his. He grasped her as he pressed his lips to hers. Mabel had no thoughts, only the sensation of Jack's lips. She changed his careful, soft graze to a bracing kiss. He drew back and searched her face, and when she moved toward him again, the kiss was deeper.

The time chimed on the radio. Mabel pulled away with a gasp. "I must … be ready for my ride."

Jack smiled. "I'll go." He got to his feet, and she stood, clutching the neck of her robe. Mabel's legs wobbled as she followed him to the door. He smiled at her and slipped out. She closed the door and stumbled to the bedroom window to watch him bound down the porch steps and trot away.

Her pulse racing from what had happened, Mabel looked at the clock and threw off the robe. With shaking hands, she pulled on and hooked her stockings. The zipper stuck half-way as she wiggled into the grey dress, and her sweaty fingers made slow work of fixing it. She smoothed on face powder and rouge without looking herself in the eye. Applying her lipstick, she ran her tongue over her lips, tasting him. Kissing Jack sent the same jitters along her spine as the times he held his arms around her to position the bat. She dropped the lipstick at the sound of the door buzzer.

Mabel threw the tube into her bag and hastened to set her hat in place. She gathered her coat and locked her door. When she stepped onto the porch, Mr. Macready wished her a good evening, took her coat, and held it as she put it on. At the curb, Mabel glanced up and down the block before she got into the car.

CHAPTER 10

The champagne sparked through Mabel as she danced with Mr. Macready. Not the daze she used to feel, but a glazed sensation she leaned on. She had accepted the glass from the waiter and gripped its chill as the guests cheered the toast raised by Jimmy's brother. The bubbles touched her lips, and she drained the glass.

The singer crooned "Prisoner of Love" and Mr. Macready's hand tightened around hers. The lyrics would make him think of Polly. Mabel gazed at the other dancers over his shoulder. Cheek-to-cheek with his bride, Jimmy murmured the song's lyrics in her ear. Others sang along, too, the tune etched in their memories from hearing it again and again on the radio. Careful in her steps lest Mr. Macready think she was tipsy, Mabel gripped his shoulder. He drew back a bit, and she met his eyes. "Could we sit?"

He guided her to their table. "Can I get you something?"

Mabel could not risk another drink while she was with him. That she considered the option scared her. "A Roy Rogers, please." The fizzy Coke in the pretend cocktail would perk her up. When he went to the bar, Mabel sat back with a sigh. She managed to smile at Jimmy and Esther sweeping by.

The song's longing for an old love brushed too close to what had happened with Jack. She had served many men who mooned with regret over old flames in drunken reveries on their "last night of freedom" before their weddings. Jack wasn't drinking when they kissed, but he was about to become a priest! Why hadn't she sent him away? She should have seen his confusion and sent him away. The champagne hadn't blurred the truth of what she had done.

Mabel searched her memories of prom night. She had accepted Jack's invitation believing he was indifferent, going to the dance only because of his status in the school. She had gotten ready in Peggy's room. The two of them made her dress from a Vogue pattern, fitting the silky fabric to fall at Mabel's ankles. Peggy had altered the bodice to deepen the neckline. When Mabel put it on, she worried it wasn't demure enough. "Oh, live a little, Mabel! You're going with the captain of the baseball team. He's not demure." Peggy knew her brother. Did she know about the crush? She must not have because, as Jack said, she would have teased them without mercy.

Peggy's attempts to pull Mabel's waves into an updo kept falling to her shoulders. Mabel took the brush and swept her hair off her face and pulled it into a tail of curls tied over her shoulder with a ribbon. When Mabel walked down the stairs, the look on Jack's face made her catch her breath. His hand shook as he fastened the corsage on her wrist.

She had felt his attention, not indifference, that evening. Now Mabel interpreted the language Jack's behavior had been speaking. He had kept his arm across the back of her chair as they sat out the dance numbers. When his teammates urged him outside for a nip, he hadn't gone and left her with the girls. He let her pull him around the party room multiple times, though he knew she wanted the other boy to see her on his arm. And at the end of the night, while the couple riding with them smooched in the back seat, he had taken one hand off the wheel and reached for hers. She had reveled in the touch of his hand. He had walked her to her door, but fearing her brothers, she had shooed him away with a quick goodnight.

Jack let Mabel's account of the evening as a "disaster" stand with Peggy. Days later, he had left for his summer work and went on to college, destined for the seminary. Mabel must have seen him at the holidays during those years, but her recollection was fuzzy. She remembered Jack walking Peggy down the aisle at her wedding, but Mabel was giddy over Al from the moment they met, paying Jack no attention.

But earlier this evening, she and Jack had slipped back to who they used to be. He admitted he carried a torch for her and asked for the kiss they might have had on prom night. Mabel would not have refused him then, and she would never have told Peggy. When he looked into her eyes tonight, everything in her desired his kiss.

He was to take the vows of priesthood in five days.

She should have said no. Mabel could only hope the kiss had helped him shrug off the wistful stabs of regret and that he would take his vows with a sincere heart.

Mr. Macready returned to the table with her drink and his own. He fingered his glass before taking a swig. A wedding reception was the last place he wanted to be, she was sure. He didn't seem to expect conversation from her. But her nerves needed a break from her racing thoughts, and his sadness tore at her. She clinked her glass against his. "Here's to Jimmy."

Mr. Macready managed a smile and raised the glass. "To Jimmy."

Mabel drew a deep drink through her straw. The band played an upbeat number, and he tapped his finger in time on the glass. "Mabel, Jimmy's not pleased about your decision, but I am."

"Thank you, Mr. Macready."

"Please call me Michael." He leaned his arms on the table. "The day you stumbled out of the rain, my gut told me you would work out as our ticket girl. But I have leaned on you too much these last months."

Mabel finished his thought in her head, *since Polly left.* "Not to worry. Michael." He smiled at his name. She leaned forward, too. "We've handled things. But I hate to see you unhappy." She hadn't meant to say that. She scolded herself again for the champagne.

He turned his head to meet her eyes. "I know who Polly is. But being a father to that little girl—that's got me staggered. She's afraid of me. And she bites."

Mabel crinkled her brow. "Oh, sorry. Betsy bit me, too." She told him what happened at Belle Isle, leaving out her sobbing breakdown. With that, the dam holding Michael's worries broke. He recounted his frustrated attempts to win Betsy over. Her biting, screaming, kicking, breaking toys. "I can't blame Madge for wanting me to leave when Betsy has a tantrum."

Mabel shook her head. "She's lashing out, but not at you."

Michael stared at her. "What do you mean?"

"She's missing her mother, and she's too young to understand."

"How do you know this?"

Was it the drink, or Michael's troubled frown and wet blue eyes? "I was that little girl." Mabel tore the cocktail napkin into shreds while telling him of her loss and confusion after her mother passed. He listened with a softness in his eyes that told Mabel he wasn't judging her.

When she went quiet, he sighed. "I am sorry for what you've been through. And you might be right about Betsy. I must figure out how to help my little girl."

"You will. Don't give up on her." They smiled at each other. The bandleader announced the bride and groom asking everyone to join them for the final number. Michael offered her his hand. "Let's see Jimmy off."

Swirling among the couples, they came next to Jimmy and Esther. Esther pulled away from Jimmy's shoulder. "This is my last chance to dance with Michael." Jimmy raised a brow at Mabel, who nodded. Michael made a slight bow to Esther and danced her away. Mabel accepted Jimmy's hand, and they picked up the steps.

He followed Esther with his eyes. "She can't wait to get to New York." He looked at Mabel. "You should be coming, too." Jimmy shook his head. "I know, I know. It's no use trying to change your mind." The number ended, and Jimmy squeezed Mabel's hand. "See you when I see you. Time for us to say goodnight to everyone." He dashed off to Esther.

Later that night, Mabel lay in the dark of her bedroom, her leg jittery under the sheet. In school, the nuns had forced her to write her wrongdoings a hundred times. Mabel arrayed her offenses on a mental chalkboard. *I will not drink.* The sips of champagne would not set her back. She'd had one weak moment.

I will not be a temptation to Jack. His affection moved her. She couldn't help wondering if he lay awake thinking about their kisses. But for his sake, when she saw him at the cathedral, she would pretend it had never happened. *I will not drink. I will not be a temptation to Jack.*

Mabel plodded through the week, repeating the phrases in her mind. Peggy did not call the theater, and Mabel took her friend's silence as a challenge to her promise to attend the ordination. On Saturday night, Mabel and Cora finished in the ticket office and lingered outside under the marquee, enjoying the air. Michael came out and began locking the theater doors. Cora waved as her ride pulled up to the curb. "Goodnight, Mabel. Mr. Macready."

Michael put the keys in his pocket and turned to Mabel. "Tomorrow, I plan to try something different with Betsy." He walked with her to the bus stop. As he talked about Betsy, the mad idea of asking him to go with her to the ordination flashed through Mabel's mind. She'd have to introduce him to Jack, Peggy, and George, but not as her boss. An illusion like the actors created on the stage.

Mabel coughed into her gloved hand to shake off the impulse. "She'll come around." They bid each other good night as she boarded the bus. Mabel plopped into a seat with a headshake of relief that she had not put him on the spot with her foolish idea. She would weather the ordination alone.

On Sunday morning, she dressed in the stunning gray wool dress with the new pumps. She frowned at her reflection as she pinned her hat in place. The outfit had been planned for impressing George, and therefore Al, with how attractive she looked, but Mabel now thought better of showing off. She couldn't risk causing Jack distress before the ceremony. His declaration to her was a weak moment, like gulping the champagne, nothing to change his course. She'd stay out of sight until afterwards, satisfy Peggy she had kept her promise, then leave.

Mabel timed her arrival at the cathedral to get inside early. The ushers kept clear an area where the archbishop and the men to be ordained would assemble for the procession. Peggy and Jack's mother would no doubt take seats up front. She took a seat in a pew at the rear near the side wall, where they weren't likely to see her. She could view the center aisle by peeking around a pillar. Sunbeams lit the stained-glass windows, and Mabel noticed she sat under a rendering of the wedding at Cana, the first miracle Jesus performed, changing water into wine. *I will not drink. I will not be a temptation to Jack.*

People crowded into the pews, and the bodies in her row crushed against her. The booming sound of the organ set her teeth on edge. When the congregation stood for the processional, Mabel stretched for a look at Jack. He walked next to Dan, both wearing red and gold vestments, hands clasped in prayer at their chests. Eyes forward, chin up, Jack was as stony as the saints and angels carved into the walls. The incense wafting from the procession thickened in her nostrils, and she dropped to her seat, bile rising in her throat. Gagging into her handkerchief, Mabel squeezed into the space between the end of the pew and the wall, inching toward the rear until she cleared the rows. An usher saw her distress and pointed to a door.

Mabel shoved it open and stumbled into the baby room. Five women holding fussing babies stood at a window looking into the nave. She ran to the restroom at the back and retched into the sink. Gripping the bowl, she tried to slow her breathing.

She palmed cold water to swish around her mouth, spit, and dried her face. Wiped away her smeared lipstick and smoothed her hair. She could not go back to her seat, but she would not wait out the ceremony with babies.

Wailing covered the click of her heels on the tile as she left the restroom and went through the door leading into the entry vestibule. Mabel scooted through an exit open to the outside.

She'd have to wait an hour or more for the end of the ceremony. She perched on the edge of the top step. A shiver came over her with the cool breeze. An usher stepped out of the cathedral and pulled a pack of cigarettes from his jacket. He lit one and gestured to her with the pack. Mabel shook her head. The man puffed a few times, ground the smoke out, and went back inside.

She began to shake with chills. Mabel forced herself to stay and prove to Peggy that she kept her word. She paced the walkway in front of the cathedral doors. George could tell Al whatever he wanted about her. Mabel didn't care. Facing Jack was the hard test. She would congratulate him in view of his family as though nothing had changed.

Sounds from the door left ajar gave her a sense of the progress of the Mass. A crescendo of applause signaled that the ceremony was complete.

Jack was a Catholic priest.

Ushers burst all the heavy wooden doors open and kicked the doorstops into place. The organ at full throttle carried the closing hymn outside. Mabel trotted down the steps and moved onto the side grass. The procession of the bishop leading the new priests came outside. She tensed at the sight of Jack bowing his head for the bishop's blessing with holy water.

The crowd of people pushing their way from inside the cathedral pooled around the priests. Mabel lost sight of Jack, but she recognized Dan's head bobbing in the crowd. She watched Peggy steer her mother to greet the bishop. Then George took the old lady's hand and said something to Peggy, who craned her neck looking for her brother among the huddles of people clustered on the steps.

Jack broke out of the throng and strode toward his family. Peggy beamed and applauded him with gloved hands. He embraced his teary mother, who kissed both his cheeks, crossed herself, and clutched him. George stepped in to shake Jack's hand.

Mabel sidled from her spot and made her way up the steps. When she came up behind Peggy, George noticed her. "We figured you didn't make it."

Peggy cowed before this puffed-up man, but he no longer intimidated Mabel. She stuck out her chin. "I'm here, as promised."

She met Jack's eyes. Arms around his mother, Jack stared at Mabel, telegraphing the feelings he had claimed when they kissed. Mabel's heart thumped. She held his gaze for the moment before Peggy pried her mother from his chest.

She grabbed Mabel and pulled her to Jack's side. "Don't you want to congratulate my brother?"

Mabel swallowed hard, intending only to shake his hand, but he put his arm around her shoulders and drew her to his chest. She breathed in the scent of his aftershave and the starch in the robes. Mabel was sure he could feel her heart. "Congratulations."

Jack whispered against her hair. "You didn't stop me."

Mabel stumbled back from his embrace. His mother wormed into the space between them, babbling about an aunt waiting to see him. Jack gave Mabel a tight smile and let his mother grip his arm and drag him away.

Mabel's stomach churned. *Why did he say that?*

Peggy dabbed at her eyes with George's handkerchief. "I'm crying like this is a wedding."

George scoffed. "Not a wedding, but they'd better have wine." He nodded toward the street. "I need a smoke. Give me a minute before we go in for the reception."

When he had melted into the crowd, Mabel gave Peggy a quick hug. "Congratulations to your family. I must leave." She moved toward the steps, but Peggy grabbed her arm.

"This *is* Jack's wedding. We're going to the reception."

Mabel shrugged her off. "I kept my promise, and now I'm leaving."

Peggy frowned and put a hand on her hip. "Jack was always meant to be a priest."

Mabel shook her head. "What are you talking about?"

Peggy moved closer to Mabel. "Whatever you imagined, it was nothing to him." Peggy's stare seared through her like a searchlight. Mabel felt her face grow hot. Peggy could be unkind, Mabel knew, but she had never spoken so harshly to her. Or accused her of what she was implying now. Had Jack been fooled into thinking Peggy didn't know his feelings for Mabel, or had Jack lied? His sister *couldn't* know he had come to her house.

Mabel backed away. Arguing with Peggy would only complicate things. She had to leave. Mabel couldn't risk facing Jack again with Peggy watching like a sentry.

"Goodbye, Peggy." Mabel turned on her heel.

Peggy called after her. "Go. I'll tell my brother you're gone."

Mabel didn't look back. She scurried to the corner of the cathedral and turned onto a path hugging the side of the building. Jack's words echoed in her mind. *You didn't stop me.* Mabel hadn't refused the kisses. Did he say that to hide his regret? In their school days, Jack would say anything to wiggle out of blame for a prank when he got cornered, using his good looks and glib excuses on the nuns to escape the ruler.

You didn't stop me. The sadness she saw in him tugged at her reasoning. Did he mean she had not stopped him from becoming a priest? *How* could she have stopped him if she wanted to? No, he had had last-minute doubts, that was all. He'd had years to consider his calling. He went through with the ordination because *he* meant to be a priest. But why say that to her?

Mabel stopped and leaned against the cathedral's stony wall. There was something else. Jack had not pulled back from their second kiss, wanting more, too. Her body was aroused from the limbo she had cocooned in since the miscarriage. With Al, she had known what the women's magazines called "married love." But the grief and the drinking had numbed her into believing those feelings were erased from her. Jack kissed her into a cascade of sensations. She enjoyed feeling that way again. *Damn, damn.* Mabel knocked her fist against the rough cement of the church.

But Jack was now a priest. Mabel feared he had not taken his vows with a sincere heart. She had no choice but to keep away from him and hope that, in time, his regret would fade. The rift between her and Peggy had widened. Mabel couldn't picture them returning to their easy way with each other. She could only hold on to her fond memories of their young years and not see either of them again.

CHAPTER 11

June 1947

Michigan Central Station's main hall teemed with travelers scurrying to and from the gates. The dispatcher's announcements echoed off the marble pillars soaring to the vaulted ceiling. The porter handed Mabel the luggage ticket for her two suitcases, and she stuffed it into her handbag. Carrying her train case, she made her way to the gate for the overnight *Wolverine* to New York.

Men with Jack's dark hair and muscular build crossed her path, causing her to hesitate in her steps. The day after the ordination, a newspaper article announced the parishes receiving the new priests. Jack's assignment was a chaplain rotating among hospitals while waiting for a church position.

Mabel sensed him moving around the city.

Fear of seeing him stalked her. She eyed the porch from her bedroom window before leaving for work in the mornings. Foregoing the late bus, she took a taxi home, driven by a friend of Tilda's, who met her at the theater's stage door and waited at the curb until she entered the house. In the ticket office, the ringing telephone startled her, and if she had to answer, she did so with gritted teeth. She stationed Cora and Bridget at the windows to sell seats and stayed out of the sight of customers. Greta was miffed by Mabel's repeated excuses for begging off going out to lunch and had stopped asking. The girls were uneasy with her strained manner and terse commands. Cora took her aside. "How can we help you?"

"Do your work," Mabel rebuffed her. The casual office chatter stopped.

Mabel's nerves had led her to the pantry, looking for the crew's cold beers. Hiding in the wardrobe room, she gulped one, emptying the bottle. Then she went to the balcony ladies' room, rinsed her mouth, and chewed a stick of gum. She told herself it was just one, she had control, turning away from the specter of Ma's frowning face in the mirror. Shame had kept her from stealing beer again.

Two days ago, when Michael called Mabel to his office, she worried he'd discovered she'd stolen the beer. At his door, she straightened her shoulders and pasted a smile on her face. He gestured for her to take a seat. "We have problems in New York."

The leased theater was far from ready to book shows. Jimmy wasn't getting the meetings he wanted, and he suspected bridges his father had burned caused him to be ignored. The girl he hired for the new office was floundering. Jimmy had no patience with her questions.

Michael shook his head. "She had good references. I don't know if she's not up to it, or he's too ornery to let her help him."

Mabel nodded in recognition of Jimmy's manner. "What can we do?"

"Jimmy's pleading for you to come sort things out." Michael figured a month in New York for Mabel to train the girl and help Jimmy get the operation on its legs. While she was away, he would oversee Cora and the typists in the ticket office.

Mabel grabbed a month's reprieve from Jack's ghost.

At the gate, the Pullman porter snapped to attention when Mabel showed her ticket. Jimmy had splurged on a sleeping compartment for her trip. She followed the man along the platform and into the first-class carriage's narrow corridor. In her compartment, Mabel sank into the comfortable, cushioned seat next to a wide, curtained window. He stowed her case on a side shelf, pointed out the restroom, and offered to place her hat on the rack above the seat. She handed over the new traveling hat Mrs. Miller had chosen. The car attendant came to the door, and the porter doffed his cap as he exited. Too late, Mabel thought to tip him. She had not traveled like this before.

The car attendant made a slight bow. "Good evening, Miss. I am at your service to New York. After the train departs Windsor, I will escort you to dinner. May I present the cocktail menu?" He offered her a stiff white card with gold lettering.

Drinking Mabel's voice was in her ear. Twelve hours on the train and no one knew her. She didn't berate herself or recite the mental promise she had already broken; she wanted to stop her racing thoughts. Reading the menu, she cringed at the Mai Tai, reminded of downing those at Peggy's wedding reception where Jack had watched her draped around Al. She ordered whiskey.

Detroit slipped out of view as the train picked up speed entering the tunnel to Windsor. Mabel could neither look back nor see ahead. The attendant brought the drink. Raising the glass to her lips, her nose twitched at the smell. She blanked her mind, took a sip, and gagged. Holding a hand to her mouth, she waited for the reflex to pass. She had scoffed at the old guys in taverns bemoaning losing their taste for the hard stuff, but maybe they were right.

The city of Windsor shot bursts of light into the car. Setting the glass aside, Mabel stretched out her legs, put her head back, and let her arms fall loose at her sides. She had let her obsession with Jack become a temptation. The whiskey, like the wedding champagne and the stolen beer, was a knee-jerk reaction to her shock at Jack's behavior and the sting of Peggy's meanness. She *had* to find another way to calm her nerves. Greta proclaimed cigarettes as the best remedy for the stress of working for Miss Barnes, but the fate of Mrs. Butler cautioned against smoking. For a month, she could rely on distance. Drinking Mabel was *not* going to New York. *I will not drink. I will not let Jack be a temptation.* Mabel tipped the unfinished whiskey into the washbasin.

When the attendant knocked for the dinner service, she took her handbag and followed him to the dining car. Couples and larger parties filled most of the tables. The white-coated waiter beckoned Mabel to a setting for one and pulled the chair out for her. She refused a drink from the bar. The waiter filled her water glass, and after glancing through the menu, she accepted his recommendation of the beef entrée.

As she waited for her meal, she overheard the diners at the nearest table conversing about plans for sightseeing in New York. She'd never been outside of Michigan except across the river to Windsor. When she agreed to the trip, Mabel's only concern had been fleeing from Jack. During the hasty time before she left, Cora and Bridget had chattered over her good luck to see the view from the top of the Empire State Building and visit the Statue of Liberty. Mabel had brushed them off. Sorry for her shortness with the girls, she would bring back souvenirs to repair the damage she had done.

Mabel skipped the coffee after dinner and returned to her compartment to find that the porter had prepared the bed for the night. She slipped out of her traveling dress, hung it on the rack, and took her robe from her case. After washing her face, she propped against the bed pillows with the sheet pulled over her legs. She clicked the wall lamp off and opened the curtain to the darkness outside. The train hurtled along the outskirts of unremarkable towns peppered with lights from houses on the backstreets. By sunrise, the train would be beyond Niagara Falls and working its way down the Hudson River from Albany to the city. The compact bed reminded her of the cot on the back porch of the farmhouse where she had passed out on summer nights. She had stumbled away from being that woman and didn't miss her. It was unlikely she'd see Tom again, but if she did, she'd thank him. The car's rhythmic rocking lulled her. After a time, she fluffed the pillows and stretched out for sleep.

Mabel woke at the sound of the porter tapping a gong in the corridor. She had her coffee with a view of the New Jersey Palisades across the Hudson River. The rising sun sparkled on the churning water, highlighting the summer lushness of the trees. The train hugged the New York waterside before tunneling under upper Manhattan for the arrival at Pennsylvania Station. Mabel hurried to repack her case and put on her hat. She tipped the car attendant and had money ready for the porter.

Stepping from the train, she emerged into the sun glaring from the iron-framed skylights high over the platform. Scurrying travelers jostled Mabel to the edge as she waited for the porter to bring her bags. He loaded them onto a cart wielded by a quick-footed Red Cap, who cut a path through the crowd, Mabel trotting in his wake. The station was immense, with a flood of people crossing the main hall in every direction. She craned her neck to look ahead and stumbled against the cart as it came to an abrupt halt.

"Miss, you going uptown or downtown?"

"Where are we now?" Mabel didn't understand what he was asking.

"Midtown. Where you headed?" She recited the office address she had memorized. "Uptown. This way."

He steered the cart through doors to a roadway tucked under a marbled overhang, darkened with soot. Taxis nosed bumper-to-bumper in two lines, people spilling from the cabs and others jostling to take them. Mabel feared the Red Cap would leave her to fend for herself, but he kept moving along the line of waiting passengers. She clutched her handbag and pulled her arms close to avoid bumping into elbows as she made her way.

A manicured hand grabbed her arm. "Mabel, is that you? Mabel, Mabel, I can't believe it." Grinning Polly threw her other arm around Mabel's neck. The bodies moving behind Mabel squeezed around them.

"Polly, what …" Mabel squirmed from Polly's grip to eye the Red Cap bobbing ahead.

"Wait a minute." Polly turned to a man next to her and cooed regrets for running off, but she *had* to see to her friend from Detroit. The man tipped his hat to Mabel as Polly took her elbow and steered them away. "You've saved me from a dull morning. Where's that man with your bags?"

Moments later, Mabel and Polly were in the back seat of a taxi careening along Eighth Avenue, the windows open to the smoggy air, and Polly shouting over the din of the street noise. "Jimmy told me you were coming. How was your trip? Welcome to New York!"

Mabel grabbed at the strap above the door as the cab jerked ahead of a truck to change lanes. "Seeing you is a surprise." If Polly talked to Jimmy, did Michael know she was in New York?

"I've been in town for two weeks, making the rounds. Driver, not here, turn at 44th. Yes, it's on the west side of Broadway." Polly kept her eyes on the driver's moves as she talked. "If I play my cards right, I'll be leaving for Los Angeles soon."

"Los Angeles?"

"My movie debut! Could be my big break. I'll tell you all about it later. Shh … say nothing to Jimmy. Oh, here we are. Driver, pull ahead to the door."

Mabel pushed out of the cab onto the curb, shading her eyes to see the building. The white brick foundation framed a double set of gleaming brass entrance doors. A grid of windows edged with black granite and brass rose eleven stories.

The frowning driver pulled her bags from the trunk and plopped them at her side. Mabel hoped the tip would smooth over his annoyance with Polly's backseat driving, but he plucked the money from her hand, slammed into his seat, and pulled away with a screech of the tires.

Polly watched him go with a hand on her hip. "We can make do without chivalry, thank you." With two hands she lifted one bag and bounced it against her thigh as she crossed the sidewalk. Mabel balanced the second suitcase in one hand and her purse and overnight case in the other, apologizing as she stumbled through the flow of walkers. Polly dropped the bag near the entrance door, then tapped on the glass. A doorman stepped out, breaking into a broad smile. "Miss Polly, delighted to see you this morning." Miss Polly fluttered her lashes and giggled her request to have the luggage stowed while they went up to Jimmy's office. The bags were whisked away, and when Polly handed Mabel a claim check, she saw Polly was not wearing her wedding ring. Mabel took the tag and looked away.

The gleaming brass and mirrored walls in the lobby reminded Mabel of the deco design in downtown Detroit sky-scrapers. From the elevator, they stepped into the seventh-floor corridor running from the front to the rear of the building. Piano notes echoed from somewhere down the hallway. Envelopes whooshed down the brass mail chute.

Polly led the way to a glass office door etched with the number in gold. Hand on the doorknob, she told Mabel, "Putting the name on the door is one of the many things he hasn't gotten around to."

The door was unlocked, and they entered to find no one at the secretary's desk near the door or at another larger desk butted into the far corner. Mabel blinked at the glare of the morning sun pouring from the two large windows. Polly fanned her face with her hand. "It's hot as hell in here." She kicked a brass stop on the door frame to prop it open, then went to the windows and jerked at the cords to bring down the blinds. Mabel set her handbag on the desk and noticed a sheet sticking up from the roller of the Remington. The words *I QUIT* ran across and down the page.

A ding of the elevator bell and heavy footsteps announced Jimmy's arrival. "You're here! Hello, Mabel. Polly, didn't expect you this morning." He wore the type of summer worsted suit from Botany 500 that Michael favored, the brown weave set off by an ivory shirt and a red and yellow striped tie, and carried a straw hat banded in the same palette.

Mabel held back a quip about his fashion change. "Hello, Jimmy. You look well."

Polly clicked on the fan set on the windowsill. "I happened to run into Mabel at the station. How do you work in this heat? Where's the girl?"

Mabel pulled the page from the typewriter and waved it at Jimmy. "She quit. Jimmy, what did you do?"

He made a face. "Good riddance. Doesn't matter."

Mabel shook her head. "It *does* matter. Who am I going to train?"

Jimmy shrugged. "You and I will get this place up to speed."

"I have only a month. You will *have* to work with *somebody* when I leave."

"One step at a time, okay?"

Mabel looked over the mess of boxes, stacks of papers, and coffee cups around the room. "It looks like a lot of steps."

"We can get started right now." He scooped the clutter on the typing desk into his arms and dumped it on a worktable at the side. Mabel rolled her eyes.

Polly stood with arms crossed. "Jimmy, Mabel's been on a train all night. Where is she going to stay?"

Jimmy went to the corner desk and rummaged among the papers there. "We'll get her a place."

Mabel frowned. "What does that mean? Michael said you'd made arrangements." She had not asked for the details in the haste of her departure.

"Esther's friends share an apartment, and we had a spot for you there, but it fell through." He picked up the telephone receiver. "Let me call her. She was going to ask her cousin."

Polly tapped her foot. "Why didn't you ask me? Mabel can stay at my place. Come with us to the lobby and tip the doorman to load her luggage into a cab. Mabel, you can have a bath and rest before Jimmy takes us to dinner."

"I'm taking you to dinner?" Polly threw him a look. "Of course, I'm taking you to dinner."

Mabel looked from one to the other, rubbing her temple, teetering between protesting and going along. Jimmy's offhand manner regarding the girl and the amount of work to be done worried her. She had no idea where to stay in New York, and he had no plan. Her weariness allowed them to lead her back to the lobby and into another taxi.

As the cab turned off Broadway and made its way along a narrow street, Polly clucked. "Jimmy. You've got your hands full with him."

Mabel held back from venting her frustration. She hadn't expected Polly to be in the middle of things, and she guessed it would surprise Michael, too. He had charged her with getting Jimmy and the office on track. If she complained to Polly before she had a chance to understand the state of the office, she might repeat her grumbling to Michael. The less said to Polly, the better. "We'll figure it out."

The cab left them outside a three-story house made of thick brown bricks carved in a way Mabel had not seen before. Steep steps led to an oak door. Polly nodded at the façade. "I'm on the first floor, those two windows next to the entrance." She grabbed one suitcase and dragged it up step-by-step to the landing. Mabel did the same with the other bag and her travel case. Polly stuck a key in the lock and shoved the door open. Together they moved the luggage inside the vestibule, where Polly parted a pair of swinging oak doors and propped one open with a suitcase. A wide staircase of the same oak led up, but Polly used a key to open a door on the right. "Welcome to the Casbah."

Her apartment was a large room longer than it was wide, with only two windows facing the street. With the shades rolled up, their height pulled light into the entire space. A davenport and two armchairs faced the windows, and a table in the corner held a Zenith radio and a lamp. No rug on the wide-plank polished wood floor. Behind the davenport, a square dining table and four chairs sat in the middle of the room. Tucked in the back right corner were two iron bedsteads, like the surplus cots sold after the war, and a folding privacy screen. Articles of clothing were strewn on the furniture, on the bed, and hanging over the screen.

Mabel set her handbag on a chair and took off her hat. Polly kicked the door shut. "I share the rent with two other girls working the road shows. It's crazy when we're all here, but lucky for you, not this week. Bathroom is behind the screen."

Mabel made her way around the screen and opened the creaky bathroom door. The toilet scrunched at the foot of a cast iron tub. At the other end, a sink with a mirror above butted between the tub and a window in the brick wall. Little light came through the frosted pane. Mabel flicked the switch and the overhead bulb dented the dimness.

When she came out, Polly was rummaging in a cupboard in the small kitchen next to the bathroom. "The other girls cook, but I don't." She opened the Kelvinator. "Looks like we can make coffee, no milk, or we can share the last beer." Polly held out the bottle.

Mabel would not make that mistake again. She shook her head. "Coffee, but could I take a bath first?"

Polly closed the refrigerator on the beer. Mabel followed her out of the kitchen. Polly pulled at garments hanging on a wardrobe rack next to the wall and tossed several empty hangers onto a cot. "Hang up your things. The towels are on the shelf in the bathroom. I'll run out for milk."

Polly took her key and left. Mabel dragged her suitcases closer to the cot. Opening one, she shook out her folded dresses and slid the sleeves over the hangers. She had to shove over the clothes already there to get hers onto the rod. There was no bureau, only a travel trunk, like the ones in the theater, its open drawers overflowing with undergarments. Leaving the rest of her things in the suitcase, she slipped out of the traveling dress and closed herself in the bathroom. Running the tap for a few minutes drew warm enough water. As Mabel stood in the tub washing with a soapy cloth, her annoyance grew. A month in this apartment with Polly would not do.

Mabel had dressed and was closing her cases when Polly came back with the milk and an egg salad sandwich to share. She perked the coffee, and they sat near the open windows, Mabel on the davenport and Polly in an armchair. A fan on the floor rotated the warm air. Mabel could see the tops of a stream of cars, taxis, and delivery trucks passing on the street outside. Polly read her thought. "It's never quiet. You get used to it."

As they nibbled the sandwich, Mabel studied Polly. She was dashing, even slouching in an armchair, a summer skirt skimming her taut legs and a sleeveless blouse highlighting her slender arms. Her dark hair had grown from the bob to her shoulders, giving her face a frame more glamorous than her old vaudeville look. The smart clothes strewn around the apartment might not all be hers, but she could wear whatever her lithe figure fancied. No wedding ring. Michael had said he understood who Polly was, but perhaps he hadn't known how low she could make him feel. Mabel pictured his sad, drawn face, his vitality drained since they had married.

Drops hit the windows, and with a clap of thunder, sheets of rain blew along the street. Polly jumped up and lowered the windows closer to the sill until she was satisfied that the rain would not blow in. The darkening outside cast the room in shadows. She made a move to pull the lamp chain, then didn't. Another thunderclap broke.

She plopped into the armchair and swung one leg over the other. "This storm will pass before we go out."

The thunder tugged at Mabel's memory. "I met Michael during a storm like this. If it hadn't rained that day, I wouldn't be here." Polly knew the story.

"You call him *Michael*? What happened to *Mr. Macready*?" Polly said his name in a squeaky tone and winked at Mabel.

"He asked me to call him Michael."

Polly nodded. "Hmm. Jimmy says you've been a rock for Michael."

"He's under a lot of pressure with Jimmy starting the New York project." Mabel lifted a shoulder. "But you probably know that." *Since you're his wife.*

"Michael's been working in this business a long time. He can handle it." Polly folded her arms across her chest and jiggled her leg.

Mabel shook her head. "From what I saw this morning, Jimmy's making things harder. He knows Michael's at his wit's end with …"

Polly's leg stopped jiggling. "At his wit's end with what?"

"You must know." Was Polly playing a game, testing for details Michael had shared with Mabel? She feared Polly knew the struggles Michael had with Betsy and didn't care.

"I'm sure you're overreacting. You don't know him like I do."

Mabel put her cup aside. "You haven't seen him in months. He hardly eats. Many nights he doesn't go home, sleeps in the theater. We see him unshaven and wearing rumpled shirts. He stays upstairs with his door closed, avoids the crew, and doesn't joke with anyone anymore. He'll disappear for hours or take an entire day off. When he's in the office, the tension is thick as mud. He goes over the numbers like a traffic cop." Mabel stopped short.

Polly's face had reddened. She sniffed. "He's the boss. He can do as he likes."

Her remark provoked Mabel. "It's what *you've* done to him." The gauntlet crashed between them.

Polly sat up straight. "What *I've* done? If he's having a hard time, it's not my fault."

Mabel leaned forward and threw up her hands. "You've left him *floundering!* It's *awful* seeing him torn up over you and Betsy!"

Polly slammed her fist on the arm of the chair. "I don't see how it's any of your business. You have *some nerve!*" She leveled her gaze at Mabel. "What's been going on between the two of you since I left Detroit?"

Mabel held her chin up. "Six days a week, I have to work around the mess you've made."

Polly hit the arm of the chair again. "You sound like a fussy wife. Or a jealous woman."

Mabel frowned, shaking her head. "That's ridiculous."

Polly scoffed. "Hah! I see what all this concern for Michael is about. You're in love with him!" She jumped up and stood before Mabel. "I've seen how you look at him! You were upset the night of our wedding. I had to push you into the photograph. You've been carrying a torch for him! Admit it."

Mabel stood and glowered at Polly. "I have not!"

Polly's voice went up in pitch. "Convince me—his wife— you're not in love with him!"

Mabel shouted at her, "He's clearly in love with you, but you've left him."

"You came here to get me out of the way!" Polly raised a fist to Mabel's face. "I tell you, Mabel, you don't want to try that."

"Are you threatening me? I didn't know you were here. Jimmy should have warned me."

"You'd like to see us break up so you can have him!" Polly's face and neck flushed with anger. "How dare you try to take my little girl's father!"

Mabel clenched her fists. "Your little girl's father is pin- ing for *you*!"

"And who are *you* pining for?"

"Jack!" Mabel fell back onto the davenport. "His name is Jack." The confession had been hiding inside, waiting to be heard, and she had just blurted it to Polly, of all people.

CHAPTER 12

Mabel played with her fork, listening to Polly banter with Esther and Jimmy. She sensed Polly biding her time for the moment to slip Mabel's confidence into the conversation. She clattered the fork on her plate. "Excuse me." As she rose from her chair, she saw the catbird expression on Polly's face. While she was away from the table, Polly would spill it.

Saying Jack's name aloud had felt like a balloon popping inside her chest, letting her tamped-down feelings for him envelop her like a mist. But his terse last words, *You didn't stop me*, pounded in her head.

Polly had jumped on her admission. "Jack? You'll have to do better than that to convince me you're not after Michael."

Mabel froze against Polly's accusation. "I have nothing more to say." She scolded herself for the weak moment that let Polly worm into her secret cracks. Polly had persisted, she refused to answer, and they had dressed for dinner in icy silence. Mabel had repacked her suitcases, aware that Polly was watching her. She set them by the door before they left the apartment, intending to send the message that she would not stay.

In the cab with Jimmy and Esther, Polly acted her breezy self. Mabel had kept her gaze on the passing blocks, feigning interest in the neighborhood. Jimmy had reserved a table at a restaurant occupying the street-level floor of a building like Polly's, which Mabel understood from Esther's chatter was called a brownstone. Mabel liked Esther, but she wondered if Jimmy got a word in when they were alone.

Esther had done most of the talking during dinner. Mabel caught Jimmy eyeing her as she left the table, and she looked away from his recognition that something was off between her and Polly.

In the ladies' room, Mabel considered reapplying her lipstick, then didn't. New York's August humidity had had its way with her hair, and she smoothed it as best she could. She straightened her skirt, braced herself, and made her way back to the table. Jimmy looked away as she approached, a signal that Polly had made him uneasy. Esther patted Mabel's chair with eagerness for her to take her seat. Mabel deliberately bumped Polly's chair as she pulled hers in, ignoring Polly's glare.

Esther grinned. "Mabel, tell me, did you leave anyone special in Detroit?" Polly blew cigarette smoke close to Mabel's face.

Mabel glanced at Polly. "What if I did? I didn't leave a child." Esther opened her mouth to respond but stopped when Jimmy laid his fingers on her arm. Polly smashed her cigarette in the ashtray and swiveled on her seat, turning her back to Mabel.

Mabel leaned her arms on the table and spoke to Jimmy. "I want a hotel room. Please." Esther assessed the tension and wiggled her eyebrows at Jimmy.

Jimmy rubbed the tablecloth with his hand. "Mm … I see. Tomorrow, we can …"

"Tonight." Mabel leveled her stare at him, aware of Polly stiffening beside her. Esther tapped her husband's arm, and they exchanged a glance.

Jimmy rose from the table. "Let me make a call." He summoned the maître d' and walked with him to the front. Esther folded her hands in her lap, a tight smile on her face.

Polly lit another cigarette and waved it at Mabel. "You have no right to judge me."

Mabel scoffed. "You have no right to accuse me." Polly threw her napkin on the table. Mabel glared at her.

Esther leaned in. "Ladies, I don't know what's happened between you, but please, for Jimmy's sake, and Michael's, can you let it go?"

Polly slapped the table. "I didn't start the catfight."

Mabel shook her head. "Of course, *you* have no responsibility."

Esther scrunched her face. "Jimmy's coming back. Be nice."

Jimmy took his chair and spoke in a firm voice. "Here's how it is—you can move to the Allerton tomorrow. Tonight, you and Polly will have to make do."

Mabel scowled. "There is no hotel in New York for tonight?"

"Not for a single woman. You must present yourself at the Allerton in the morning."

Mabel folded her arms and tapped her foot. Polly crunched her cigarette pack in her hand. Esther pushed back her chair. Jimmy took the cue. "I'll get a cab." He left the table. Polly grabbed her handbag and followed Jimmy.

Esther patted Mabel's arm. "It's only one night."

Mabel sighed. Jimmy should never have put her in this position, but it was no use complaining to Esther. "Let's go." They gathered their handbags and made their way to the street.

When the taxi pulled up, Jimmy grabbed the front seat with the driver, and Polly slid into the back seat. Esther looked at Mabel and got in next, and for a moment, Mabel thought about closing the cab door and letting them drive away without her. But she squeezed in, and Jimmy gave the driver Polly's address. Esther's attempt at small talk during the ride got no response, and she went silent.

The taxi pulled to the curb outside Polly's building, and Jimmy leapt out to open the rear door. Polly lurched from the seat and marched to the stoop. Esther slid out to allow Mabel to exit, then got back in. Mabel bade them goodnight and Jimmy tipped his hat. "I'll send a cab at nine tomorrow to take you to the Allerton. I'll meet you there." He slid in beside Esther and the cab sped away.

Mabel hustled up the steps to come behind Polly opening the door, fearing she would lock her out. She pushed through the doors, ignoring Mabel. Inside the apartment, Polly clicked on a lamp, pointed to one of the cots, and shut herself in the bathroom.

Mabel glowered at the closed door and sat to take off her shoes. She vowed not to say another word during the hours they had to spend together. With her suitcases already packed, she opened the overnight bag she had used on the train. She slipped off her skirt and blouse, folded them over the bed frame, and buttoned into her robe. Polly emerged from the bathroom in a flimsy short nightgown and went into the kitchen. Giving the bathroom door a hard shut, Mabel locked herself inside. She steeled her intention to ignore Polly's theatrics.

Mabel came out of the bathroom to find Polly had clicked off the lamp and was lying on her cot with an arm flung over her face. The raised window shades allowed streaks of light from the street to guide Mabel to her cot. It was too hot to bother turning down the sheet. She laid her head on the lumpy pillow with her back to Polly.

Noise from the street dwindled to snippets of conversation from passing walkers, cats howling their fights, and the hum of traffic on the avenue a block away. Mabel held her wristwatch to the dim light. Midnight. She had gotten through harder nights than this. She closed her eyes.

"I should not have said those things to you." Like a dog with a bone, Polly was not letting things go. Mabel opened her eyes and bit her lip.

Polly persisted. "But you shouldn't judge me either." Mabel's pulse quickened. Her fingers tightened on the edge of the cot. *Ignore her.*

But Polly sensed Mabel listening. "I met Michael at the place we had dinner tonight. I used to work there between shows as the cigarette girl." Polly chuckled. "He was with Jimmy. Neither of them smoked, but Jimmy kept calling me over to their table. First, he asked my name and tipped me. Next, the old line, hadn't he seen me in something? I had broken into vaudeville then, and we had Detroit in common. Another tip. Third time, he introduced me to Michael." Mabel pictured the scene, Polly costumed in the short tulle skirt and skimpy vest, elegant Michael standing and taking her hand in his.

"I don't believe in love at first sight. Attraction, sure. We had attraction. Those blue eyes. He was the most refined man I had ever met." Mabel held still, caught up in the story, lest any movement would break the spell Polly had cast. "The hat-check girl told me he managed a Broadway theater, and that got me hoping Jimmy would call me over again. But they left."

"I thought that was it. But when I got off, he was waiting outside. I pretended for a minute not to remember him, but he saw through me. We went for a drink and ended up talking for hours. He told me about the offer to work for Jimmy's father in Detroit and his mixed feelings about taking the job. I had left Detroit to break into New York theater, so I understood." Polly sighed. "It was relaxed and easy, as if we had known each other for a long time. When we called it a night, he got me a cab and asked how to reach me. My agent's office takes messages for me, and I gave him that number."

Polly rose from her cot. Mabel heard the crinkle of the cigarette pack and the strike of the match. "I don't take men seriously, especially in show business. As much as I liked him, I toyed with him at the beginning." She walked into Mabel's view and sat on a straight-backed chair next to the wardrobe rack. The light caught her long bare legs crossed, and the glowing tip of her smoke.

Mabel made a slight move to relieve the cramp in her arm. Polly waved the lit smoke in her direction and continued. "Men want so much from women, and they take it, but not Michael. He acted as if he had to *prove* that I should keep seeing him. I had a singing part in a small show downtown, and he had long hours at his theater, giving us little time together. But one day, he made a picnic and rowed me around the lake in Central Park. On nights we both had off, he took me to hear music he liked in the clubs on 52nd Street. Other nights, just to see each other, we'd meet at my stage door and eat from a box." Mabel heard a longing in her tone, as if she was talking about someone gone from her life.

Polly got up to squash her cigarette in an ashtray on the table. Then she plopped onto the end of Mabel's cot. She sighed, leaning on one hand. "I got my first *good* part in a road show on short notice. My big break, or so I thought. He was excited for me. We had a last evening together. I knew what was going to happen between us. You won't believe me, but Michael was the first man I was with." Polly wore her emotions on her sleeve, and her sincere tone underlined that she was revealing the truth.

Mabel shifted onto her back to face Polly. "I believe you."

Polly reached out and squeezed Mabel's arm. "He talked about our future, but I could only see mine. I kissed him good-bye and boarded the train. Town after town, the show was a hit on the road, and I was smitten with the spotlight and my rave reviews. He was reading about me in *Variety*, but we weren't keeping in touch." She pursed her lips. "What I mean is, *I* wasn't keeping in touch. His letters reached me at the theaters. I still have them. Why didn't I even telegraph him? The life of a would-be starlet blinded me."

Polly shook her head. "By the time I knew for sure about the baby, I'd let things go so long, I couldn't tell him. I never blamed him. The truth is, I wanted to get it over with and go back to the show. I thought I'd give her up for adoption, but my sister wouldn't stand for that." She went silent for a few moments.

Polly's candor watered down the blame Mabel had laid on her. She reflected on Polly's decision not to let the wild card of her affair with Michael stand in the way of her dreams. Mabel had answered her desire for Al by eloping with him three weeks after they met. Her distaste for Peggy's deference to George told her she might not have been happy as a homemaker. If she hadn't rushed to marry, how different might her life have been?

Mabel sat up and leaned against the pillow. "But now you *have* told him *and* married him."

Polly went for another cigarette. The pack was empty. She tossed it away and came back to the cot. "Michael is better than I deserve, but Betsy *does* deserve him, and I realized he can do more for her than I can. Has he told you about his family?" Mabel shook her head. "Upstate New York wealth from generations in the shipping business. Michael came to the city to make his own way, got a foothold in a big theater, and he's good at managing. The monogrammed cuffs and expensive suits don't hurt." She chuckled. "His family pesters him to come to his senses. I bet he hasn't told them about Betsy, but she will benefit from his money."

Mabel nodded. "I shouldn't have been so hard on you."

Polly shrugged. "I beat myself up every day. Hasn't worked. I'm still an absent wife and mother." She paused. "You're hard on yourself, too, aren't you?"

In the darkened room, Mabel saw a tunnel she kept running through, searching for the end. She cleared her dry throat. "I gave my husband no choice but to divorce me."

"Jack was your husband?"

"No. *Al* divorced me. *Jack* is the Catholic priest I kissed."

Polly grabbed her arm. "Oh, Mabel. What are you saying?"

For a second, Mabel had an impulse to push Polly off the cot and pull the sheet over her to hide the shame of her own past. In the hospital, the psychiatrist urged her to talk, but her fear of unbottling the darkness inside held her silent. But sharing it with Polly in the dim glow from the streetlight offered Mabel a pathway through her despair.

She swallowed hard. "I met Al at my best friend's wedding." The story of Mabel's past unfolded as if she were narrating her role in a movie. When Mabel's tears flowed, Polly slid her hand over Mabel's and held it tight. After Mabel described the recent events with Jack, Polly stretched her legs. "Whew! I wish I had more cigarettes."

Mabel shook her head. "I don't know what will happen if I see him again. Or I do. That's what scares me."

Polly stood and went for the ashtray. "Mm. But a secret romance with a priest is exciting." She rummaged for a butt and lit one.

Mabel snorted. "Exciting?"

"Forbidden fruit." She blew out the smoke. "How long before you go back?"

"Michael figured a month to sort out the office. But Jimmy lost the girl, so who knows?"

Polly pulled the chair over and sat by Mabel. "Something tells me you should make him decide what he really wants."

"Didn't he decide that when he was ordained?"

Polly stubbed out the cigarette. "Maybe. But don't you want to know for sure?"

Mabel lay back and folded her arms. "I'm afraid to know what either of us wants."

"When I decided to tell Michael he was Betsy's father, I was terrified he'd refuse to believe me. It put everything between us on the line. I could have lost him forever. Then I realized the person he is would not reject Betsy. Your Jack sounds like a man who will own up to the truth."

Mabel sighed. "Maybe you're right." Jack had always been straight with her, which made his last words to her so upsetting.

Was he struggling with the truth of his feelings, or his anger at letting her distract him?

Polly yawned. She got up and walked over to her cot. "I need some sleep."

Mabel turned onto her side, punched the pillow under her neck, and closed her eyes. She didn't want her mind to drift to where the worry lived. Instead, she pictured her hand in Jack's, leaning against his shoulder, and rested there. The next thing she knew, Polly was tapping her shoulder and calling her name. She opened her eyes to the sun glinting off the windowpanes.

"If you're meeting Jimmy at the Allerton, you've got to get going. I made coffee." Polly was dressed and holding a mug. The confidences they had shared in the dark had erased Mabel's bitterness toward Polly, and she blushed thinking of her rude demand for Jimmy to get her a hotel room.

Polly spared her the embarrassment of apologizing. "You're welcome to stay here, but one of the girls might come to town, and there's no space for your things. You'll be more comfortable at the Allerton."

Mabel swung her feet to the floor. "I'll go. Thanks, Polly, for … everything."

"Likewise. C'mon, get a move on. I'll help you with those bags, then I've got to run to a meeting." She winked. "The movie's casting director is in town."

A short time later, the two of them were bumping Mabel's luggage down the brownstone steps when the taxi Jimmy had arranged pulled to the curb. The driver loaded the suitcases, and Mabel hugged Polly goodbye. She waved from the back seat as the cab headed to the end of the block. The driver made the turn onto Eighth Avenue amidst a crush of trucks, cars, and buses inching north. Pedestrians and delivery carts ignored the signals and zig-zagged across the avenue between idling vehicles. Drivers honked and yelled at others. She asked the cabbie how far they had to travel. "Ten blocks to 57th, then east to Lex. We'll get there." He spat out the window.

Fumes mixed with the rising temperature as the cab crawled and braked in the traffic. Mabel covered her nose with a handkerchief. The twenty-four hours she'd been in New York seemed longer. Telling her story to Polly had felt like the sting of picking at a peeling sunburn and exposing tender skin. She hadn't asked for secrecy, but she had a feeling Polly would keep it to herself. Mabel tucked Polly's advice to make Jack decide what he wanted into the back of her mind. She must tackle the immediate business of fixing the mess in Jimmy's office.

At last, the taxi lurched to a stop at the arched entrance of a towering building of dark red brick. Jimmy, pacing on the sidewalk, moved ahead of a doorman and yanked the taxi door open. "Morning, Mabel. Let's get you settled and go on to the office." He reached through the open front seat window and paid the driver. Mabel stepped out and blinked against the sun's glare. He spoke to the doorman about her suitcases, and Mabel followed him inside.

At first glance, the grand lobby with its marble columns and staircase winding to a mezzanine reminded her of the Lafayette. But the furnishings created the impression of a grand home. Seating areas with deep carpets and cushioned chairs invited reading or chatting. Vases of fresh flowers adorned pedestals and tabletops. Women dressed for work hurried from the elevators.

Mabel walked with Jimmy to the main desk where a middle-aged woman waited with a smile. "Hello again, sir. I presume this is the young lady you registered?"

Jimmy introduced Mabel to the manager, Mrs. Blumer. The women looked each other over as Mrs. Blumer pushed a clipboard toward Mabel. "Welcome. We have the office address where you will be working. If you could fill in your home address and the other lines, please." Mabel added the information, and when she finished, Mrs. Blumer rang for the bellhop and passed her a key for a room on the tenth floor.

Mrs. Blumer reached under the counter and brought out a pamphlet. "We do need to ensure you understand the rules of our residence and agree to comply. Read this over and stop by to chat with me later." Mabel took the booklet and agreed to meet Mrs. Blumer. A bellhop came with her luggage on a cart, tipped his cap, and asked Mabel to follow him.

"Jimmy, give me a few minutes."

He looked at his watch. "I'll be waiting."

At the elevator, the bellhop wheeled the cart into an empty car and pushed the button for the tenth floor. As they ascended, the aroma of brewing coffee filled the car. He pointed out the floor directory attached to the elevator wall. "Miss, you'll find the dining room on three, the library on four, and the sunroom and porch on fifteen."

She longed for a cup of coffee but didn't dare test Jimmy's patience by stopping. On the tenth floor, the bellman took her key to unlock the door and led her into a tidy room with two large windows, flowered curtains open to the sky. On one side sat a single bed made up with several pillows and a new-looking spread, and a sink was tucked into the corner. Opposite was a sitting area with an armchair, a coffee table, and a side table with a reading lamp. A bureau with ample drawers had a spot next to the double closet. The bellhop set the suitcases near the bureau, placed her key there, and asked if he could be of further service. Mabel handed him a tip, and he left her with a click of the door.

She tossed her purse onto the bed, longing to sink into its softness after the night on the cot. She sighed and wrangled a suitcase open to shake out her dresses and hang them in the closet. Hurrying to change into a fresh blouse and skirt and brush out her hair, she wondered what her stay cost, but she didn't care. Jimmy would have to cover it. With sunglasses and purse in hand, she locked the room and, on the way to the elevator, found the shower and toilet room. When she reached the lobby, he was in a telephone booth and waved her over. He plunked the receiver on the hook.

Mabel put on her sunglasses. "The hotel will do nicely, Jimmy."

He was already on his way to the street door. "It's a busy day. Let's go."

Jimmy tutored Mabel as they taxied to the office building. "First thing to understand is our aim is to own theaters. Yeah, we want the good shows, but with the real estate, we control our costs." He tipped his hat back. "I've got my hooks into one old place and there's a second wreck none of them want. Locations are good. We aren't gonna' make palaces. We'll spend enough to pass inspection and get them open." He rattled off the first names of the owners of rival theaters, none of them familiar to Mabel. She knew better than to interrupt, giving him meaningful nods when he paused.

The cab rolled along Broadway to the building. Jimmy thrust money at the driver and threw open the door, at the last second remembering to hold it for Mabel sliding out. She had seen him tanked up on ambition before, but his manner had elevated. She caught his energy, her stride becoming a march alongside his purposeful gait from the curb to the door.

The Lafayette office had shipped boxes to New York with ledgers and files for setting up the books and record-keeping of a ticket office. Mabel's challenge, though, was organizing the theater renovation project while acting as secretary for Jimmy's producer pursuits. In between telephone calls, he replied to her questions with sketchy instructions. She suspected he created impromptu excuses to break away from her putting him on the spot to provide details. By the third day, she realized it was just as well there was no girl to train, as the scope of the operation overwhelmed her.

Jimmy was out getting sandwiches when Michael telephoned to ask how she was faring. Mabel's frustration answered. "Honestly, I don't know. The real estate agent for the new theater sent a fifty-page contract for review. I'm a fish out of water."

"We have a copy here as well. Jimmy's father and I will go over it. He's not leaving this all to his son."

"That's a relief." Mabel waited for the question she knew he would ask.

"Is she all right?"

"She looks wonderful."

Michael's sigh came over the wire. "Thank you." He cleared his throat and changed the subject. "I've asked the architect for the renovation to walk you through the theater. Jimmy isn't going to buckle down on the details. Work with the architect and you'll get on top of it." Mabel thanked him, though she had doubts.

They said their goodbyes, and as the line disconnected, a commotion at the office door announced Jimmy's return, with a paper bag of sandwiches and a young man. "Here she is. Mabel, meet Thomas Lamb, our architect."

◆

CHAPTER 13

June 1948 (one year later)

Polly sashayed through the lobby door toward Mabel and the barman taking inventory of a liquor delivery. Mabel set her clipboard on the counter, wiped her hands on a towel, and came around to hug Polly, who whispered, "Should you be doing this?"

Mabel shrugged. "I make sure we get what we paid for." She asked the barman to finish stowing the bottles.

Polly took a look around the lobby. "I've come to see what Jimmy's done with this place before we start rehearsals."

For the New York theater's debut shows, Michael talked Jimmy into booking Gilbert and Sullivan comic operas, reasoning that known crowd pleasers would sell seats at a pace to make their operating budget during the initial season. Jimmy was not a fan of the shows but agreed with the logic. Mabel understood Michael's underlying motive when the casting director hired Polly to sing a supporting role in the first production.

Polly's venture into the movie business had been a mixed bag. Out in Hollywood, she had starred in a film about a doomed vaudeville queen. The reviews were fair enough, but the box office was dismal. Her agent said the movie men didn't see her star quality, and no further contracts had been offered. The dying vaudeville circuit presented nothing worth doing. She had drifted back to New York by playing a small part in a musical's road company.

Mabel steered Polly across the lobby to the doors behind the orchestra section. "Seeing this place now, you can't imagine the mess Thomas had to deal with."

Jimmy had bought an old vaudeville house sandwiched in the middle of a block between a tenement and a two-story garment factory. The most that could be said for the structure was that the roof was sound, the exterior doors were intact, and on the façade, the vertical marquee surrounded by broken light bulbs could be relit.

The day Mabel had first gone inside with Thomas Lamb, an army of workmen were chipping at falling plaster, hauling debris, and setting up scaffolding. She'd clutched a handkerchief to her nose while following Thomas on a careful walk along a wood-plank pathway laid through the rubble. A thousand seats with moth-eaten upholstery, worn carpet, dangerous old lighting, warped stage floorboards, the mildewed curtain, missing pulleys and broken backstage gear, and a warren of old wardrobe and dressing rooms inhabited by mice.

Thomas feasted on the challenge to restore the space. "We shall make a beautiful theater together, Mabel."

Mabel's head swam with the daunting list of repairs. She feared the work could not be done within the bare-bones budget

Jimmy allowed. And certainly, the renovation would not be completed within the one month she had agreed to stay in New York. "How long will it take, do you think?"

"Jimmy gives us only six months. He is booking shows."

She saw through Jimmy's guise. He had planned all along for the project to lure her into staying permanently in New York. Back at the office, she confronted him.

"I swear I'm not trying to paint you into a corner, but why not be a part of what we're doing here? Michael talked Greta into coming to work at the Lafayette, so you don't have to return … soon."

"*Both* of you *assumed* I would stay here!" Jimmy shrugged off the implication.

Mabel picked up the telephone and dialed Michael. He'd said, of course, he'd honor the original deal if she wanted to spend only a month. But she might consider the opportunity, working alongside Thomas, to learn from the experience of refurbishing a New York theater. And he suggested that time away from Detroit would give her a different perspective.

Mabel took his meaning: Polly had told him about Jack. Michael was handing her a reason to leave the muddle behind. She had to swallow the chagrin of him knowing about her foolishness. Mabel hitched herself to Jimmy's plan and held on tight in its wake like a dinghy tied to a speedboat.

The top-to-bottom restoration had taken nine months of hard work and a third more money than Jimmy had budgeted, but he gained the attention he craved. The opening reviews lauded Thomas's gift for design. With close inspection, patrons might notice the patched seats and the mismatched paint on the second balcony, but he achieved a striking overall effect unique among Broadway houses.

Polly admired the style as they walked down the main aisle to the stage. "Thank goodness it's refined, not gaudy like a movie palace."

Mabel nodded. "Thomas believes Broadway houses should have none of that fussiness." She led the way through an alcove to the backstage dressing rooms.

Polly smirked. "What else does Thomas believe? Tell me about him."

"He's moved on to the next project Jimmy's got cooking." She hadn't seen him in weeks. His departure left her missing the many ways Thomas had filled her off-hours.

Their cordial working relationship, forged through twelve-hour days, had turned into a friendship during the snowstorm that shut down the city at Christmas. Esther and Jimmy had asked them both to their apartment for dinner but explained they were *not* celebrating Christmas. Esther fretted over offending her, but Mabel assured her that a not-Christmas dinner was a perfect way to spend the day.

A thick snow had been falling when Mabel traveled uptown to their apartment building on Riverside Drive. Thomas, his coat covered with white flakes, was in the vestibule when she arrived, and they laughed about bringing a snowman with them in the elevator.

Within an hour, the storm was a raging blizzard. The radio news announced nothing could move through the streets drifting with snowbanks. Mabel and Thomas ended up marooned in Jimmy's and Esther's apartment, playing cards, talking, waiting out the storm for that night and another day before taxis could move on Broadway.

Polly cocked an eyebrow. "Esther says he's handsome."

Thomas had his own style. He favored bright-colored shirts worn with a contrasting vest, no tie, and an open collar. Tortoiseshell glasses sat on a good-looking face. His dark hair made Mabel think of Cary Grant's, sleek and unperturbed when he took off his hat. He was the same age as Al, but his proper manners reminded Mabel of older gentlemen. Esther would sometimes eye Thomas when the four of them were together and later tease Mabel about him.

Mabel scoffed. "Esther is lovely, but she's a busybody."

Polly smiled a knowing smile and patted Mabel's arm. "It's nice that you've met someone."

Among the single women at the Allerton who plodded off each morning to secretarial pools, or clerking, or department store sales, she was Mabel who worked in the theater and could nab tickets for a popular show. Thomas had been the subject of speculation among the women she was friendly with, and she enjoyed letting them think whatever they assumed. Mabel would sometimes see a wry smile turn up his mouth at noticing the girls giggling when he called for her, but he never commented and was always gracious.

On Sundays, Thomas studied the architecture of New York City and asked Mabel to explore it with him. Through his practiced eyes, she learned to admire the structures defining the city. He talked his way into an empty office on an upper floor of a skyscraper, and they spent a morning in full view of the construction site of the new United Nations Headquarters. They tramped through the streets of lower Manhattan as he photographed tenements. He introduced her to Chinese food, and the pasta they ate in tiny storefront kitchens in Little Italy made her remember meals at Luna. Hearing that she did not drink alcohol, he didn't drink when he was with her, adding to her relaxation around him.

He had not tried to kiss or fondle her, never more than take her arm. There were moments when her regard for him leaned into flirtation, but neither of them pursued it. She believed he enjoyed her company as much as she enjoyed his, but he hadn't asked her, and she never probed, about relationships. Her long hours split between the Broadway office and the theater kept her social footprint light. The seclusion she had fostered closed her in like a too-tight girdle she pretended wasn't squeezing her. Thomas had filled her Sundays, and she was grateful for that.

"Will you stop? Thomas is not *someone*."

Polly pulled back. "Okay, if you say so. It's just that I hoped a year away from Detroit had changed things for you." They came to the dressing room with Polly's name printed on the plate. "Tell me, Mabel, how many dates have you been on?"

Mabel sensed Polly setting her up to talk about Jack. Feelings for him stayed buried under her workload, and she would not dredge up the emotions for Polly's curiosity. She folded her arms. "Tell me, Polly, how many times have you seen Betsy?"

Polly shoved her way into the dressing room. Mabel expected her to slam the door in her face, but Polly plopped into the chair before the makeup mirror and flicked on its lights. "I traveled to New York by way of Detroit, for your information."

Mabel leaned against the wall. "Cora told me you'd been to the Lafayette."

"Michael is thinking about bringing Betsy here to see me perform." Polly looked at herself in the reflection. "I *am* trying, Mabel."

Mabel smiled and waved an arm at the room to change the subject. "Sorry, but you'll be sharing this dressing room."

Polly shrugged. "I figured as much. God, I was such a fool about the movies. This town is making me claw my way back."

"Jimmy's in your corner. He's making his mark. And Michael believes in you."

"I don't know where I'd be without them. I'll make the most of this. Can you come with me for lunch before my costume fitting?"

Mabel looked at her wristwatch and, for a moment, worried she was late, then remembered. She had quit the meetings. During her first weeks in New York, the stress of the job inflamed her cravings to drink. She feared her weak control would give way, and she would let Michael down. A poster plastered outside a tavern, of all places, led her to the meetings. Though she had misgivings about joining the gathering of anonymous people, she went down into the musty church basement. Sitting in a circle of hard-backed chairs, they spoke of livelihoods ruined, families lost, and the degradation of their bodies and souls, all because of alcohol.

She had been the only woman in the group. The man leading the meetings had been nervous about her participation, admitting he had no experience with "females in the program." The men snubbed her as though she were an invader. She sat in silence through a few meetings, not knowing what she'd say Until one night, overwhelmed with sadness by the story of a man's family dying in a house fire while he was in a tavern, Mabel began sobbing. Men pulled out their handkerchiefs and thrust them at her. When she took a deep breath and dried her face, the man next to her patted her leg. She had pushed his hand away and blurted, "My name is Mabel, and I am an alcoholic." As her story spilled out, their faces told her she had passed the initiation. She was as much of a drunk as any of them.

Mabel had hidden her misgivings about the steps and their references to God. Overcoming alcohol's grip was supposed to depend on admitting she had no power to stop drinking unless she accepted God's power. If an all-powerful God was in charge, had he not abandoned her long ago?

Listening to the army vets had stopped her from believing she was weak. Chain-smoking and plopping the butts into the dregs of their coffee, some had a jiggle in their legs that never stopped; others sat rigid, legs splayed. Regular guys whose lives were derailed by a catastrophe they had no way to control. War had heaped guilt and grief on them. If the burliest, bravest, men had turned to alcohol in their misery, she was no pushover.

Now, her grief burrowed like a splinter under her skin, the fleeting pain from a random bump flaring then subsiding. The control she had developed as a child against her brothers' tortures returned to her. When dark moments from her drunken days pushed into her dreams, waking her with bile in her throat, she shook them off with gratitude for having survived what she had done. Her body had filled out, not like the voluptuous Miss Front End, but her clothes fit well and energy carried her through each day. She had stopped worrying about drinking, so stocking the theater's bar was a task like any other. Nonetheless, she did not tempt herself by going to taverns.

Polly knew a tucked-away place for lunch where actors and stagehands with tight budgets went for a hot meal. The place was homey like a diner and as dark as a tavern, the window shades kept closed at all hours. The start of the afternoon baseball game blared from the radio on the counter. In a booth at the back, Mabel and Polly ordered hamburgers. Polly lit a cigarette while they waited for the food.

"You never heard from him?" Polly was circling back to Jack. Mabel shook her head. "No. I didn't expect to. He's a priest."

"What about his sister?"

"I put my Christmas card to her in the Lafayette pouch and Cora posted it in Detroit. Peggy didn't reply." What she didn't tell Polly was that Cora had forwarded a card received at the Lafayette from Dan, Jack's seminary roommate. The postmark was from a town in the UP on Lake Superior. He wrote that he prayed for her to find peace in her heart. She couldn't help but read between the lines. Jack had talked to him about her. She kept the card, but didn't respond to Dan.

"Are you going back?"

Mabel jerked her head up at the question. "Why are you asking me that? Has Michael said something to you?" Mabel talked with Michael on the telephone most days, and he had not raised the subject.

"No. I'm wondering what you want to do. Is New York your home now?"

Mabel sat back. The word home sounded like an unfamiliar language. "I don't know."

The waitress brought their hamburgers. Polly tried to lighten the moment by clinking her Coke bottle against Mabel's "Here's to my debut in Jimmy's theater." Mabel smiled and took a sip. But the question stayed at the side of her mind as she listened to Polly's small talk.

They did not linger to have coffee. After paying the bill, Mabel walked Polly back to the theater for her costume fitting, then continued the few blocks to the office. The blue-sky afternoon had edged up in temperature, and Mabel peeled off her cardigan. Office workers crowded the sidewalk along Broadway, reluctant to end the lunch hour and go inside. Entering the lobby, Mabel blinked away her squinting against the sun. At the elevator, she exchanged greetings with the postman, a heavy sack hefted over his shoulder. They got into the car together; the elevator ascended, and he tipped his cap when she got off at her floor. "See you in a bit, Miss." His routine was to begin deliveries on the top floor and work his way down.

Jimmy's secretary, Rose, looked up from her typewriter when Mabel entered the office, then clacked the end of a sentence and stood. "Can I run to the ladies' before we go over things?" She nodded, and Rose scurried out. Mabel went to Jimmy's desk and checked his calendar. Jimmy's habit was to take meetings over an extended lunch period, leaving the office to Mabel and Rose until he returned later to hear anything they needed to tell him.

Rose returned and held the door open to shove the doorstop into place with her foot. "It's gotten warm in here." A semi-cool breeze blew in from the hall, along with the tinkling sounds of the piano in the rehearsal room at the far end of the corridor.

Mabel sat in Jimmy's chair; Rose swiveled her chair close to the desk and handed Mabel a typed sheet. "This is the report I've been working up." While Rose reviewed the numbers, Mabel listened and nodded, grateful for Rose's organization and quick mind. New York brimmed with competent secretaries, many experienced in the theater business, but few could have navigated Jimmy's choppy waters as well as Rose. Middle-aged, neatly coiffed, always wearing a string of pearls, she had a way of responding to Jimmy's manic style that satisfied him, and then made sure to take care of every detail he didn't fathom.

The postman appeared in the doorway with a bundle of city mail and the mail pouch from Detroit. Rose accepted the bundle from him, and he flipped the pouch onto her desk and left. Mabel stood and stretched. "How about I get us some Cokes?"

Rose smiled. "Good idea. I'll see what we have here."

Mabel gathered some change and rode down to the lobby canteen. She came back ten minutes later with two icy bottles and set one on Rose's desk. She held a parchment envelope out to Mabel. "This is addressed to you personally. Looks official."

Mabel took the envelope and, flipping it over, noted the return address on the back flap as the Wendell Brown law firm in Detroit. She plopped into Jimmy's chair, sliced the envelope top with his leather-handled opener, and pulled several typewritten pages from inside.

Mabel gasped, then pressed her palm to her mouth. It was too late to pretend she hadn't received the envelope, to write "Return to sender," and give it back to the postman. She had to keep reading.

It is our sad duty to inform you… Ma had passed three weeks ago. *Oh, Ma, Ma, my Ma.* Tears pulsed behind Mabel's eyes. Twisting her fist in her lap, she imagined punching Al and screaming, *Why didn't you tell me?*

Mabel propped her head on her knuckles and continued reading through watery eyes. The firm was carrying out Ma's instructions for her estate. She had done well financially, expanding her property from the diner to owning the entire block and building a pie factory. Mabel couldn't help thinking,

Of course she did, in only a year. That was Ma. She had left her business assets to her partners.

Al was in charge. Mabel tapped her foot in anger. He had buried Ma without her and left it to a lawyer to give her the news. She couldn't begrudge him the benefit of his hard work, but not telling her Ma had died was unforgivable. He knew from Peggy that Mabel worked at the Lafayette. He could have telegraphed. Mabel's hand shook, turning to the letter's next page.

As for her personal property, Ma willed her house and all its contents to Mabel. *House?* Mabel read it again in disbelief. The lawyers wished to know if she intended to occupy the home or to sell it. In either case, she must appear in person to complete the papers to transfer the deed and settle related matters.

Ma had not forgotten her. Mabel laid her head on the desk and sobbed.

◆

CHAPTER 14

"**S**ign here, and here." Mabel took the ink pen and, with a flourish, signed her name, then capped the pen and sat back. Mrs. Nelson blotted the signatures, shuffled the papers into a parchment folder, and handed it to a waiting clerk. "Miss Hunt, congratulations on your new home."

The man who owned the law firm wrote the letter Mabel received, but his daughter took charge of Ma's legal affairs. Enterprising Ma had sought out one of the few women attorneys in Detroit. Mrs. Nelson managed the firm's real estate practice. "I wanted to take criminal cases, but the courts here won't allow women attorneys to appear." She was young, smart, and feisty, with a plump face, tousled curls, and a fondness for oatmeal cookies, with a few always on her desk.

Mrs. Nelson's firm handshake and warm smile had set Mabel at ease. "Ma was a grand lady and a good businesswoman. I am at your service, Miss Hunt."

Her diligence included changing Mabel's legal identification on her Michigan driver's license, allowing the legal transfer of

Ma's house deed to Mabel Hunt. Punching Al in the nose was Mabel's recurring fantasy, but she at least had the satisfaction of erasing his name.

Mrs. Nelson pushed a key ring across the desk. "As I explained, the furniture and any personal effects on the premises remain as they were. We checked the property yesterday and the utilities are operating."

Mabel took the keys. "I cannot thank you enough, Mrs. Nelson."

"We will contact you twice a year to review the use of the fund Ma established for the upkeep of the home. Telephone me if any need arises." She stood and opened the office door for Mabel. "Enjoy your new home, Miss Hunt." Mabel repeated that intention to herself as she rode the down elevator to the lobby of the Penobscot Building in downtown Detroit.

She had acted on instinct in the moments after she'd read the letter from the law office. Pulling away from concerned Rose at her side, she wiped away her tears, commanding, "Get your steno pad."

Jimmy walked in while she was snapping a to-do list at Rose. "What's going on?"

"I am leaving for Detroit as soon as I can." She waved the letter at him. "There's been a death ... in my family." She had folded the letter into her handbag, added a final instruction for Rose, and walked out of the office. As the door clicked shut, she heard Jimmy say, "What the hell?"

Mabel had plunged into the sidewalk crowd on Broadway, thinking of Ma's arms around her the last time they were together. If only she had had another chance to tell Ma how much she loved her. Had she suffered? The brief letter gave no details. Mabel clenched her hand on her bag. She would never forgive Al for this. No matter what their agreement, he should have made sure Mabel received word about Ma.

Her angry stride propelled her to walk the entire way to the Allerton. Before she went to her room, she used a telephone in the third-floor lounge to reserve a seat on a train heading for Detroit the next afternoon. Hand on the receiver, she considered leaving a message at the theater for Polly, but didn't. Nor did she call Michael. Jimmy would have done that.

In the hotel's basement luggage room, she dusted off her two suitcases stored there. The larger wardrobe she had gathered in New York would not fit in those. Mabel swapped the suitcases for a travel trunk left in the "unclaimed" locker. She didn't wait for a bellman but toted the trunk herself onto the service elevator. Mabel had no appetite for dinner and let the hour pass as she folded and crammed clothing into the trunk. A message from Esther, asking her to call, was slipped under her door; Mabel crumpled and tossed it into the trash.

Her closet and drawers emptied, the trunk closed, Mabel spent the last of the evening gazing at the city from the Allerton's roof terrace. At that height, the din receded, and the sparkling lights patterned the streets and bridges. Her grief about Ma and her anger pushed away any nostalgia for her experiences in the Big Apple. She would make Al pay for his transgression; their agreement be damned.

The next afternoon, she strode through Pennsylvania Station like a wave dragging sand in the undertow. Before boarding the train, Mabel inquired at the travel agent's desk about booking a hotel room in Detroit. She wasn't concerned with the cost, having saved most of her salary over the months in New York.

While Mrs. Nelson finalized the house details, Mabel resided at the Hotel Statler and took her meals in the dining room. The waiters learned to seat her away from others and not to offer anything from the bar. The hotel was distant enough from the Lafayette to avoid running into anyone she knew. She didn't call the theater. Michael could wait until she had settled her mind—and her grievance—about Ma.

Mabel had stood in the doorway across the street from the diner, the spot from where she had last seen Ma, watching the comings and goings on the block over several mornings. The diner had its morning crowd, and trucks unloaded and delivered supplies. Early on the fourth day, Al drove down the block and pulled into the alley next to his old tavern, which had become the pie sales office. Mabel trotted across the street to sneak down the alley.

She lurked at the corner of the building until he parked the sedan, then stepped toward the car. Al opened his door, got out, and blanched at seeing scowling Mabel.

She shouted, "How could you be so heartless?" He took a step toward her, and she held out her arm. "Do not come near me."

Al backed up. "Okay, okay. Mabel, what are you doing here?"

"What am I doing here? You heartless bastard! Did you think I wouldn't care?"

"Mabel, you must understand …"

"No! None of you had the decency to telephone me when she passed. You buried Ma without telling me!"

He looked away, then met her eyes. "I'm sorry."

"Sorry? She was the only family I had. She belonged to me long before I met you."

"I can only say … I'm sorry."

Mabel clenched her fists and shook them at Al. "You can tell me how she died. Tell me."

He sighed. "She collapsed in the diner. Patsy was there. She went quick."

Mabel leaned her head on her fists. "I want to punch you."

Al stepped closer. "If it will make you feel better, punch me."

Mabel looked into the eyes of the man she had once loved with all her heart. The lingering hold she'd let him have on her blew away. "I will never forgive you."

He opened his mouth to speak, then stopped and only nodded.

Damn him! He wasn't sorry. The slight she saw in his eyes, saying he had given her no thought, angered her more. Mabel pointed her finger past him toward the rear of the diner. "I am going inside the diner to talk to Patsy. You will not follow me." She was sure he knew Ma had left the house to her, and that she was taking possession of it. She stuck her chin out and aimed the finger at him. "And understand this—I will come here whenever I please, and you will not get in my way."

He nodded. "Understood. I won't."

She spun on her heel, stomped through the alley to the sidewalk, and ran past the old tavern to reach the front of the diner. Mabel pushed open the door to the familiar tinkling of the bell. At the sight of Mabel, Patsy came around the counter and they fell into each other's arms. Patsy had not known Mabel as a girl, having worked for Ma only in recent years. But Patsy had fast become Ma's confidante, and Mabel trusted her. Crying on Patsy's shoulder, she pretended for a moment that Ma held her.

Once they brushed away the tears, Patsy made grilled cheese sandwiches, Ma's cure for any upset. Side-by-side on counter stools, they crunched on the toasted bread around the gooey cheese, a ritual of deeper comfort than any church could ever be.

"She was fine those days before; gave no sense that anything was wrong. I don't fret, and you shouldn't either, about her suffering. I got hold of her before she hit the floor, and she was already gone." Patsy crossed herself. "They gave her a beautiful funeral. Al took her Up North where she wanted to be buried. Will you go there?"

"I don't know."

"I could go with you."

"Thanks, Patsy. After I settle into the house, maybe we will."

"I miss her." Patsy wiped a napkin across her face.

"Me, too."

"She gave me a place here when I was down and out."

"Me, too." Mabel patted her arm. "What happens to the diner now?"

Patsy looked at her. "Al is the principal owner. Got to give him credit for what he's done. He asked me to keep the diner going, and I want to. The factory makes the pies, and I can handle this place." She had moved into the upstairs apartment.

Mabel smiled. "I believe Ma is happy with that arrangement. I'll come in for grilled cheese."

"You're not staying away?"

"I'm not staying away. I let that go too long." Mabel had played a strong hand against Al. She would be discreet, not announce herself to his family, but she would visit Patsy as often as she pleased.

Mrs. Nelson had offered a tour of the house before the signing, and Mabel politely declined, saving her first view for when her deed was official. Now, with the keys in her handbag, Mabel asked at the hotel for a taxi to take her to the house. Mabel had pin-pointed the street on her Detroit map, near Livernois and Seven Mile Road. The driver loaded her trunk and noted the address with a nod. "I don't mind driving to that pretty neighborhood."

When the cab turned off the main road and slowed to a glide along the block of homes, Mabel gazed at the trees. Michigan trees in summer were densely lush, but this was indeed a forest. The homes nestled among the trees were just as impressive, their brick facades rising two and three stories, flanked by manicured lawns and gardens. The driver peered at house numbers and pulled into a driveway curving in front of one such home. "This is it."

Mabel stuck her head out of the open window and gaped at the structure. The façade was made of something smooth, off-white, not brick. The two stories soared taller than in a frame house and stretched across a wide lawn. Red clay tiles lapping over each other covered the roof. Flower beds bordered by red brick traced the front on either side of the entry. She had never seen a house like this.

The driver hauled her trunk out and set it on the entry stoop. She clambered out of the cab and fumbled for the money to pay him. He handed her his call card. "If you need another ride. Want me to put that inside?"

"If you would, please. Let me get the door open." She slipped the key into the ornate lock on the wood-planked front door, painted red and hinged with black iron fittings. Pushing it open, she stepped through a vestibule into a tiled foyer soaring to a high ceiling.

The driver came behind her with the trunk and plopped it in the middle of the space. Hands on his hips, he looked around and whistled. "Spanish. Beautiful ironwork. Watch that roof, though. Replacing the tiles is tricky."

Mabel stared at him. "How do you know this?"

"My brother is a handyman, and I work for him when I'm not driving. We've worked in the hoity-toity neighborhoods. This is a grand Spanish-style stucco. Bet there's four or five bedrooms."

Mabel blew out her breath. "I have no idea."

He put on his cap and stepped out. "Good day, Miss. You have my card."

Mabel stood at the door, fingering his card. "Thanks. I don't have a car." He tipped his cap and got into the cab.

She closed the door and leaned against it. The foyer was the size of the living room and bedroom together in her old Corktown place. A wrought-iron chandelier crafted with spirals around the bulbs hung from the ceiling far above. She opened a door to a musty-smelling coat closet, and another door under the staircase surprised her with a powder room.

Mabel crossed the foyer and stepped down onto a carpeted floor in the large living room, spanning the house from front to back. Six floor-to-ceiling windows with black iron grilles gave a view of the trees. A wide marble hearth and mantle set in the wall reached above her shoulders. A davenport and chairs were grouped by the front windows, with more chairs near the fireplace. Mabel ran a hand along a mahogany lamp table and came up with dusty fingers. Sealed packing boxes were stacked along one wall. French doors at the far end of the room opened onto a screened summer porch.

Mabel needed to use the powder room. She sat on the porcelain toilet, gazing at wallpaper grapevines. What had Ma been thinking, buying this house? It was the opposite of the Ma who spent summers roughing it in an army surplus tent at a lake up north. Whatever Ma's intention, Mabel felt like Cinderella in the fairy tale.

Leaving the powder room, she started up the staircase, pausing on the landing with a leaded-glass window. On the second floor, more packing boxes stood in the wide hallway. Mabel looked into three good-sized bedrooms, two linen closets, and the main bathroom, with two sinks, a tub, and a shower. All the rooms had large iron-bordered windows, cranked open to pull in the air.

Mabel flung open the closed door to the fourth bedroom. She could see things of Ma's on the bureau, and her old footlocker sat at the foot of the bed. She pulled the bedroom door shut. For now, she'd take one of the other bedrooms.

Mabel steadied her walk down the staircase with a hand on the polished banister. At the bottom of the stairs, a short passage on the right led to a library. Built-in bookcases lined one wall across from a marble fireplace half the size of the one in the living room. Centered in the room was a desk as large as the one Michael used in the theater. Atop the blotter was an envelope bearing Mabel's name written in Ma's hand.

Mabel slipped a finger under the flap to open the envelope. Taking the page from inside, she imagined hearing Ma's voice as she read.

> *Mabel, my girl,*
> *You're reading this because I have passed. You've met*
> *Mrs. Nelson, and you can understand she wouldn't*
> *let me buy this house, or go another year of building*

*the pie business, without making a will. She drives
a hard bargain. I don't expect you'll be reading this
for a long time yet, but whenever you do, think of
me standing next to you, wagging my finger, as I
know I do.*

*From the day I found you in the back of your
father's truck, you have been my great joy. You got
the short end of the stick in life, and the money from
the pies made it possible for me to do right by you.
This house is for you.*

*Make a home, Mabel. Think of me, but don't
get all mushy.*

All my love,

Ma

Mabel swiped at her face. She folded the letter into the envelope, then placed it in the top drawer of the desk. She stared into the cold marble fireplace, dirty with old ashes. *Make a home.*

Leaving the library, she peeked into the dining room. A long table flanked by twelve chairs, lit by another iron chandelier. Four oversized windows looked into the backyard garden, and a swinging door in the corner led to the kitchen. A slight movement of the door caught her eye. Mabel pulled its brass knob and came face-to-face with a young girl, hair in braids, wearing farmer overalls and a checked sleeveless shirt, her hands black with dirt. They stared at each other.

"What are you doing in my house?"

"I was in the garden and didn't hear you come in. I'm Iris." She went to the sink and began washing the dirt off her hands.

She glanced over her shoulder and saw Mabel's puzzled look. "I come with the house."

"How did you get in here?" Mrs. Nelson had mentioned the money for upkeep, but not a girl.

"With a key, a course."

"Why didn't Mrs. Nelson tell me about you?"

Iris dried her hands with a dish towel. "I don't know any Mrs. Nelson. Ma hired me. I was the kitchen girl at the diner." She opened a cupboard and rummaged inside. "You hungry? I'm starved."

Mabel shook her head. "This is my house now. I don't need a girl. Just get your things and leave."

Iris closed the cupboard and folded her arms. "Don't be hasty. It's a big house to clean. Not counting the garden. And I cook."

Mabel looked around the kitchen. On three sides, cupboards lined the walls. A stove as large as the one in the diner, and a new refrigerator, were set amid ample work counters. At the far end, a table and four chairs sat in a windowed nook, next to a doorway into a mudroom.

Iris followed Mabel's gaze. "Did they tell you there are two fireplaces and four bathrooms?"

"Mrs. Nelson said they checked the house yesterday. Why didn't she know about you?"

"Maybe I was out when they came?"

Mabel folded her arms. "*Maybe* you broke in here! Where's the key you used?"

Iris backed away. "It's under the mat at the backyard door, where she left it."

"You *did* break in! No one gave you permission!" Mabel marched through the kitchen and into the mudroom. Outside the yard door, she pulled the key from under the mat.

Iris came up behind her. "I was getting the house ready for ya."

Mabel put the key in her pocket. "You didn't know I was coming." Where she stood, backstairs led up from the mudroom. Mabel started up and Iris trotted behind her. At the top, one door led through to the bedroom in the back corner of the house. Another door at the side was ajar. Mabel shoved it open. The room spanned the length and width of the two-car garage below. "Iris, are you living up here?"

A sleeping pallet lay in the corner under the windows, and clothes hung from pegs set in the wall. At the far end, Mabel peered into a tiny bathroom with towels draped over a half-tub. She pointed at the clothes. "You can have lunch, then pack your things."

The girl looked as if she would cry. She clomped down the stairs to the kitchen.

Mabel stood gazing at the branches on one of the backyard trees poking at the screened window. This house, this girl; what was she supposed to do? The place charmed Mabel, and Ma's letter reinforced her decision to own it. But Iris had a point about the effort to maintain the many rooms with their nooks and crannies. How would she manage it? Perhaps she *had* been hasty in telling the girl to leave, but how could she trust someone who broke in?

Mabel made her way down to the kitchen, where Iris was stirring iced tea in a pitcher. Mabel slid into a chair at the table in the nook. The windows were open to the back garden.

Birdsong wafted in with the breeze. A plate of egg salad sandwiches and thick slices of tomato sat in the center. Iris poured the iced tea into glasses and sat down. Mabel bit into half of a sandwich, the egg salad tangy with diced pickles, like Ma made. She glanced up to see Iris, wide brown eyes brimming with tears, staring at her.

"I have no place to go. The cops are after me."

Mabel choked on the bread in her mouth and spat it into her hand.

CHAPTER 15

Mabel lay on her side in bed, comforted by the silly notion that Ma talked to her through the steady, low hoot of an owl in a nearby tree. Leaving the window open to the chilly night air so as not to disturb its roosting, she pulled the blankets tighter around her neck.

What would Ma say about the girl sleeping over the garage?

Iris had pleaded her case to Mabel. "I knew where Ma hid the key to this place because she paid me to help her move in. She kept me on at the diner, but I up and followed a stupid boy to Chicago." She twisted her braid in her fist. "He made off with his robber crew and left me in the street."

Mabel stared at the girl. "You did a robbery?"

Iris shook her head. "No, not me. But the police might think I did. I got outta' there, but people seen me with those guys." She hooked her fingers into the straps of her overalls. "I hitched my way to the diner. Patsy told me Ma had passed."

Mabel pictured the girl on the highway. It was a wonder she'd made it back. "Don't you have family here?"

Iris scoffed. "Who do you think kicked me out soon as I showed up?" She crossed her arms. "If you're not gonna' let me stay, pay me for what I already done."

Mabel crossed her arms. "I want to hear what Patsy thinks about you." Behind the closed library door, she dialed the diner's number.

Patsy confirmed Iris had worked for Ma. "I don't know what happened when she ran off, but up to then, Ma trusted her. I have to say she rubbed me the wrong way. Snippy."

Mabel was torn. "Should I let her stay?"

A brief silence. "Up to you."

Mabel ended the call and considered. Iris *was* snippy, and she had been foolish, but she didn't seem like a criminal. Ma had given her a chance. Mabel had been a slapdash housekeeper in her small apartment. She had no time to care for a large house. Mrs. Nelson's funding included help in the house.

Mabel opened the library door to find Iris waiting. "Don't make me regret letting you stay."

The girl clasped her hands together in thanks. "You will like my cooking."

"This is temporary while I get settled."

Iris worked hard, busy on her hands and knees in the house or the garden before Mabel had her morning coffee. She tacked her list of chores to the wall in the mudroom, and for each one she completed, added more to do. A neighbor's kitchen girl told her where to order the groceries on a house account. The dairyman delivered milk and eggs every morning.

Mabel had no energy for keeping up with Iris's frenzy. She had arrived first each morning in the theater office, but now found it a struggle to open her eyes before ten. Her daily wardrobe reverted to an old pair of trousers and a flannel shirt. She walked barefoot on the tile floors, wandering through the rooms, opening one of Ma's boxes, then closing it. In Ma's bedroom, she had run her hands over the dented footlocker, then sat on it and cried. The meals Iris prepared proved she cooked as well as Ma had, but Mabel left most of the food on her plate. She passed the days bundled in a blanket in the wicker rocker on the screened porch, watching the birds flit among the branches, the squirrels scurrying for acorns, the wind blowing across the garden. *Make a home.* What did that mean for her?

One morning, as she fumbled with the coffee pot Iris had left for her on the stove, Mabel saw the wall calendar page turned to September and gasped. She had walked out on Jimmy and Rose in June. What did they tell Michael? She had never called him to explain her abrupt disappearance. No one at the theater knew where to find her. After this long absence, did she still have a job? Work had been her lifeline, and she had abandoned it.

Panic jolted Mabel into action. She took her cup to the desk in the library, downed the last of the coffee, and picked up the telephone receiver with a trembling hand. She racked her brain to pull up the Lafayette's number and started dialing. What could she say to make Michael understand? Her grief over Ma had paralyzed her. If Polly had told him Mabel's secrets, he might be sympathetic. *Or* he could assume she had gone on a binge. If Polly had said nothing, he'd be angry she had gone AWOL from the business, after all he had done for her. Mabel dropped the receiver into the cradle before the line could ring. She would go in person to beg his forgiveness.

Running up the staircase, she shouted for Iris. "I need the ironing board!" She was in her bedroom flinging undergarments from a drawer when Iris carried in the board and the iron. Mabel nodded her head at the closet. "Hurry and iron the blue dress!"

Iris pawed through the closet and brought out the blue dress. "If I might say so, this is a sundress. It's September."

"You're giving me fashion advice?"

Iris shrugged. "It's too chilly for this thin dress, that's all."

Stomping to the closet, Mabel grabbed a wool checked plaid skirt and a white blouse. She tossed the clothes onto the ironing board and hurried to the bathroom.

Mabel gazed at her reflection in the mirror as she pinned back her hair. Her skin looked as sallow as it had the day she first stumbled into the Lafayette. She was *not* that girl Michael had first met. He had believed in her, and she would make good on that belief. Scrubbing her face, she searched for the words to convince him she deserved her job. She brushed out her hair and smoothed powder and rouge on her face. She *must* make him see.

Iris stood in the foyer as Mabel squared her shoulders to leave. "Will you be back for dinner?"

Buttoning a wool jacket over the skirt and blouse, conscious of the garters poking into her thighs, Mabel wobbled in the heels she wasn't used to wearing. "I don't know when I will be back."

When she opened the front door, a hard wind blew her hair askew. Iris had been right about the weather. She grabbed a scarf from the coat closet and wound it around her hair, then went out. Mabel stood on the porch for a moment to get her bearings. Her house was at the northern end of the city, a long commute to the theater. She tucked her purse under her arm and trudged into the wind to the bus stop at the end of the block. She was shivering by the time the bus pulled up. The driver quoted the fare to ride along Seven Mile Road to Woodward and change for the downtown line. She fished coins from her handbag to drop into the fare box, then found a window seat.

At Woodward Avenue, the next bus was waiting at the stop, and she quickly boarded. Her mind worked on her speech to Michael, not noticing the passing landmarks, until the bus lurched to a halt across the avenue from the cathedral. She stared at the steps and saw a reenactment of Jack embracing her, whispering, "You didn't stop me."

The torment that had driven her away from Detroit churned her stomach. Hundreds of times, alone in her room at the Allerton, she had dreamt scenarios where she *had* stopped him. The relentless workdays in New York had overpowered those fantasies and left them simmering in her dreams. Her fear of seeing him collided with her desire for his kisses. Jack was behind the million excuses she had given herself for not returning to the Lafayette.

The bus moved on. She took deep breaths and forced her mind to focus on meeting Michael. Despite the wind, Mabel got off before her stop and walked the last few blocks to the theater. In the Lafayette vestibule, she unwound the scarf and smoothed her hair. She had forgotten lipstick. Mabel bit her lips and strode through the lobby to the ticket office door. With another deep breath, she pushed inside.

Cora jumped up from her chair. "Oh, Mabel, thank goodness! We've been worried about you."

"I'm back." Mabel glanced at the empty typing desks. "Where are the girls?"

Cora shook her head. "They're working only two days a week."

Mabel frowned. "I don't understand. I'll go up and see Michael."

"Mabel, he's in New York. He took Betsy to see Polly in the show, and they stayed on."

"He's not here? *Who* is managing the Lafayette?"

"Michael brought Greta over from the Cass."

Mabel pointed above. "Is she upstairs?" At Cora's nod, Mabel strode into the inner corridor and stomped up the stairs. If the typists were on a short week, that could only mean tickets were not selling. How could Michael stay away? A fair question for her, as well.

Greta met her at the door to Michael's office. "Nice to see you, Mabel. I wondered if you might show up."

Mabel heard the sarcastic tone. "I'm here, Greta. Tell me what's going on."

"Do you still work here? Has Mr. Macready said so?" Greta folded her arms.

Mabel shook her head. "I haven't spoken to him. Yet."

"Exactly. No one knew where you were. *I* have been holding the fort. So, please, do not waltz in here and ask me to explain anything." She turned and went to sit behind Michael's desk.

Mabel followed her and took the chair in front of the desk. "Greta, you're right. I should have talked to Mi … Mr. Macready." She sat up straight, her hands fidgeting in her lap. "Please don't give me the brush-off. I was thrown for a loop by the death in my family. I let things go too long."

The telephone on the desk rang. Greta shrugged. "You'll have to explain to him. This is the call I'm expecting from the New York office." She picked up the receiver and exchanged greetings with Rose. "You won't believe who's here with me." She thrust the handset at Mabel.

Mabel pretended calm as she took the handset. "Hello, Rose. Yes, it's Mabel. Is Jimmy or Michael in the office?"

Jimmy came on the line. "Mabel. Esther was saying just last night that your 'situation' must be difficult, or you would have called. And I told Esther, in the theater business, the show must go on, no matter what. Of all times for you to disappear. What do you have to say?"

Mabel feigned an upbeat tone. "Jimmy, I am so sorry. The death in my family was a blow. But I've sorted myself out."

"My sympathies, but we're gearing up for the biggest show the Lafayette has ever had. Michael put Greta in charge. I'm not changing that."

"I see. Where is Michael?"

"He's training a manager to run the theater you walked away from."

Mabel accepted the deserved arrow and kept her voice even. "Does he plan to return to the Lafayette?"

"You're in no position to question what Michael may be doing."

"What do you want me to do?"

"Michael didn't fire you, but putting you back on the payroll is up to Greta."

"I understand. Thanks, Jimmy."

"Don't mention it. Put Greta on, will you?"

Mabel handed the receiver to Greta. Whatever he was saying made her avert her eyes from Mabel. Getting up from the chair, Mabel folded her arms and stood looking out the window. At the rear of the theater, the crew unloaded crates from two idling trucks. She turned when she heard Greta hang up the call.

Greta sighed. "Mabel, neither of us expected to be in this position, but we can make the best of it."

Mabel nodded. "What is the show coming in?" She pointed at the window. "They're loading in down there."

Greta smiled. "Jimmy contracted for *Annie Get Your Gun.*"

Mabel gasped. "That's wonderful! I knew he went after it, but …"

"He got it, but he had to make concessions on the timing. The set is arriving now, but the cast will not be ready to open here for another month. He had to negotiate around changes to the leads, which we had no control over. To avoid going dark, he got his father to use the Lafayette as a concert stage for the Opera House. They booked a vocal series to give the Lafayette revenue while we wait to open *Annie.*"

Mabel shook her head. "Jimmy *can* make deals. I assume the Opera House sold the tickets, and you didn't need the girls."

"Right. But Mr. Kelly promised to assign the typists here starting next week when the *Annie* tickets go on sale." Greta shifted in her seat. "Look, Mabel, I don't want things to be awkward between us. I'll put you on the payroll as ticket girl."

Mabel had no standing to expect anything more. She'd have to wait for Michael's return to discuss her future. She nodded. "Thanks."

"While you were in New York, I got married." Greta held up her ringed left hand.

"Congratulations! I'm happy for you."

"He's in the crew at the Cass. We want to buy a house. *Need* to buy a house. I'm expecting."

"Oh, Greta." Mabel felt embarrassed that she hadn't kept up their friendship, and this news meant Greta had moved on. "When?"

"I'm only three months. No one here knows, so please don't say."

"Of course not."

Greta rose from the desk, and Mabel stiffened at noticing the slight bulge under her skirt. Three months pregnant, as Mabel had been when she miscarried. What a terrible term that was, implying she had made a careless blunder. Yet she *had* blamed herself and spiraled into drinking. The loss would always be a torment. But now she had no urge to escape from it with alcohol.

"I'm telling you because I will have to quit when it becomes obvious. Maybe you'll get this job if that's what you want." She put her hand on Mabel's arm. "I *am* happy to see you, Mabel."

Mabel took her hand. "Thank you. And I'm happy you're doing so well."

"Tomorrow, get here by ten." Greta's lips turned up in a smirk, and Mabel returned the gesture. They had broken the ice.

"I'll be here." Mabel collected her bag and turned to the door.

Greta went back to her chair. "Oh, I almost forgot. Jimmy said to tell you that Thomas is in Detroit. You know him, right?"

Mabel spun around. "Thomas, the architect?"

"That's him. Jimmy's dad asked him to design renovations for the Opera House. He comes to the office for a typist when he needs one."

"Thanks again, Greta. See you tomorrow." Mabel took the stairs at a quick pace, anxious to find out more from Cora. She stopped typing when Mabel came into the office.

"Mabel, pardon me for asking … are you well?"

Mabel cringed at having left Cora, as well as Michael and Jimmy, in the dark about her absence. "I am doing better, thanks. And I apologize for not being in touch."

Cora smiled. "If you're okay, no need to apologize." She looked around the empty desks. "Maybe you know more than I do about our jobs. Mr. Kelly can reassign me, but I really like working in this theater."

"Greta will put me on the payroll as ticket girl tomorrow. She says the typists are coming back next week."

Cora scoffed. "Ticket girl? After all you've done in New York?"

"Not to worry. Our job is to get the tickets into people's hands." She glanced at the full coffee pot. "Let's have a cup and you can fill me in on where we are with *Annie* sales."

"Better yet, we've got load-in sandwiches in the pantry. Want to walk backstage and say hello to the crew?"

Tilda welcomed her, and the men smiled and tipped their caps, then got on with hauling crates from the trucks. While Mabel and Cora were in the pantry bundling their sandwiches into napkins, Thomas Lamb walked in.

"Mabel! What a delight to see you." He made a slight bow and extended his hand.

Mabel smiled and gave him her hand, which he held for a moment. "It's wonderful to see you again, Thomas." She was aware of Cora's playful smile.

Cora gathered the sandwiches. "Thomas, if you have typing for me, join us for a sandwich."

He motioned toward the stage. "Thank you, but I'm here to meet the construction chief before we go to the Opera House."

His lively eyes looked at Mabel from behind the spectacles. "Mabel, would you have supper with me?"

She had missed his charm. "I'd love to."

"I'll come for you when we finish at the Opera House." Thomas waved and left the pantry.

Tilda waddled in. "If ya got a minute, Mabel, I need to speak to ya."

Mabel looked at Cora, who took their sandwiches and left the pantry. Tilda shuffled from one foot to the other. "The gout's bad today." She plopped into a chair and pulled an envelope from her apron pocket. "My sister kept this mail for ya." She slapped it on the table.

The smudged handwriting on the envelope was Jack's. Postmarked in Detroit in April, months ago. "Why didn't you send this to me in the pouch?"

Tilda shrugged. "She put it aside for a time. When she give it to me, I forgot it in my apron pocket when the crew laundry went out. They just give it back to me." She shook her head. "It's my fault. Sorry."

Mabel sighed. "Okay, Tilda. Thanks."

The cleaner pushed up from the chair and shuffled out of the pantry. Mabel fingered the envelope, excited yet reluctant to know its contents. Jack may have written because he was still vexed with her, or to scold her on Peggy's behalf. But the letter had come a year after the ordination. Strange that she had passed that spot and received this letter on the same day. Mabel walked along the backstage passageway lined with dressing rooms, found an empty one, and closed the door. She tore at the flap of the envelope. No return address.

In his script, Jack had written:

Dear Mabel,
When you read this, I will have left the city. The bishop granted me a sabbatical leave from my duties. I don't know what my future is. I hope to figure that out.
Take care of yourself.
Jack

Mabel groaned. *Oh, Jack.* The turmoil he must be in. But why tell her this? They had had no contact for a year when he wrote the letter. A flare of resentment rose in her. Was he saying that *she* caused his confusion? That was not fair.

She read his words again. It was possible he had written to her as a friend. If she had reached out to her friends instead of the bottle, she might not have ruined the life she had with Al. But what could she do for Jack? Jack didn't say where he was going. Peggy must know he'd taken a leave, and Mabel guessed she'd not be happy about it. Peggy's silence had signaled her unwillingness to repair their relationship, and Mabel didn't want to open that can of worms, especially after Ma's death. There was nothing Mabel could do. She folded the letter into her skirt pocket.

In the office, Cora had set out their sandwiches with Cokes on an empty desk. Mabel did her best to follow Cora's chatter about the girls. She seemed able to forget, or at least forgive, Mabel's curt approach to supervising in the past. Mabel got the impression that the office atmosphere had been more formal under Greta's supervision than the typists cared for. Mabel avoided judging Greta's leadership. Michael had put her in a tough spot, and she had done her best to keep the ship afloat.

Cora maneuvered the conversation to her curiosity about the architect. "I've enjoyed doing the typing for Thomas. He's got big plans for the Opera House. I hear the New York theater is quite a gem."

"Thomas did a wonderful job with the budget he squeezed from Jimmy."

"Rose told me she thought you were involved with him."

Mabel shook her head. "We worked together while he renovated the theater. He was kind to show me around the city." Before Cora could respond, Mabel changed the subject. "Let's get to the ticket sales, shall we?" Cora took the cue and cleared away the sandwich wrappers.

As they walked through the plans for sales, Mabel recognized Greta's meticulous organization and the imprint of Miss Barnes's training at the Cass. A blitz of radio and newspaper advertising was scheduled. The Lafayette had expanded its number of subscription patrons. The list of automobile dealers, reliable sources of block sales, was up to date. With such a big show, it was reasonable to expect every performance to sell out.

Mabel had gone with Thomas to see the amazing Ethel Merman perform *Annie* in New York. Starstruck Polly had used her crew connections to worm her way backstage to watch Merman every night for a week. Mary Martin would headline the road show, and her reviews all but guaranteed Detroit theatergoers would come out in numbers that would make the run profitable by a good margin.

When Cora ran out to the ladies' room, Mabel looked around the office with a satisfied feeling. It was good to be back in the swing of ticket sales. Whatever it might take, she would prove herself again in this office. And she resolved to be kinder to Cora and the girls.

When Thomas came into the office, ready to take her out, Mabel had an idea. "I'd like to show you my house, Mr. Architect."

$$\bullet \blacklozenge \bullet$$

CHAPTER 16

"Ah, the Spanish style," Thomas murmured as the taxi pulled into the drive. For an hour, he inspected the facade and ironwork, ran his hands over the stucco walls, took the height of the arcade doorways, and viewed the tiled roof from the second-floor balcony of the garage. Mabel left him to roam on his own while she worked on the dinner preparations. Iris got busy at the stove, rising to the occasion of a formal meal rather than the usual kitchen table supper. Thomas strode into the kitchen from the backstairs and looked over her shoulder. "Smells delicious." She blushed red to her hairline.

Mabel was setting the dining room table as he came through the kitchen door. Thomas watched with hands in his pockets. "The detail in this house is remarkable for the Midwest. Sturdy and stately. A local architect drove me around the city before I started work on the Opera House. This neighborhood dates back to the twenties. What made you choose it?"

"I inherited the house, sight unseen. I've lived here for only about six weeks."

"The house has been maintained well."

"I know little about taking care of a house, especially a house like this."

"The men working on the theater restoration will know which craftsmen in the city have expertise with this style." Thomas waved a hand. "That tile roof can be tricky to repair."

"I've heard that. I appreciate the advice." She gestured to the chairs. "Please have a seat. I'll check on dinner."

In the kitchen, Iris ladled the steaming first course into two soup plates. She winked at Mabel. "When you told me you were bringing a guest home for dinner, you didn't mention he's a dish."

Mabel frowned. "Watch yourself." Picking up the servings, she backed out of the kitchen door with a glare at Iris. She set a bowl at each place, then filled their water glasses from the pitcher on the sideboard. She picked up her spoon to signal that he should begin eating.

Thomas tasted the soup and nodded. "When you inherited this house, did you think about selling it?"

"No. I had nowhere to live."

"I figured you for a rolling stone, like me. Not one to settle down."

"But you're settled in New York, aren't you?"

"Not for the long run. My plan is to travel the world of architecture, taking on projects as I go." He looked around the dining room. "This house would fetch a good sum."

She had not shared her past with Thomas, but he had detected her remnants without knowing how close he was to the truth. She eloped with Al to get away from her father's house. After running from her marriage, she slept on a cot in the farmhouse where she drank. In New York, the Allerton had been a good enough way station.

"I've never had a proper home. The woman who was like my grandma left this house to me, hoping I would settle down."

He smiled. "If that's what you want."

"I think I want to try."

"I presume you'll work at the Lafayette?"

Mabel nodded. "Yes. Jimmy's got a Broadway show booked."

Iris peeked from the kitchen door, then came to take the soup plates. Thomas cleared his throat and adjusted his napkin on his lap. Mabel gulped water. When they were together in New York, conversations flowed easily between them. Sitting with him now, she felt she had nothing to say that would interest him.

Iris returned with the plates of roasted chicken and potatoes. After asking if they needed anything else, she scooted back to the kitchen. Thomas waited for Mabel to raise her knife and fork over the chicken, and he did the same. While they ate, he amused her with tales from the refurbishing of the Opera House. Jimmy and his father had come to blows more than once during the project. He chuckled. "As I recall, you went toe-to-toe with Jimmy quite a few times."

"He's not happy that I left New York."

"Are you happy?" Those kind eyes gazed at her from behind the spectacles.

For a moment, she didn't know how to answer. Then she said, "I want to be happy."

Iris interrupted to take away their plates and offer coffee. Thomas refused, looking at his watch. "I must go to the Opera House to look in on the night crew. There is still much to be done in a short time."

Mabel led him to the desk in the library to use the telephone to call a taxi. While they waited, he admired the cabinetry in the library. When the cab pulled up, Mabel saw him to the door.

Thomas took her hand. "Thank you for a delightful evening, Mabel. Your home is lovely, and I hope it brings you much happiness."

Mabel smiled. "Thank you, Thomas. You are always welcome here. If you need anything before you leave town, call me at the Lafayette. Cora enjoys doing your typing."

He grinned, donned his hat, and went outside to climb into the cab. Mabel closed the door and leaned against it. *Are you happy?* Fortunate to own the house, lucky to have her job back. More than that, she couldn't say.

The clatter of pots propelled Mabel into the kitchen. Iris was up to her elbows in suds at the sink. Mabel grabbed a clean dishtowel and waited as Iris rinsed a pot, then took it and rubbed it dry. They worked in silence until the pots were gleaming in their cupboards; the silverware replaced in the sideboard; the stove wiped down.

Mabel hung the dishtowel on the drying rack, then leaned against the counter. Iris swept the floor. "Iris, I'm going back to work tomorrow."

"What time will you want dinner?"

Mabel explained the theater schedule. Iris was quick to adjust. "We'll have a bigger breakfast; I'll pack your lunch and leave a plate on the stove for the late nights."

"Thanks, and thanks for tonight. I won't be bringing anyone else home."

"Why not?"

She couldn't answer. Why not indeed? Mabel hid her confusion by turning to leave the kitchen. "I'm going upstairs. Good night."

She flicked the switch for the foyer light off and made her way up the stairs. Standing in the second-floor hallway, Mabel stared at the doors to the four bedrooms. What dream had built this house? She imagined children scooting among these rooms, giggling behind the closed doors, a whoosh of footsteps running past her down the stairs. The late hour weighed on her. She shook off the vision and dragged through preparing for bed.

Sleep didn't come, and she lay awake thinking about Jack's note, her bedside alarm clock ticking away the minutes. The darkness made it easier to confront what her heart held. The night she confided in Polly, Mabel realized her feelings for him were genuine. His letter was a sign that he was struggling as a priest. The sabbatical was his version of running away after what had happened between them. What if he wanted to change his future? Polly may have been right about making Jack declare his feelings.

Mabel threw off the bedcovers and went to the bureau. She flicked the lamp on and pulled out the bottom drawer. Inside was the jumble of papers from her room at the Allerton she had thrown into her trunk in her haste to leave. She rummaged until she found the envelope sent from the UP with Dan's Christmas card. He would know where Jack was.

Mabel put on her robe, tucked the envelope into the pocket, and went downstairs to the library desk. She pulled out writing paper and held the pen, unsure of the proper words. Dan was Jack's friend, but he too was a priest, and he might not wish to be involved. She could only hope he'd help.

Dear Dan,

I apologize for not writing since receiving your Christmas card. I was away from Detroit for a year, but I am back and living at a new address. Last April, Jack sent me a note that reached me just this week. He wrote about the sabbatical and considering his future. Do you have an address where I can write to him? I hope all is well with you.

> *Sincerely,*
> *Mabel Hunt*

She wrote her address on Canterbury Road at the bottom of the letter and on the back flap of the envelope. Mabel propped the sealed letter next to her handbag and clicked the lamp off. She took the stairs two at a time and went back to bed. Her eyes closed, and she slept until the alarm jangled her awake.

On her way to the theater, she slipped the letter into the mailbox at the corner and marched to the bus stop with a satisfied feeling. Dan would reply, she was sure. As the bus passed the cathedral, she shook away the ghosts of Mabel and Jack on the steps. Ghosts had no future.

The brisk September morning quickened her walk from the bus to the Lafayette. Out front, men on ladders were hanging the marquee message: *Get tickets now for Annie Get Your Gun.* The office would be humming.

Mabel entered to a chorus of greetings from the typists busy at the desks. Cora was standing with a clipboard and raised her brows with a nod to the rear.

Michael sat at Mabel's desk.

Mabel gave him a wave then turned away to unbutton her jacket and hang it on the rack. Her heart pounded. She straightened her skirt and forced a smile as she approached the desk.

He stood with raised brows and folded arms, reminding her of the nuns waiting for her to explain herself with the punishment already decided. She hadn't seen him for months. New lines etched his forehead, and his face was as somber as the day Mrs. Butler died.

Mabel met his eyes. "Hello, Michael."

He nodded. "Cora, Mabel and I will be upstairs." He made for the door to the corridor, and Mabel followed with a glance at Cora, who crossed her fingers.

In the hallway, Mabel stood beside him. "Michael, before you say anything, please know that I am very sorry for leaving the way I did."

He started up the stairs without responding.

Mabel plodded behind. He was not going to make this easy. She expected to see Greta in his office, but was surprised instead by Polly, who hugged her. "Mabel, are you all right? We were worried sick, weren't we, Michael?"

"Thanks, Polly. I'm fine now." Mabel stole a glance at Michael standing rigid next to his desk chair.

"Polly, Mabel and I have business to discuss."

"The most important thing is Mabel is back, and she's fine."

Polly was trying to soften Michael's annoyance. Mabel played along. "How is Betsy? Did she enjoy your show in New York?"

Polly beamed. "She loved it! We had a wonderful time together."

Michael cleared his throat. Polly gathered her handbag and hat. "Can you believe it, Mabel? I'm auditioning for a part in *Annie*! The road company is still casting. Wish me luck." Polly blew a kiss to Michael and swept from the office, her heels clacking down the steps.

Mabel stood before Michael's desk. "I hope Polly gets the part."

Michael ran a hand across his brow. "Yes, of course. See here, Mabel, Jimmy and I are concerned. What do you intend us to think when you show up here after disappearing for two months?"

Mabel twisted her hands. "Please do not lose confidence in me. I was wrong to run off without talking to you. The death in my family hit me like a ton of bricks. But I should have telephoned. I am so sorry."

He sighed. "There's a lot to be sorry about. You walked out, leaving the operation running on bare bones. We burned a bridge at the Cass by taking Greta from them."

Mabel bristled. "If I may say, that had nothing to do with me. You made that decision before you took Betsy to New York."

Michael reddened and tapped a pen on the desk. "That's not the whole story. If you had talked to me, I would have asked you about coming back to the Lafayette and Greta taking the job in New York, which she wanted. I had to get her on the payroll first."

Mabel would not give Greta's condition away, but he had a point even if it would not have worked out. She tried a different tack. "Look, I was grieving, and I made a mistake, okay? You gave me a chance when I was at the end of my rope, and I will do whatever it takes to prove to you I want this job." She leveled her gaze at him. "I spent a year in New York because you and Jimmy needed me. Now, I'm back in Detroit. I've inherited a house. I am here to stay."

His expression softened, and he sat down. "I am sorry for your loss. You inherited a house?"

Mabel perched on the chair beside his desk. She told him about Canterbury Road. He had an old school friend in the neighborhood. Mabel promised to invite him and Polly to visit. He said he would enjoy that. They looked at each other.

Michael smiled. "Welcome back, Mabel. Don't ever run off like that again."

Mabel grinned. "Thank you, Michael. I won't."

He sighed. "Jimmy is making big moves, as you know. We've got tickets to sell."

"Greta assigned me as ticket girl."

Michael nodded. "Greta called in sick today. She's been running a tight ship downstairs. I'd like you to keep the office humming."

Mabel nodded, wondering how much longer Greta could keep her secret. She wanted to ask Michael more about Polly and Betsy, but thought it best to get to work. His telephone rang, and she rose to go downstairs, glancing back. She would not let him down again.

Mabel gave silent thanks to organized Greta as they launched sales of the *Annie* tickets. She telephoned subscribers and filled in the seating charts for dates with sold-out seats. Extra telephone lines installed in the office rang steadily. In a blur of two weeks, the Lafayette sold out the show. Cora and the typists cheered when Michael allowed them to pick dates to see the show in the house seats.

Greta did not return to work. After a week of sick days, she telephoned Mabel at the office. "My ankles are twice their size, nothing fits me, and eating makes me nauseous. Put me through to Michael. I have to tell him."

Michael assumed Mabel knew about Greta's condition but did not blame her for keeping the secret. "Greta did us a great service by coming over to the Lafayette. If she wants to work with us again someday, we'll be happy to have her." He was more concerned with following the *Annie* success with another hit. "I'll make trips to New York to help Jimmy with negotiations."

Polly won an ensemble role in the *Annie* cast, playing two characters in different scenes. "I'm understudy for Mary Martin, unofficially. If she goes down, I'll be ready." Mabel smiled at her confidence as they ate sandwiches in the pantry during a rehearsal break. Polly was also feeling assured of her marriage. "Michael rented a house for us near the school Betsy will go to. He hasn't seen a property he wants to own. Madge got herself into college, did you hear? We have a girl to cook and look after Betsy." She lowered her voice. "What's going on with the priest since you've been back in town?"

Mabel shook her head. "Nothing." Polly didn't know about Jack's letter, or that Mabel had written to Dan. She wasn't ready for her chewing on those details. Every night, she checked the mail Iris left on her desk in the library. Nothing from Dan. The mail delivery in the UP was slower than in the city, and October snow was falling in the far north. But it had been a month, and she was losing hope Dan would reply.

Polly threw up her hands. "You'll end up sorry if you don't put that to rest one way or another."

Mabel crumpled the wax paper from her sandwich. "How about you give it a rest?" She checked her wristwatch. "I must get back to the office."

Polly shook her head. "I hit a nerve."

Jimmy and Esther made the train trip for the *Annie* opening at the Lafayette. The grand reviews in the Detroit papers kept the telephones in the ticket office ringing, though they could offer only standby tickets for will call seats not claimed for a performance.

While Jimmy was in town, he and Michael spent hours on the telephone with New York producers. The tense negotiations soured Jimmy's mood. He was curt with Cora, no jokes or teasing the girls. The office pressure eased when he cut his Detroit stay short and flew back to New York.

Mabel anticipated Michael following Jimmy, and it was no surprise when he announced his travel. "I'll leave on the first of November." He paused, and Mabel looked up from scribbling notes on her pad. "Polly insists we take Betsy trick-or-treating on Halloween. It falls on Sunday this year, and the theater will be dark."

Mabel blurted an impromptu invitation. "Come to my neighborhood for trick-or-treating." The pumpkins Iris bought from a passing farm truck sat on the back porch, waiting for carving. Cut-outs of witches and ghosts decorated the windows of houses on her street, and when night fell, the dense trees created a spooky effect. Halloween was the perfect occasion for them to visit her house. "We'll make it a party."

Michael liked the idea. "Polly has a costume in mind for Betsy, and also for me." He shifted in his chair. "This is not my forte. She finds it ludicrous that I work in theater and hate dressing in costume."

Mabel chuckled. "I'll keep a check on the costuming."

When Polly heard the party plans, she clapped her hands. Betsy wanted to be a fairy princess, and the wardrobe mistress had sewn yards of tulle and satin into a flowy dress. "Should Michael and I wear something matching? Let's raid the wardrobe room."

"What are you thinking?" Mabel followed her, angling to protect Michael from the extremes of Polly's ideas.

"Dorothy and Scarecrow from the Wizard of Oz." Polly flipped open a trunk and pulled out a gingham dress. "I could make this work for Dorothy."

Mabel shook her head. "How about something simpler?"

Polly snapped her fingers. "I'll be a black cat. Look at this." She held up a form-fitting black leotard. "I can add a cap with ears and a tail. I'll paint whiskers on my cheeks."

Mabel grabbed a black fedora from a hat tree. "Make ears to sit on the brim of this hat, and Michael can wear it with a black turtleneck." Polly studied the hat. Mabel pushed her idea. "You'll match well enough to escort Betsy. She's the star of the show on Halloween."

"You're right. He doesn't enjoy dressing in costume, but I can sell him on this." Polly gathered the leotard into a bundle with the hat. Relieved, Mabel grabbed a witch's hat for herself.

Mabel went around inviting everyone who worked in the theater to a Halloween party at her house. When she announced this to Iris, her eyes widened. "I thought you were bringing no one home."

Mabel shrugged. "I changed my mind."

Iris chuckled. "What shall we serve?" They settled on a simple array of finger sandwiches, pickles, gingerbread, nuts, and sugar cookies as a buffet in the dining room for guests to nibble during the evening. Cora and the girls would bring popcorn balls and candied apples. They found a huge punchbowl in the sideboard for the apple cider mulled with cinnamon and cloves.

As the day drew near, Iris scrubbed, polished, and dusted. One evening, Mabel came home to find her at the kitchen table cutting silhouettes of bats and ghosts from pieces of construction paper. "We'll put these on the windows and on the front door."

Mabel uncovered the dinner plate on the stove and cleared a space on the table of paper shreds. "Having a party takes more work than I realized."

Iris nodded at a basket holding paper pouches and a sack of candy corn. "If you want to help, you can stuff the bags for the trick-or-treaters."

"I can do that." Mabel finished her supper, washed her plate at the sink, and got to work on the basket. Iris had made an extra effort with the preparations, and at the theater, the girls talked excitedly about their costumes and looked forward to a fun evening. It was too late to call off the party. But she worried. At backstage parties, beers loosened the stiffness among roles and rank in the theater pecking order. At her house, there would be no alcohol.

Mabel shared her nervousness with Polly. "It was silly to ask the staff to get together with their boss. What if no one talks? What if no one shows up?"

Polly modelled her black cat outfit for Mabel, strutting around the dressing room. She had sweet-talked Michael into wearing the male version of the costume, minus the tail. She pooh-poohed Mabel's concerns. "A party is what the doctor ordered for this crew. Believe me, no one is afraid of talking to Michael. And I'll be there."

On Halloween, Mabel donned a full-length black velvet cape borrowed from the wardrobe room. She buttoned it closed and tied the ruffled collar, sweeping it around her legs clad in black tights. The witch's hat with black fabric strings of "hair" attached all around covered her blond curls tucked under the brim. She sat for Iris to smudge a green tint on her cheeks and circle her eyes with gray. Then they did a walk-around of the living room and dining room to make sure all was ready for the party.

Mabel squeezed Iris's arm. "The decorations are perfect. Everything you've done is wonderful."

Iris beamed. "You have a home to be proud of. Let's light the fire."

The evening weather was clear and crisp. Clusters of costumed children scampered along the sidewalks, parents leading the smallest ones. Candles inside carved pumpkins glowed on Mabel's porch and porches down the block. Mabel stood outside, giving the candy pouches to the trick-or-treaters as she awaited her guests. The papier mâché bats Iris wired to a low branch spooked the kids risking the walk to take a treat from the witch.

Michael's sedan pulled into the drive, and Polly jumped out to lift Betsy from the back seat. The fairy princess carried a pillowcase for collecting treats. Mabel squatted to hear her say, "Trick or treat," and wave her wand.

"Here's your first treat. Are you ready to get more?"

Betsy nodded. Michael pulled his lanky frame from the driver's seat and greeted Mabel. Polly, clad in the leotard and a furry cap tied under her chin, plunked the hat with ears atop her husband's curls. She struck a pose with a hand on her hip and with the other took Michael's arm. "Aren't we a pair of black cats?"

Michael raised his brows as though daring Mabel to make a smart remark about his costume. She grinned. "We'll get a snapshot of you later." He shook his head.

Betsy wiggled her impatience to start trick or treating. Polly took her hand and kept the other around Michael's arm. "We'll wear her out and come back for the party."

Cora and the girls arrived dressed in the glittery garb they had scrounged from the theater and the dramatic face makeup they had painted on each other. They wanted to take turns on the porch with the candy basket, and Mabel gave it over. She greeted the other guests as they walked into the foyer.

Polly had been right. The costumes provoked laughs and lightened the mood. Tilda and her sister, holding masks to their faces, shouted "Boo!" at everyone. Tilda came to Mabel's side and whispered, "Ya done all right for yourself with this place. Now, get the husband." Mabel smiled and offered her a sandwich. Someone tuned the console radio in the living room to dance music, and partners paired up. Men from the crew stepped onto the back porch to smoke. Mabel suspected they passed a flask around and let them be. Iris, dressed as a clown, introduced herself as she bustled between the dining room and kitchen. Mabel slipped into the kitchen to help. "It's going well, don't you think?" A loud burst of laughter came from the dining room. Iris put more sandwiches on a platter. "I'd say so, by the amount they're eating."

Before long, the black-cat couple returned with the sleepy Fairy Princess Betsy cradled in Michael's arms. Polly slung the treat-filled pillowcase over her shoulder. Mabel led them upstairs to settle Betsy on a bed. Once she snoozed, they hurried to the dining room, Polly's tail swishing back and forth.

Michael said to Mabel, "Betsy had a lot of fun, and Polly was in her glory out there. This was a great idea."

Mabel smiled. "Happy Halloween. Have some food." She watched as the crew and the girls greeted Michael and Polly with jokes and laughs. She needn't have worried. Michael was a fair and kind boss, and the staff liked him. He moved around talking, taking playful gibes about his costume from the crew, and complimenting the girls in his easy manner. Mabel chatted and kept an eye on the food. She lost track of the time until ten o'clock, when some people said their goodnights, and she saw them out. The basket of candy corn bags was empty, and Mabel turned off the porch light to signal no more treats.

The remaining group lolled on the davenport and chairs, costumes awry. Polly started a word game that generated giggles. After a few rounds, Michael bowed out of the game and asked Mabel if he could go upstairs to check on Betsy. She rose to go with him.

As they went up the staircase, Michael admired the window. "This is a beautiful home, Mabel. Walking around this neighborhood got me thinking about buying a house."

"Thomas thought I could get a good price for this house."

"Would you sell?"

Mabel shrugged. "I think not. But nothing is permanent."

"Fatherhood lasts forever." They looked at each other. She had spoken without considering his commitment. He eased into the room where Betsy slept. She dozed on her side with the costume dress bunched under her legs. Michael brushed his daughter's hair back from her face. "She won't like me waking her up to drive home."

The front doorbell chimed. Mabel frowned. "It's too late for trick-or-treaters."

Polly called up the stairs. "I'm getting it."

Michael picked up Betsy's shoes from the floor. "I'll wake her so we can leave."

Mabel reached for the shoes. "Give me her things and I'll tell Polly." Gathering the fairy cape and wand, too, Mabel trotted down the stairs.

Polly emerged from the entry vestibule and came to Mabel's side. "Trick or Treat. Your Jack is on the porch."

CHAPTER 17

Mabel stumbled off the bottom step and dropped the fairy wand. Polly grabbed Betsy's things and prodded Mabel toward the door. "Go talk with him. I will hold everyone back for a few minutes." She whispered something to Michael coming down the stairs with the little girl.

Mabel stepped into the vestibule and shut the door behind her. She pulled open the outer door. With the porch light off, faint strips of light from the streetlamp filtered through the tree branches. The candles flickered in the pumpkins on the stoop. Letting the door click shut, she leaned against it while her eyes adjusted to the dimness. No one was there.

"Mabel, I'm here." Jack stepped out of the shadows at the corner of the house. She tried to swallow away the tightness in her throat.

"What are you doing here?" She had sought him out, and he had appeared, like a wish granted by a fairy or a dark spell cast by a wicked witch. But the last time he had shown up on her porch, it had cost her two drinks and months of anxiety. A longing to be with him competed with the panic she used to feel as a kid when flinging herself off the tire swing into the lake.

He stood before her. A full beard and hair curling at his ears meant he had not been to the barber for some time. There was a worn-down look about him, as if he had not been sleeping. He reached out as though to touch her cheek, then dropped his hand.

"Your face is green." Jack shoved his hands into the pockets of his zippered tweed jacket.

"Dan said you were looking for me."

"I asked him for an address to write to you, not for him to give you mine."

"If you want me to leave, I will. But I'd like to talk with you if you will let me."

"Your last words to me were not kind." They looked at each other.

"I regret what I said to you. I'm sorry."

Voices behind the door meant Polly had stalled the group as long as she could. No way was Mabel introducing Jack to Michael or anyone else.

He nodded at the house. "I've disturbed your party."

"My friends are ready to leave." She waved a hand toward the driveway. "Wait for me at the side door.

With a nod, he turned and followed the walkway around the corner of the house. Mabel breathed deep and opened the front door onto Polly and the typists clustered in the vestibule. Polly stared at Mabel with wide eyes. "While you were outside, Iris made treat bags to take home."

Mabel forced a bright smile. "Time to say good night, then, is it?" She shook hands, pecked, and patted backs as her guests filed out, saying thanks and good night. Michael, carrying Betsy, raised fingers in a wave. Polly, last, as Mabel knew she would be, whispered in her ear, "He is better looking than you let on."

Mabel grabbed her arm. "Not a word to Michael. I will sort this out."

Polly nodded. "Find out what you need to know." She hustled to Michael's sedan.

Mabel stood on the porch until the cars had pulled away. The street went quiet. She used a twig to snuff the candles inside the pumpkins. What to say to Iris about the man at her side door?

She heard the clang of the garbage can lids and made her way around the corner of the house. There Iris and Jack were stuffing paper bags into the cans, Iris giggling at something he said. When she saw Mabel, Iris clamped a lid closed and wiped her hands on the apron tied over the clown trousers. "Mabel, your friend Jack hasn't had supper. I'll gather some leftovers." She hurried up the stoop and held the screen door open.

Mabel cleared her throat. "Fine, yes, let's go inside." Jack moved to take hold of the door, and Iris stepped inside. As Mabel passed him, he said, "Thank you."

In the kitchen, Iris offered Jack a chair at the table as she bustled about getting a plate and arranging the sandwiches and bits of fruit left from the party. Mabel perspired under the heavy cape. She rubbed at a trickle of wetness along her neck, and the melting green makeup stained her fingers. Mumbling, "Excuse me," Mabel left the kitchen and ran up the front stairway.

When she flicked on the light over the bathroom mirror, she gasped at the mess on her face. Flinging the cape to the floor, she peeled off the tights and black leotard and bundled her hair into a ponytail. She scrubbed at her skin until the water ran clear of the green. Then Mabel bundled the costume into her arms and scampered across the dark hallway to her bedroom.

She pulled on high-waisted trousers and a long-sleeved wool sweater. Slipping her feet into moccasins, Mabel loosened her hair and brushed it off her face. Standing at the mirror, she tapped the brush against her palm. Jack said he came because she was looking for him. This was the time for him to declare his intentions. She scoffed at the silliness of that old phrase popping into her head. But she held the upper hand; he was in her house.

Downstairs, Mabel found Jack at the kitchen sink, washing the last of the dishes. Iris, with the broom and dustpan, made a quick sweep of the floor, then turned toward the mudroom. "I'll be saying goodnight." She winked at Mabel behind Jack's back.

Mabel waved her off. "Thanks for your help with the party. Goodnight." Iris clomped up the back stairs to her room over the garage. Jack dried his hands with a dishtowel and leaned back against the counter, looking at her. "Come with me," Mabel said. She flicked off the switch for the kitchen light and led him through the foyer to the living room.

The small lamp atop the radio console cast a dim light. The fire had gone to embers. Mabel shivered and hugged her arms against the room's chill. Jack used the fireplace poker to stoke the flames. He took a log from the basket at the side and placed it on the grate.

Stepping back, he came face to face with her and grasped her hands in his. "Hello, Mabel."

Looking into his eyes, she imagined his warm hands sliding under her sweater. This would not do. She inched back, and he let go of her hands. "Jack. Tell me why you've come to my house." She tugged an armless chair closer to the fire and sat down.

Jack stretched out on the rug between her feet and the fire. "Things went awry tonight, and I took a chance coming here." He looked into flames running along the log. "Peggy kicked me out of her house. My mother has disowned me." He turned his face toward her. "I've made a formal request to the bishop to leave the priesthood."

Mabel covered her mouth with her hand. Jack nodded, the weight of his words hanging between them. "My family refuses to accept my decision." His eyes teared. "I hurt them. They're ashamed of me."

She slid off the chair onto the rug and stretched her legs next to his. "Tell me what happened."

"I've been lying for years. I let it go too far." Jack sighed. "I should not have gone through with the ordination." He drew his legs up to his chest and rested his chin on his knees, staring into the flames. "I ran away from my duties." His voice caught as if he might cry. "Dan, good man that he is, stood by me. He knew the pain I've been in. Gave me a refuge up north to sort myself out. I've spent the last six months in the woods, confronting my lies."

Mabel longed to say something to comfort him, but she kept silent. She recognized the need to tell the truth of his mistakes, as she had in the circle of alcoholics. If he could bear being honest, she could bear listening to him.

He cleared his throat and leaned against the chair, shoulder to shoulder with her. "I wasn't called to a vocation the way the priest told us altar boys it came about. As far back as I can remember, my mother said that when I grew up, I would be a priest. I was in grade school when she gave our pastor my father's place in our house, coming for dinner, lecturing me and Peggy about sin. Peggy laughed it off, but for me it was dead serious. Every day after school, I went to the sacristy to prepare what the priests needed for Mass. On Saturdays, my mother took me with her to help clean and reset the altar while the priests heard confessions. It was as if she promised me to the priesthood, like an arranged marriage. And my obedience to her, and the rituals, carried me along. Until high school."

"You know I loved playing baseball. I was good enough to be scouted by a major league team. Not the Tigers, but a real chance to get into the game. One guy on my team found out my mother shut that down with the scout without telling me. When I confronted her, begged her to let me try out, she called the priest to talk sense into me." He clenched his fists at the memory. "You might remember the time I went away on 'retreat.' He forced me to stay alone in a room at the seminary for 'prayer and reflection.' Given only bread and water, alone, scared, I caved. I played my part. Captain of the baseball team on his way to the priesthood."

Mabel and the other girls used to line the fence to watch handsome Jack play baseball. Her heart ached hearing about the sadness he had secretly carried. Had that been an unspoken connection between them back then? They had both been wounded and hounded in their family homes. Both of them pretended and went along.

She said, "I wish you had been able to talk about how you felt. To Peggy at least."

He scoffed. "I would never have told Peggy. She was sold on me being a priest. And you know her. She'd have no sympathy for me." He looked at her. "Many times, I wanted to tell you. I wish I had." If he had, what difference might it have made? But they were here now.

The burning log split, sending sparks up the chimney. Jack went on with his story. "When I got out of the house, things got better. In college, and over the summers I worked in the forest conservation corps, people didn't know that I was supposed to be a priest. I was one of the guys." He chuckled. "I dated a few smart girls who had ideas for their lives. Girls with ambition, studying for careers. I realized what I was missing. Don't get me wrong, I don't mean sex."

"I had missed the part where *you* decide what you want to be when you grow up, who you are. I didn't have answers to those questions, but I understood it was my choice to make. When Peggy announced her wedding, I planned to come back and tell them I wasn't going to the seminary."

He turned his face to Mabel. "I also planned to throw myself at you. To see if there was a chance for us to be more than friends." He shook his head. "Seeing you at the wedding thrilled me but seeing you with Al flipped me on my head. So, I got drunk. I didn't fight for you and I didn't have the guts to stand up to the family. Instead, I let the charade continue."

In the seminary, the doubts and fears he'd bottled inside cracked his pretense. "The other men fell into line. I zig-zagged between flaunting authority by breaking rules and then remorseful pious streaks when I went numb. It was as if I was living a bad dream." He ran a hand through his hair. "Then Peggy told me you were back in town." He kicked at the hearthstone. "When she told me what you'd gone through ... I was so sorry I had let you go."

"What you heard from Peggy was not the worst of what I did." Mabel had not told Peggy the whole truth of her downfall after she ran from the hospital. As far as she knew, Tom had said nothing about the state he found her in at the farmhouse, and neither Peggy nor Ma had pried for the details from Mabel.

He looked at her. "The night I met you at the rooming house, I told you I didn't judge you. You looked beaten down, but also real, if that makes sense."

"That night, you prayed over dinner and talked about becoming a priest. Now you're saying that wasn't real."

Jack sighed. "You were toughing out your situation; told me to leave you alone. I fell back on my pretense. I kicked myself for not being as strong as you were. But I couldn't walk away from you. Thoughts of you flooded me no matter what I did."

He shook his head. "Dan figured it out after the afternoon we spent with you. Gave me a man-to-man talk about being truthful. But I told him he was mistaken and plowed ahead. The ordination was scheduled. I lived in my mother's house for the week before the ceremony. Lying on the bed in my old room, I watched the ghosts play."

"I convinced myself I only had to kiss you to make my obsession end. Why did you let me in when I came to your apartment that night?"

Mabel shrugged. "I had never seen you so flustered. I thought something terrible must have happened for you to show up at my door like that."

"I made up my mind to tell you. After, I treasured our kisses."

"But at the ordination, your words to me were not kind." She had enjoyed the kisses, too, tangled up with regret. But she wouldn't admit that.

"I should not have said it. I'm sorry. Being ordained was the worst mistake I've made in my life."

Mabel folded her arms. "You made that choice and you dragged me with you! It was not up to me to stop you."

Jack nodded. "You have a right to be angry with me. I'm sorry, so sorry." He reached for her arm. "But I know what's true now. I love you, Mabel."

He had said the words she longed to hear, and it would be easy to take his face in her hands and kiss him. She could have him. But he was not free to make that choice with her.

She shook her head. "Oh, Jack. I accept that you're sorry. But love? How can you know that?"

He gazed at her. "I want to know love with you. If you'll let me."

Her heart pinged with the same want, tempered by her judgement. *I will not be a temptation to Jack.* She stiffened her tone. "You are not in a position to want that."

He understood her meaning. "The bishop will hold a hearing on my petition."

"You don't know who you are. And I am not high school Mabel. She's long gone."

"Please don't freeze me out."

She looked him in the eye. "I'm not freezing you out. But you have to figure out your life."

He was quiet with the truth of what she had said. The mantel clock chimed. Mabel nudged him. "It's midnight. I have work tomorrow."

She stood and crossed the room into the foyer, and he followed. As he zipped his jacket closed, Jack said, "I heard this house was Ma's gift to you. I'm sorry you lost her."

"She was good to me. Thank you." Mabel opened the door.

As he moved past her, Jack touched her cheek and smiled. "Good night, Mabel." The kiss held back sparked between them.

"Good night, Jack." He slipped out, and she locked the door. Mabel snuffed out the last of the fire and turned off the lamp in the living room. Exhausted, she wanted no more thinking, only to hold on to his words, *I want to know love with you.* In the darkness of her bedroom, she pulled off her clothes, and the longing for him inched along her frame. She snuggled under the covers and let her senses imagine his touch.

CHAPTER 18

In the first half of November, the overnight temperatures dropped close to freezing. Drafts of frigid air greeted Mabel when she rose in the mornings. The bathroom radiator spat enough steam that her teeth didn't chatter as she washed, but in the larger rooms, the radiators cranking against the cold drafts seeping from the windows made little difference.

One morning, Iris laid a small fire in the library and brought Mabel's coffee and toast on a tray. "The oil man said the house will stay warmer if we put up the storm windows." She saw Mabel's puzzled look. "On the outside. They're in the garage."

They went into the mudroom, and Iris opened the door connected to the garage. Cold air whooshed over them. Mabel walked down the cement steps into the space, sized for parking two sedans. The yard tools and push mower cluttered the nearest corner. A jumble of clay pots, emptied of their summer flowers, and sacks of peat moss sat in the middle. The storm window frames in assorted sizes and shapes leaned against the back wall. Brushing past cobwebs hanging from the rafters, Mabel hugged her arms around herself and studied the pile. Lifting the heavy panes was not a job they could manage. Shivering, she shooed Iris back inside the mudroom and jumped up the steps, closing the door against the chill. "We need some help."

In the library, Mabel fished inside the desk drawer for the card from the taxi man who worked on houses. Iris plucked it from her hand. "Leave it with me. We'll get the windows up afore it snows."

Mabel plodded to the bus stop, glad for the lack of snow, dismayed she had overlooked the windows. She had been in a daze since seeing Jack. Iris's chatter about chores for the coming winter—canning vegetables, ordering firewood, hiring boys on the block to shovel snow, seeing to the oil delivery for the furnace—had gone over her head. A pile of unpaid bills had sat untouched on the library desk until Iris waved the pages in front of her, saying the grocer held their order.

Jack floated in the back of her mind. When she lay in bed, his words replayed like a radio station she could not switch off. Unable to sleep, she'd get up and pad to the kitchen, fix a mug of hot milk, and sit huddled under a blanket in the armchair in the library. Iris had found her, head lolled back, and shaken her awake enough times to wonder, "Are you having the grief again?"

Mabel feared her distraction would cause mistakes in the ticket office. Her bleary eyes watered from checking and rechecking the ledgers. Michael had gone to New York, and she telephoned him each day with the treasury report. She sat on the edge of her chair, her leg shaking, until he was satisfied with the details, avoiding Cora's concerned glances.

Polly had, of course, been keen to pry from her what happened on Halloween. "I still think forbidden fruit is sweet. And now you know where he stands."

Mabel frowned. "Where does that leave me?"

"In a romance with a handsome man."

"Who is still a priest."

"Give him a chance to come round."

She didn't tell Polly she could hardly tolerate the limbo of waiting for him. True, she had made the overture of writing to Dan. But what Jack had declared unnerved her. Sending him away was right for both their sakes. Unless … she hated second-guessing herself.

Mabel fell back into her terse tone with the typists, and the camaraderie of the Halloween party faded. But the girls perked up with excitement when they heard Michael's announcement of the date for the theater Christmas party. They anticipated a rollicking affair since the *Annie* cast would join in. Gleeful Jimmy had extended the show's run at the Lafayette through January because a fire in a Chicago theater kept the road company from moving on. More tickets to sell.

Speaking with Mabel from New York, Michael confided his delight about the run keeping Polly in Detroit. "We'll have a family Christmas. The three of us, and Madge, if she wants to join us."

Mabel's spirit sank further at the thought of moping about on the holiday, the house empty except for her ghosts. With company, she might keep them at bay.

"All of you *must* stay at my house on Christmas Eve. Betsy can wake up there on Christmas morning and find what Santa has brought her." Bringing to life the Christmas morning she never had as a child would be a bonus.

Michael was pleased. "That's a wonderful invitation. A row of stockings hanging on that beautiful fireplace. Talk with Polly, and we'll firm up the plans when I return."

To Mabel's relief, Polly loved the idea. "Betsy *will* believe Santa can come down your chimney! We don't even have a fireplace."

Iris, too, was happy about the plan. "We'll make a wonderland for the little girl." They had the money to be generous. Mrs. Nelson's accounting of the house fund proved Iris's frugal care. Mabel told her, "Invite whomever you'd like to join us. This is your home, too."

Iris accepted Mabel's declaration with a half-curtsy. "Appreciate that, Mabel. Got one person in mind. Patsy called asking for you and me to give her a hand on Thanksgiving. She's openin' the diner for the folks on the block who got nowhere to eat, like Ma used to do. What say we show up for her and she comes here for Christmas?"

"That's kind of her. But I thought you and Patsy didn't get along."

"Aw, that was before. She asked me nice."

Patsy's following of Ma's tradition comforted Mabel. "Yes. Let Patsy know we'll be there."

Now, Mabel entered the Lafayette's lobby to find a small crowd waiting for the ticket windows to open. It had been like this since the extended run was advertised. She tapped on the office door, and Cora slid open the peephole, then unlocked it and held it ajar for Mabel to slide inside.

"Are we ready to open a window?" Mabel asked as she unwound her scarf and hung her coat on the rack. Cora handed her a mug of black coffee with a raised brow, and Mabel bit her lip in chagrin. "Thanks. Good morning, girls. Are we ready to open a window?"

Cora nodded. "Yes, and you have a visitor." She gestured toward the lobby. "A priest knocked on the office door asking for you. I showed him to the bench by the candy concession."

The *nerve* of him to show up at her office. Her hand shaking slopped coffee over the rim of the mug. Cora pried the mug from her fingers and offered her a tissue for the drips. Mabel crushed the tissue between her palms.

She made her tone as even as she could. "Go ahead and open the window. I'll be right back." Tossing the tissue into the wastebasket, she went through the inside corridor to the door for the lobby. Cracking it ajar, she peered out. The end of the candy counter was in sight, but not the bench. Mabel slipped around the door and inched along the wall until she got a look at the bench.

Jesus. Father Dan. He saw her and stood.

"Mabel, good morning. Nice to see you again." He held a black fedora and a pair of gloves. His chin doubled over the white clerical collar. The black robe swirling around his legs reminded her of the nuns.

"Dan, what are you doing here?" She stiffened against hearing the answer. It had to be about Jack.

"I am on my way to Michigan Central to go back to my parish up north. I took a chance to stop and talk with you." He gestured toward the bench. "Can we sit?"

Mabel glanced up and down the hallway to be sure they were alone. "For a few minutes. We have a line for the ticket windows." She held her skirt taut and sat down at one end of the bench. He took the other, swiveling to face her.

She crossed her arms. "Jack showed up at my house because you gave him my address." She looked him in the eye to make a point of her dismay.

"I showed him your letter, but not until *after* he had made his formal petition. He was determined to find you when he came back to the city. He would have come here."

Dan fingered the hat in his lap. "The bishop sat for Jack's petition hearing yesterday. I was summoned to appear with him."

"What happened at the hearing?" Mabel dug her fingers into her arms. She had never ridden a roller coaster because watching the downward plunge made her shake with terror. Peggy and Jack laughed through it, but no amount of cajoling could get her to go with them. Now she held her breath for the drop.

"The bishop delivered a long, angry lecture about the disgrace of his actions. But he will forward the petition to the Pope. It could take months, but it's likely Jack's withdrawal from the priesthood will be granted."

Oh, Jack. Mabel shook her head. "I had no idea he would do this. I hadn't seen him since the ordination. It's not my fault."

Dan tapped the fedora on his knee. "Mabel, listen to me. He didn't quit because of you. Jack is following his heart in turning away from the priesthood. That's my honest belief. I testified on his behalf. Whatever happens between the two of you is separate from his decision." He looked at his wristwatch. "I must get to the train station."

They stood and walked in silence to the front lobby. Mabel glanced at Dan's profile. He was a stand-up guy, and a priest. If he testified for Jack, he must be sure. But his words were not proof.

Before leaving, Dan smiled at her. "You know how to reach me."

"Yes. Thank you, Dan, for coming to see me."

"He's a good man, Mabel." He donned his hat and went out.

She stood by the door as Dan got into a taxi idling at the curb. Jack would be at loose ends waiting for the word from Rome. His family, more upset. But this was not her problem to solve. Jack must stand on his own, just as she had.

Shrieks came from inside the ticket office. The patrons still waiting in line craned their necks to see what caused the commotion. Mabel hustled to the locked door and pounded until it opened, and she burst inside.

Polly, in costume, threw her arms around Mabel. "I'm the lead! Mary's down. I'm the lead!"

Cora waved a sheet of paper. "The director ordered stuffers for tonight's program. Once the stencil's cut, we'll run them on the mimeograph."

Mabel grinned at Polly. "Break a leg! Now get out of our hair while we work on the programs."

Polly grabbed Mabel by the shoulders. "House seats for Madge and Betsy." She twirled and ran to the corridor going backstage.

The girls twittered about Polly's good fortune. They cleared a worktable and started the routine for a cast change. The typist preparing the stencil gently pulled it from the typewriter and held the fragile sheet with both hands as Mabel looked over the wording and okayed it for copying. Cora refilled the machine with ink. Two of the girls loaded the stencil and worked the lever to squeeze ink over the stencil as the drum rotated.

Cora held up a hand to pause after the first copies slid into the drying tray. She checked the still-damp pages for blots, then nodded. The girls restarted the drum and printed sheets rolled off. As they dried, others cut the pages into strips and handed them to those stuffing the programs.

Michael entered the office, eyeing the running mimeograph. He had returned from New York the day before. "Have you changed the lobby message board?"

Mabel took chalk and an eraser from the counter. "I'll do that now."

"Walk with me." He opened the door to the lobby. The cluster of ticket buyers was gone. Next to the windows, a chalkboard perched on an easel. They had had no cast changes for weeks, using the board only to post the box office hours. Mabel erased the board and began writing in block letters, *Tonight the role of Annie*, aware of Michael pacing behind her.

"Our star refused to have an understudy. The director made Polly stand by for *all* the female roles. She says she's ready to play Annie, but ..."

Mabel paused the writing. "She asked for the house seats for Madge and Betsy."

He nodded. "I'll drive home later to pick them up." His forehead crinkled, and he sighed. "I'm the nervous one. Polly's thrilled."

Mabel poised the chalk over the board. "You know she'll give it everything she's got. We'll cheer her on."

"Put the girls somewhere in the first balcony to do that." He turned and climbed the staircase to the boxes. He'd watch Polly's rehearsal from there.

Mabel returned to the office to locate the evening's open seats for the girls. The balcony had been sold out, but seats here and there from returned subscriptions remained. She pulled the tickets and made the complimentary notes in the treasury binder. They had done well enough in the run to absorb the cost, but Michael would pay from his own pocket.

At their normal quitting time, the typists went out to eat supper before the curtain. Cora stayed behind to help cover the window and telephones. With no tickets to sell, they opened only the will call window ahead of show time. At the first gong calling patrons to their seats, Mabel shooed Cora out to the balcony. The last of the will call patrons claimed their tickets, and Mabel closed the window.

The orchestra began the overture as she scurried through the backstage door. She had a folding chair waiting in a hidden spot in the wings.

If anyone in the audience that evening had been disappointed reading the stuffer announcing Polly as the lead, they forgot about it when she sang "You Can't Get a Man with a Gun." She embodied the character of Annie Oakley in her own Polly way, whipping the rifle from side to side and strutting along the footlights. Her voice was clear and strong. The audience went wild with applause. Mabel cheered, too. Michael had to be relieved and delighted.

In the wings, the crew hustled with scenery and prop changes. The seamstress stood ready with the dressers for any last-minute costume adjustments Polly needed. At the intermission, the stage manager reminded her of the blocking for the numbers in the second act. Mabel heard Polly's confident "I got it."

In the second act, Polly's singing of the ballad, "I Got Lost in His Arms," cast a trance over Mabel. Like Annie in the play, she couldn't say how it happened, but the lost feeling embedded within her eased when she was close to Jack. She hungered for him to hold her in his arms and to kiss him again. As the song ended, applause filled the house, but Mabel sat with tears streaming. A song had turned her to mush. What was she to do about him?

The Annie character had her happy ending, and so did Polly, taking multiple bows to the roars of the crowd. When the ushers had cleared the house, Mabel made her way to Polly's dressing room. Michael stood in the narrow hallway, beaming and shaking hands with passing cast and crew members. Mabel poked her head around the door, taking in the fragrance from the vases of red roses Michael had had delivered. Polly, Betsy on her lap, surrounded by well-wishers, waved. Mabel blew her a kiss. Cora and the girls bustled in with their programs for Polly to autograph. As she passed him on her way to the office for closing, Mabel's eyes met Michael's in a mix of shared relief and elation.

The next day, the morning paper reported the star had missed a performance, with speculation about her condition and no mention of Polly. At lunchtime, she appeared in the office, wearing dark glasses and looking for coffee. The girls burst into applause, and Cora jumped up to pour a mug. Polly made a little bow and took rapid sips of the brew Cora handed her.

The celebrating had gone into the wee hours. "Michael put Madge and Betsy into a cab at midnight. When the crew chief kicked us out, a bunch of us ended up at that little burger place down the street that's open all night." She tilted her head at Mabel. "Walk backstage with me."

As they ambled down the hallway, Mabel said, "You were wonderful. I'll remember it always."

Polly sighed. "I had a moment, didn't I?"

Mabel looked at her. "What did the director have to say?"

"He's an old hand, jaded. He cared only that I didn't bomb. But the assistant told me he actually applauded a few times."

"What will happen tonight?"

"She's here, recovered. Back to my corner." Polly noticed Mabel's pouting lips. "It's okay. Last night took a lot out of me, and I'm not talking about the party. The lead is like gymnastics for three hours." Polly took the sunglasses off and looked at Mabel. "Big surprise—I'm pregnant."

CHAPTER 19

"**D**on't watch me!" A piece of apple pie fell from the fork Polly stuffed into her mouth. "Is there pumpkin, too?" She mopped her lips with her hand.

Half of the mini-pies Mabel had taken to the pantry for the crew were gone. She suspected Polly had eaten most of them. Watching her lick up crumbs, Mabel asked, "Is there room in your costumes for all this pie?"

Polly sat back with a shrug. "Barely. But I tipped the seamstress to alter them." She shook her head. "The first time, I couldn't look at food without retching. Now, I can't stop eating." She looked at Mabel. "Are you okay with me talking about it?"

Mabel pulled the pie tin to her side of the table. "Eating pie helps." She took a forkful.

"Yes, it does. And these pies are the best." Polly dug her fork in once more.

Mabel's feelings about Polly's pregnancy flip-flopped like balls ricocheting in a pinball machine. She kept to their routine of taking an afternoon break together, sometimes going numb as Polly prattled about the baby, and sometimes braving it for inoculation against her old anguish, like having the measles. Mabel's heart swelled at seeing Michael's elation when Polly took his hand and placed it on her belly. But when her own hands shook and the tears welled during the girls' chatter about throwing a stork shower, she shut down the talk by pointing out mistakes and calling for silence. Cora's face told her it wasn't fair to let her sadness take away the others' joy.

Helping Patsy with the neighborhood Thanksgiving dinner had been a welcome respite. Mabel and Iris arrived at the diner early to find Patsy already busy in the kitchen, draped in an apron from bosom to knees. "Happy Thanksgiving! Warm yourselves up with coffee, then I'll put you to work."

The radio played upbeat music while waiting to broadcast from the parade on Woodward. Gripping a hot mug, Mabel warmed her hands and breathed in the savory aroma wafting from the kitchen. Iris downed her coffee and chewed on a donut as she donned a clean apron and tossed one to Mabel. Patsy stuck her head out of the kitchen door to hurry them. "Iris, come and work on the potatoes. Mabel, get all them tables set. It'll be a full house."

Mabel, get all them tables set. Ma's voice was in her ear. Fork left, knife right, spoon by the knife, folded napkin in the middle. The last time she had set out the silverware for Thanksgiving, though, had not been in the diner. It had been at Peggy's house, their last year of high school. Her own family had given up all holiday rituals, and Peggy's mother always had a place for her at their table. Jack had sat across from her that day, and she recalled how he stiffened when the parish priest intoned the grace with a special prayer for God to bless the young man's vocation.

Mabel wondered where Jack was this Thanksgiving. She hadn't thought to ask Jack where he would stay while he waited for the decision from Rome. The seminary wouldn't allow him there, and his family had banished him from their homes. She hoped he was not facing the same agony of a lonely holiday she had known in her first sober months. But the time alone had made her reflect on her actions. He had said the same about his stay up north with Dan. She could only hope that his heart was at peace.

As they opened the diner to their guests, a quick headcount had Mabel setting extra places at the counter. Patsy's big heart had reached into the neighborhood, as Ma had, to bring food and company to those who were alone or too feeble to cook. A few of the old ladies remembered Mabel, but they didn't pry past asking where she worked and saying wasn't it just like Ma to leave her the house. When an old timer pointed his finger, saying, "You was that Miss Front End," as she poured his coffee, she didn't get flustered, only smiled, and moved on.

After they ushered the last people out and locked the door, Mabel sat at the counter with Patsy and Iris to eat their own dinner. Mabel raised her glass of mulled cider. "Happy Thanksgiving. Cheers to you, Patsy, for your kindness to the neighborhood."

"It's only right. The people around here supported Ma from the start. If it weren't for her, I mighta' been on the street."

Iris chimed in. "Patsy, thanks for not holding nothing against me."

Patsy looked at her. "Everybody makes mistakes, girl. We go on. All we can do." Then she raised her glass. "A toast to Ma." They nodded to Ma, smiling from the photo on the wall, and drank the toast.

On the way home, Iris said, "You laughed a lot with the folks today. Looked good on you."

"What are you saying?" Mabel blushed at knowing Iris watched her.

"Looked like you had a happy day, that's all." Iris shrugged. "Nice to see."

Mabel had learned to trust Iris's knack for reading people. That mirror turned on her brought the realization that making the effort for the joy of others had moved her sadness into a corner.

She and Polly polished off another pie. Pushing the tin aside, Polly took cigarettes from her pocket, then tossed the pack into the wastebasket. "I'm giving those up. Make me gag."

"Have you talked to the director?"

"He made it official. They can't keep me in the cast when the show moves to Chicago. In a year, if I have no baby fat, my agent says I can try for something. But he's letting me down easy. We both know the score." She sighed. "I'll be here, starring in the role of mother and wife. Don't know if it'll be a comedy or a tragedy."

"Oh, Polly." First Greta, now Polly, giving up their dreams. Or beginning new dreams?

"There's no script for this, no music to dance to."

"But there are others who have starred in the role." Polly raised her brows, waiting for an example of outstanding motherhood. Mabel shrugged, no one coming to mind. They looked at each other.

Polly shifted in her chair. "Michael's fussing over me, insisting on regular doctor checkups. Would you go with me to the first one?"

"I can't leave the office."

"Yes, you can. I need you."

"You are fearless on stage, yet you need me for the doctor's office?"

Polly reached over for Mabel's arm. "One time. Please." She was nervous about seeing the doctor, but she was using it to drag Mabel closer to her own fears.

Mabel twisted away from Polly. "I know what you're doing. One time."

Polly gave her a satisfied head-bob. "The appointment is set for Monday afternoon."

On Sunday morning, Iris broached the subject of the closed-door bedroom upstairs. "You want me to sort out the things Ma left? If your friends are to stay here on Christmas Eve, I've got to clean the room and set it nice for them."

Of course, Iris was right, but it wasn't fair to leave it to her. "Let's get it over with."

When Mabel opened the bedroom door, she shivered. The radiators in the room were shut off. Iris twisted the knobs open, and the pipes clanked as they heated. Ma's footlocker sat like a little coffin at the foot of the bed. Mabel dragged it to her bedroom and shoved it in the closet; it could wait until the day she felt strong enough to open it. Iris was emptying the bureau drawers and Mabel sorted out the closet. Ma's kitchen dresses reeked of cooking smells despite laundering, and Iris put those in the rag bag. They bundled Ma's few other dresses, trousers, and shoes for the charity collection, setting aside a thick wool coat to offer to Patsy. Iris went to clear the cabinet in the bathroom.

Mabel sat in the armchair, gazing out the window. Ma was not a ghost in this room or the clothes. She was a memory to call on for strength.

Iris came out of the bathroom. "I can get the rest of this done during the week. What will they need? Anything in particular?"

"Michael and Polly will want Betsy to sleep in here. Is there an extra cot in the basement, or should we bring in the one from the sewing room?"

"Let's move the cot from the sewing room. That will open space to hide the presents Santa ordered from Hudson's." Michael and Polly had given Mabel a lengthy list of the expected deliveries.

When she entered the theater on Monday morning, Mabel ran into Michael, valise in hand. "Last-minute trip to New York. I hope to return by the end of the week. You'll go to the doctor with Polly this afternoon, right?"

She wanted to back out, but he counted on her going. During his frequent absences, he expected her to look after the business, and since the pregnancy, also Polly, while he was away.

"Yes. Don't worry."

He nodded and donned his hat. "I'll telephone tomorrow."

The afternoon's bitter wind blew a few flurries. Polly took the wheel of Michael's sedan for the drive to the midtown Women's Hospital. As they pulled into traffic, she said, "I'm seeing the doctor who took care of me for Betsy. It's the only place in the city that would attend an unmarried woman having a baby. No one there looked down their nose at me."

Mabel clung to the seat cushion and kept her eyes on the street. Polly glanced at Mabel. "You look a little green around the edges."

Her stomach churning and sweating inside her coat, Mabel rolled the window down an inch for air. "I'm fine. Get us there in one piece."

When they reached the hospital parking lot, Polly angled the car into a space, and they made a brisk walk to a three-story brick building housing the medical offices. After checking the register for the doctor's office number, they rode the elevator to the fifth floor. Before opening the frosted glass door, Polly looked at Mabel. "Are you okay?" Mabel wiggled her hand to go in.

The windowless waiting room held two rows of cushioned chairs with arms, like those around Michael's conference table, facing a nurse seated at a reception desk. The bland beige walls were bare, and the linoleum floor was scrubbed clean. A table along the wall held pamphlets and magazines. A young woman with a belly filling a maternity blouse rose from a chair and waddled to the water cooler in the corner.

At the desk, Polly gave her name to the nurse, who handed her a clipboard of papers. She slipped out of her fur coat, a gift from Michael after her starring performance, and Mabel hung it with her modest wool on the rack near the door. They took seats, and Polly began filling in the forms.

Mabel whispered in Polly's ear, "This is as far as I go."

Polly muttered as she continued writing, "I meant for you to be with me for the exam."

"Nope."

"You have to."

"Never said I would."

Polly huffed and rose with the clipboard. "I'm going to tell the nurse I want you with me."

"Don't you dare."

At that moment, the nurse came over to take the clipboard. "The doctor's ready for you."

Polly frowned at Mabel and followed the nurse.

Mabel drank a cup of water drawn from the cooler, then went to the table hoping for the distraction of a fashion magazine. To her dismay, blissful portraits of mothers and babies gazed at her from the spread of tattered covers. The pregnant woman came up behind her and tossed a copy of *Parents'* on the pile. She rummaged through issues of *Your New Baby* with the comment, "They're no help when you're walking the floor with a screaming infant." She glanced at Mabel. "First one?"

"Oh, no. I'm here for my friend."

"Mm. Sooner or later, it'll be your turn."

"I'm not planning that."

"I wasn't either. Then the right guy came along, and we're on number three."

How lightly she spoke despite the huge crack in the floor opening between them. Mabel shook away the dark vision and wiggled out of the conversation. "I must go to the restroom."

The nurse directed Mabel to the ladies' room in the hallway. After splashing water on her face, she held the hand towel over her eyes. She was not as immune to babies as she had hoped. A nurse scurried in for a quick use of the toilet and left. Alone in the restroom, Mabel stretched out the time to reapply her face powder and lipstick. While she fluffed up her waves with her comb, she thought about going down to the lobby coffee shop, but Polly wouldn't know where to look for her.

When she had blotted her lipstick a second time, Mabel closed her handbag and stepped into the hallway. Near the elevator, she dawdled by reading the directory of doctors' offices on the floor, all of them obstetricians. Before the miscarriage, she hadn't yet seen a doctor. Afterwards, the doctor who cared for her in the hospital told her she'd soon want to try again, as if she was throwing darts in a fairway game. *Breathe.*

The elevator bell dinged, and the doors opened to let out the passengers. Mabel focused her eyes on the directory as a group of women walked past her, dispersing to different offices. She startled at a familiar voice behind her.

"Well, well, well. If it isn't the tainted woman who led my brother astray."

Mabel turned to see red-faced Peggy, her lips sneering and eyes narrowed. She wore a green and black plaid winter coat in the fuller style, with only the top two buttons closed, the gap revealing her rounded belly. She stepped closer to Mabel, backing her against the wall.

Tainted woman. That Peggy would use that term stunned her. "Peggy, listen to me. You are mistaken."

That didn't satisfy Peggy's mean streak. "I don't think so, Mabel. You destroyed my family."

"I've done nothing to you." The interruption of another elevator arriving gave Mabel the advantage to step around Peggy and start walking among the women moving down the hall.

Peggy followed, stepping next to her and grabbing her arm. Mabel squirmed to break free from her grip. Peggy's jaw clenched in a distorted smile until the hallway cleared and they were alone. "My mother's taken to her bed. She won't eat, and she cries all the time! Jack broke her heart—because of you!"

Mabel stiffened. Her heart sank over how shaken their mother must have been at Jack's abandonment of the priesthood. "I didn't know what he was doing."

Peggy raised a fisted leather glove at Mabel. "Don't stand there pretending you didn't know, or that it's not your fault. He's killing my mother, and for what? To be with a drunk!"

Mabel drew back with a gasp. When they were young, Mabel had often witnessed the satisfaction Peggy got from hounding those who angered her. But she had never turned on Mabel in this way. She imagined shaking Peggy by the shoulders. But even if she did and shoved past her, scowling Peggy would never take back the shameful accusation.

Mabel steadied her voice as forcefully as she could. "You have *no* right to say such things to me! I had *nothing* to do with Jack's decision. *Nothing.* Now I am walking away from you." Shaking, she turned her back on Peggy and made for the door to Polly's doctor. Peggy tailed her.

"I am not finished with you, Mabel."

Before Mabel could open the door, Polly stepped out. "There you are. I'm ready to go."

Mabel flashed an alarmed frown toward Polly and pointed over her shoulder. "This is Peggy. Jack's sister."

Peggy scoffed. "Who's this? Another drunk?"

At that, Polly stepped around Mabel. "I beg your pardon. You have something to say?"

"I am talking to Mabel, if you please."

"It sounded like a quarrel to me." She exchanged a glance with Mabel, who clutched her bag to her chest as if it were a shield.

Peggy hissed at Mabel, "You should have seen the look on Jack's face when I told him you snuck into Al's place to hide your drunken binges, and cheapened yourself in barrooms so the police had to haul you out. Tom spilled all the ugly details. How he found you filthy and sloshed, living with *two* men!"

Polly took a step forward. "Now, just a minute here, you …"

Peggy cut her off, scowling at Mabel. "I gave Jack an earful about you. He knows what you really are!"

Mabel's heart pounded in her ears. "Stop! Peggy, stop!"

Polly stepped in, nose to nose with Peggy. "That's enough. Peggy, move on with whatever business you have. We're finished." At that, Polly took Mabel's arm, standing like a sentry against Peggy's next move. "Walk away, Peggy. I warn you."

"Warn me of what?" Peggy shook her fist at Mabel. "He'll go back to the priesthood. He'd never take up with you!" With that, she spun on her heel and marched down the hallway.

Polly nudged Mabel through the door into the office. When she had shut it behind them, she blew out her breath. "Whew! She's on the warpath for you." Seeing the nurse's puzzled look, Polly waved to her. "We're just getting our coats."

In a daze, Mabel reached for her coat. Winding her scarf around her neck, she whispered, "Peggy blames me for what Jack's done. I know her. She will *never* see it another way."

Polly shrugged into her fur. "Maybe. But what matters is what he thinks."

"What do you imagine he thinks? She gave him a nasty taste."

"But he knew what happened, and he said he loved you."

"I didn't tell him the *whole* truth. But it sounds like Peggy did."

CHAPTER 20

Father Dan replied to Mabel's telegram within a day. When the Western Union operator relayed the message, Mabel asked her to repeat it.

Ignoring the ringing telephones, she scribbled on a pad, head down. Jack was living in the rooming house where she had sought refuge.

After they left the doctor's office, Polly had advised her to talk with Jack at once. "Don't let his sister's lies gnaw at him."

Peggy's fury worried Mabel more than she had let on to Polly. It was not the pounding of the final nail in what used to be their friendship, as much as the danger that the venom Peggy poured into Jack's ear had sown mistrust that could not be undone. Now that she knew where to find him, Mabel was less sure of facing him. Jack might look upon her through the taint of what he had heard.

Jack was familiar with Peggy's worst side. When they were growing up, she had often aimed her bitter sneering to hurt Jack, but he put up a defense against it. Many times, Mabel had seen him frustrate his sister's meanness with his cool practice of refusing to appear upset. In the moment, the tactic threw her off balance. He may have used that shield against her accusations about Mabel, but he might be left wondering why, when he professed his love, Mabel had not told him the whole truth.

Polly came into the office seeking donuts at the same time Cora hung up a call and waved for Mabel's attention. "We have another sorry subscriber."

The Lafayette had offered the seats for the extended weeks of *Annie* performances only at the window, no mail orders. Because of the high demand, Michael allowed subscribers to return their tickets for resale at the window. When a subscriber regretted selling the hottest theater ticket in town, the girls scrambled to find another seat.

Polly plopped into the chair next to Mabel's desk. "What news on the Rialto?" Her code for asking if Mabel had learned Jack's location.

Mabel rose to go to Cora. "I have an address, but …"

Polly shook her head. "Go today while you can. Michael returns tomorrow on the early train."

Mabel waved away Polly's advice and went to Cora. Michael's absence created a series of excuses to stay in the office. She lurched from one problem to another, missing her lunchtime. It was mid-afternoon when she nibbled on a sandwich between telephone calls. She talked herself out of going to the rooming house. Even if she did duck out, a private conversation was impossible in the place's shabby lobby with scruffy men looking on. In the frigid weather, where would they go to be alone?

Then she thought of Luna. He'd probably take his dinner there.

But she had to cover Michael's duties before the eight o'clock curtain. Since her stint in the New York theater, the crew in the back of the house recognized her as Michael's stand-in. She did the final walk-through alongside the stage manager before he cued the lights down. As the overture began, Mabel hurried from backstage to the office for her coat. Her hands trembled doing the buttons. She had never left her post before the end of the performance while Michael was away. But her leaving didn't bother Cora, who waved at her with wishes for a good evening. Still, Mabel paused in the lobby to quiz the lead usher about the coverage of the aisle doors, check the concession stand, and call for Tilda to mop up a spilled soft drink. At last, she was on the sidewalk, hailing a cab.

By the time Mabel arrived at Luna, the tables were empty, and Mrs. Marini had her sons washing pots. She bustled over to greet Mabel. "You want to eat? Sit. I bring you a plate."

"I'm too late. You're ready to close."

"No, no. Sit." She pulled out a chair at a table along the wall. Mabel hung her coat on a peg and took the seat. One son brought the breadbasket, followed by Mrs. Marini holding a plate heaped with spaghetti and meatballs. She set it before Mabel. "All right, I sit with you?"

Mabel nodded. She waited for the older woman to sit, then took up her fork. "Mrs. Marini, thank you." She dug into the spaghetti, wondering how to ask about Jack in a casual way.

"You don't come in much anymore."

"I have a house now, and after work, I go home."

Mrs. Marini clasped her hands at her chest. "Ah, good for you. A home is the most important thing." She leaned in. "Father Jack don't come neither."

Mabel wiped her mouth with her napkin. "You haven't seen him?"

"No. He tell me goodbye, move out of the seminary. He not gonna be a priest."

"I know."

"He tell me he loves a girl. Is that you?" Jack had been certain enough of his love to tell Mrs. Marini.

Mabel clattered her fork on the plate. Looking into Mrs. Marini's kind eyes, in that moment, she knew. "Oh, Mrs. Marini, I hope it's me."

The old woman grabbed her hand. She said something in Italian that sounded like a blessing. Then she stood up. "When you find him, bring him to see us." She patted Mabel's shoulder. "You eat while we clean."

Mabel ate the pasta with a lighter heart, despite her lingering worry about Peggy's damage. When she left the restaurant, the cold, and the late hour, had reduced the foot traffic on the street. She walked to the corner scanning for a cab but then turned down the block where the rooming house stood. From across the street, the lobby's dark windows reminded her the door was locked at ten. Gazing at the rooms above, she imagined Jack stretched out on a lumpy bed and wished him a good night.

Riding in the taxi she hailed, Mabel decided to send a note the next day asking him to meet her outside the rooming house on Sunday afternoon. They would walk to Luna, and she would unravel the knots of her past in her own telling. Jack would understand; she trusted his word not to judge her.

At home, Mabel tucked the covered plate on the stove into the refrigerator and shut off the lights. Upstairs, before going into her room, she peeked in the bedroom suite. Iris had layered cozy blankets on the bed, and a stuffed bear waited on the cot for Betsy. Living in this house was like she had gone from the earth to the moon in the two years since Tom found her in the farmhouse. What might the next two years bring? Mabel went to sleep pondering how Jack fit into that future.

She woke with a start. For a moment, Mabel couldn't recognize the noise. She threw off the covers and opened her bedroom door. Downstairs, the doorbell rang and rang, and someone pounded on the front door. In bare feet, Mabel dashed down the staircase. Before she reached the bottom step, the kitchen light went on, and Iris rushed into the foyer, pulling a sweater over her nightshirt. "What the …"

Mabel scooted across the cold tiles and cracked the vestibule door open to slip around it. In the entry, bitter cold air seeped from under the outside door. Shivering, she put her eye to the peephole. "Oh, no. Iris, come quick!"

Mabel fumbled with the lock and yanked the door open. In a blast of frigid air, Polly, with wailing Betsy clinging to her neck, fell against her. "We had nowhere else to go!" Her bare hands extended from the wide sleeves of her fur coat. Underneath, a nightdress clung to her legs. One foot wore a slipper, the other a boot.

Mabel pulled them into the foyer. "Oh, Polly! What happened?"

Iris rushed to close both doors. Before she did, a teenage girl holding Polly's other boot dashed inside. She flung the boot on the floor and threw her arms around Betsy and Polly. Betsy lifted her head and let out a scream.

Polly raised her teary face to Mabel. "If it weren't for Millie, we'd be dead." She sagged under Betsy's weight, and Iris reached to take the sobbing child. But the girl, Millie, enfolded Betsy in her arms, rocking her.

"The house caught fire!" Polly grabbed at her hair. "Millie saved us!" She fell back against Mabel. "She pulled Betsy from her bed and woke me." Choking on tears, she moaned and pushed a hand under her coat, rubbing the flannel covering her belly.

Betsy's wails ebbed to gulping sobs. Millie whispered in her ear, and the child let her take off the pink wool coat covering her sleeper pajamas. Millie wore trousers under a nightdress and only socks on her feet.

Mabel, alarmed, kept a grip on Polly as she spoke to Iris. "Warm baths. I've got Polly."

Iris nodded and took Millie's arm, steadying her to walk up the stairs carrying Betsy. Polly called to Betsy, "It's okay, honey. Millie's got you. I'll be there soon."

When they had gone, Mabel asked Polly, "Are you bleeding?"

"I don't think so. Oh, Mabel, I can't tell you how horrible it was! Betsy screamed and screamed. We ran to the curb and jumped into the sedan. Millie was brave! She ran back inside for our coats and the car keys. The smoke! The firemen made me pull away." Trembling, she grasped at the stair railing. "Getting here was all I could do."

"Of course. You're safe now."

Mabel grasped the collar of Polly's fur and tugged her coat down one arm, then the other. Tossing it aside, Mabel circled her arm around Polly and turned her to start up the stairs. As they crossed the second-floor hallway, the cadence of Millie's voice calming Betsy leaked from behind the closed bathroom door.

Polly sighed. "Betsy will never get over this."

Mabel shushed her. "You'll all feel better soon." Leading her into the bedroom suite, Mabel sat Polly on a stool with a glass of water while she drew the bath. When the hot tub had filled part-way, she went to Polly. "I'll leave you to soak."

"Stay with me, please." Polly pulled her nightgown over her head and stepped out of her panties. Mabel's heart pounded as they both looked. No blood.

Mabel kept her eyes on the floor as Polly lowered into the warm water, holding her belly. Leaning back against the tub, she held her head in one hand and cried. Mabel sensed the tears arose from Polly blaming herself, even if it wasn't her fault. She sat on the lid of the toilet and waited. After a few minutes, Polly splashed water at her face and took a deep breath. "Help me out. I want to go to Betsy."

Mabel pulled a towel from the rack and extended her hand to Polly. As she stepped out of the tub, Polly's eyes widened. She grabbed Mabel's hand and flattened it against her belly. "There. My baby is kicking." They locked eyes.

Mabel sucked in her breath at a faint pulsation under her fingers. Her own pregnancy hadn't lasted long enough to feel what the doctor in the emergency room called "quickening." She lay on the gurney, crying, watching his eyes above his mask, his fingers between her legs, as he told her it was for the best.

Trembling, Mabel took her hand away and leaned over the tub to pull the stopper, letting the water drain. Polly swabbed the towel over her body, mumbling, "We're okay, we're okay."

Later, after Polly fell asleep curled up with Betsy in the double bed, and Millie dozed on the cot, Mabel sat at the kitchen table with a mug of coffee, recalling the moment in the bathroom. The sensation of the baby moving was a bittersweet wonder, but a wonder. It had doused Mabel's immediate fear, but she felt a ballooning responsibility to protect Michael's family. They were in her house.

Iris came through from the foyer, carrying the smoky-smelling pink coat and the fur. "I'll hang these in the basement to air." When she came back, she poured a cup and sat with Mabel. "What a night." She repeated what Millie had told her about the fire. "Got so she'd check every night to be sure Polly didn't fall asleep with a smoke, but that's not what happened tonight. Something in the kitchen started it, and Millie's beating herself up with blame. But she can't figure it, because nothing was on the stove. When they drove away, most of the house was afire."

Mabel shook her head. "They'll need … everything. When she's up to it, show Polly into my room for clothes. Something will fit her."

Iris nodded. "Millie's about my size. The little girl … we'll figure it out."

Mabel finished her coffee and looked at the clock. "I'll get dressed and drive the sedan to the theater. Michael will come here when he hears what happened." His train was due in a few hours. His usual practice was to come to the office before going home to freshen up from the journey. She dreaded having to tell him about the fire. "They'll stay here as long as they want. Order what you need."

Mabel left Iris at the table, scribbling on the grocery list. She dragged her legs up the staircase, and in the bathroom, revived her tired face by washing with hot, then cold, water. Dressed in a trouser suit and her face made up, she went downstairs to find the keys to the sedan.

Iris handed them over. "I emptied the pockets in that fur."

Mabel bundled into her coat and scarf and went to the car. It had been four years since she drove, and once she started the engine, she fumbled with the levers to position the seat and the mirrors. The wipers had frozen, and she stood in the wind to hack the ice with the scraper. When the engine was warm, Mabel jerked out of the driveway, unfamiliar with shifting the sedan's gears.

Stuck in the early traffic, wiping at the fogging windshield with her glove, the heater making little difference in the frigid interior, Mabel longed for her usual bus ride. At last, she pulled the sedan into the lot behind the Lafayette. As she entered the stage door, the watchman greeted her. "Miss, never seen you here this early."

Mabel told him about the fire at Michael's house. Then she left messages for the director and stage manager that Polly's status for the evening's performance was unknown. Mabel hoped she'd skip it to rest with Betsy.

In the office, Mabel made a pot of coffee and nibbled the muffin Iris had thrust at her as she left the house. Her eyes kept checking the clock. When Cora came in, followed by the typists, Mabel learned they knew about the fire from the morning paper. The headline read, *Mother and child escape burning house,* with the address, but no names. Cora knew it from sending Michael's rent check each month.

For once, Mabel did not try to stop the girls chattering. They started a collection to buy clothes for Betsy. Everyone knew Michael came from money, but even so, the girls planned lunch-time shopping to put together "a little care package" for Betsy, wishing to return some of the generosity Mr. Macready had shown them. Cora proclaimed, "We're a family here, through thick and thin."

Mabel sat with that thought as she watched the door for Michael. The telephone rang, and she got only two words out before his voice shouted, "Where are they? Tell me! Where are they? What hospital?" He had seen the paper at Michigan Central.

She talked over his frantic rambling. "Michael, listen. Polly and Betsy are at *my* house. They're fine. They are *not* hurt." In the background, she heard the stationmaster call a train. "Your car is here, at the theater. I will come get you."

"No." He stifled a sob. "A taxi will be quicker. Call, will you, and tell Polly I'm on my way." The line went dead.

As she replaced the receiver in the cradle, Mabel looked up to see the girls all staring at her. She held up a hand. "Mr. Macready is taking a taxi to my house." She blew out her breath. "Let's do our best today holding the fort and not worry him with business." Cora nudged the girls back to work and gave Mabel a thumbs up.

When Mabel telephoned the house, Iris took the message and reported on Polly. "She came down for coffee, then went back to bed. I'll watch for the taxi."

The day moved on, and Mabel took it as a good sign there had been no calls from the house. At the afternoon break, Mabel went backstage to the pantry and poured another cup of the coffee that was doing nothing to keep her lack of sleep from catching up with her. She was leaning toward taking a quick nap in one of the dressing rooms when the stage manager stuck his head in. Polly would not perform that evening. He handed Mabel the cast list naming the actress the taking over her roles. Relieved, she dumped the last of her coffee in the sink and made her way to the office.

In the corridor, she saw Cora with her eye against the peephole in the door to the lobby. "What's going on?"

Cora grasped the doorknob. "The Red Cross has a package for the family burned out last night. The landlord gave them Mr. Macready's work address. Their deliveryman is here." She pulled the door open.

Mabel gasped. Jack stood there, a bulky box in his arms. She recognized his field jacket as the same as Tom had worn for civilian war service, with the Military Welfare insignia woven on the sleeve. He wore dungarees and work boots, no hat or gloves. His hands were chapped from the cold.

His eyes widened at seeing Mabel. He cleared his throat and spoke to Cora. "Miss, where would you like me to set this box?"

Cora pointed to the corner, but Mabel put a hand on her arm. "Cora, we should stow the box in Mr. Macready's car. I have the keys. Can you run into the office and get my handbag, please?"

Cora trotted away, and Mabel motioned Jack into the corridor, then closed the door. He set the box on the floor. She checked to be sure they were alone, and said, "How is it you …?"

"Work for the Red Cross? They took me on for the Christmas season, to deliver boxes to folks down and out." He nudged the carton with his boot and looked away. Of course he would need work since abandoning his priestly duties.

"The Macready family is staying at my house. They're shaken up but not hurt. You met Polly on Halloween."

"Polly is …"

"Mrs. Macready. It's a long story." Mabel lowered her voice. "Are you comfortable in the rooming house?"

Jack's eyes flashed, and he stuck out his chin. "You checked on me with Dan?"

"I was hoping to talk with you." His tone was pushing her away. But if she missed this moment, she might not get another. "I ran into Peggy. Can we talk about … that?"

A frown flitted across his face, and he checked it with a shrug. Footsteps signaled Cora's return with the handbag. Jack stepped closer to the box and stood with hands folded behind his back, looking away, as though they had not been speaking.

Mabel reached for the purse and took the keys from it, saying, "Thanks. I'll walk with him to the sedan." When they were alone, she would invite him to meet her for Sunday dinner.

Cora said, "Mr. Macready left word for you to telephone right away. I can do this."

Mabel looked from Cora to Jack. "Will you wait for me?" He ran a hand through his hair, then nodded. Handing the keys to Cora, she pretended not to see her puzzled look. "Show him to the car, then take him to the pantry. I won't be long."

She smiled at Jack, but he looked away and stooped down to grasp the box.

$$\bullet\!-\!\blacklozenge\!-\!\bullet$$

CHAPTER 21

Jack didn't wait.

After telephoning Michael, Mabel had hurried to the pantry, but he was not there. She ran through the lobby to the street, looking for the Red Cross van. She stood in the freezing wind, staring at the empty curb space. Back inside, she rubbed her numb, stiff hands over a radiator and called Cora over.

"Mr. Macready wants his sedan right away. I must drive home."

"The girls made a basket for Betsy." Cora pointed to a wicker hamper brimming with packages, tied at the top with pink ribbon.

Mabel called for attention. "Girls! Listen up." At their desks, the women froze. "You have outdone yourselves. I'm proud of you. Thank you."

The typists grinned and applauded. Mabel blushed, realizing this was the first praise they had heard from her. Cora patted her on the back.

When Mabel had alerted the stage manager that she would be out until curtain time, and brought the car around front, Cora came outside with a stagehand who carried the gift basket. With it stowed in the back, Mabel pulled into the traffic. Dismayed that Jack had left before they could talk, she drove while lost in her thoughts. The coolness of his manner surprised her. He might resent her asking Dan for his whereabouts, but she worried the edginess stemmed from something more serious. He had gone without even leaving her a message.

She pulled the car into her driveway with little recollection of getting there. Michael stepped outside and came around to open her car door. He was the sad twin of the man she first met that stormy day, paler, unshaven, with more lines etched in his handsome face. "Mabel, I don't know how to thank you. I …"

She pushed out of the sedan and touched his arm. "Michael, there's no need to say anything. How are they?"

"Polly is holding up. We've been trying to settle Betsy."

Mabel gestured to the packages in the sedan. "The girls made a basket for Betsy, with clothes and toys. The box is from the Red Cross."

She thought he was going to cry, but he pulled his shoulders back and grabbed the bundles. "Polly's made a list of things to shop for. We'll open these first."

Clad in a pair of Mabel's knee socks and her long bathrobe, Polly met them inside, her finger to her lips. "Betsy fell asleep on the davenport." She eyed the Red Cross box. "Are we official refugees?" Mabel explained the gift of the hamper. Polly tugged Michael's arm. "Your people are wonderful."

Michael carried the packages to the dining room table. As he and Polly started opening the box, Mabel went through the kitchen door looking for Iris. She was tending a pot on the stove, and Millie stood at the sink, washing dishes. Iris clamped the lid onto the pot.

"Are you staying for supper? We've got a stew cooking."

"Smells delicious, but I must get back to the theater for curtain call. Any problems here?"

Millie turned, and she and Iris exchanged a glance. Iris shrugged. "We've managed. With the mister in the house, Millie's bunking over the garage with me. Polly let me wipe the bathroom, but they stayed in their bedroom until now." She looked at Millie. "Betsy cries a lot."

Polly poked her head around the swinging door. "Millie, come see the clothes for Betsy. Mabel, the girls sent just the right things." She let the door close, and they heard her murmuring to Michael. Millie nodded at Mabel and went through to join Polly and Michael.

Iris leaned closer. "They been arguing about staying here. He's saying they should move to a hotel." She busied herself at the stove as Michael strode in from the dining room.

"We've got basic things for tonight. I'll take Polly shopping tomorrow." He glanced at the kitchen clock. "I'll go to the theater to manage the performance and check in with the crew. You take tonight off." Seeing the shake of her head, he put up a hand. "I insist."

Mabel followed him into the foyer, advising him of the cast change made in Polly's absence. After seeing him out, she took stock of the clutter in the dining room. As she gathered the discarded wrappings, she looked up to see Betsy standing in the doorway, staring. Mabel waved to her.

"Hello, Betsy." The girl didn't scream or cry. After a moment, she waved back. Mabel smiled. "Do you want to help me clean up?" She wadded up some paper and threw it into the empty box. Betsy came forward and picked up wrapping paper, crumpling it in her fists.

Then Iris burst through the swinging door, and Betsy ran. Mabel started after her, but the little girl was fast, scrambling up the steps, yelling for Millie. Mabel let her go. Iris shrugged. "That's livelier than she's been all day."

Millie came down the steps with Betsy by the hand. "Iris, can we feed Betsy now, so's we can get her in bed?"

Iris nodded. "Sure. Let's set her up in the kitchen, and we'll eat, too." She looked at Mabel. "When you and the missus are ready, I'll bring dinner in."

Mabel went upstairs and knocked on Polly's bedroom door. She opened it, wearing an oversized man's flannel shirt over a pair of Mabel's trousers, unbuttoned, held up by a sash tied around her middle, and the knee socks. She waved Mabel inside and closed the door, saying, "I must ask you something."

Michael's travel case was open on the floor, and a suit jacket hung on the back of the armchair. The cot was tidy with fresh sheets, but the bed was a jumble of blankets and pillows.

Mabel nodded. "I came up to talk. You first."

"Are you sure we can stay here as long as we want to?"

"Yes, you can." Mabel had no hesitation about opening her home to them.

Polly folded her arms. "Michael says we should move to a hotel."

"Why does he want to do that?"

"He won't admit it, but his he-man side is taking charge. He's feeling guilty about not being home when the fire broke out, and his pride is dented. As the boss, he's uneasy about mixing you up in our personal drama. He intends to find a new house, buy furniture, everything, right away."

Mabel knew the practical side of things was Michael's natural habitat, but his worry about her was surprising. "If he took all of that on, plus the traveling to New York, it would be harder for me to manage than all of you staying here."

"It's too much for any of us." She sighed. "Moving fast can't make us forget what happened. I tell you, Mabel, coming that close to losing my child rattled me." Polly's instinct to protect her child had brushed up against its cousin, the grief of loss.

Mabel nodded. "What can I do?"

"Help me work on him."

Mabel sighed. "How?" She wasn't keen on getting between her boss and his wife. But she wanted to help them weather the shock of the fire.

Polly waved her hand. "Just back me up. I've told him we should relax over the holidays, take care of Betsy, and sort things out about the fire. When the new year begins, I won't be on stage, and we can look for a home. We'll stay here until we find it."

"If he wants my opinion, I will back you up."

"Thanks." Polly tugged at her shirt. "I *must* buy new clothes. This Red Cross stuff is an awful costume."

"That's what I want to tell you. It was *Jack* who delivered the Red Cross box." Mabel paced the room as she reported her talk with Mrs. Marini and the unexpected encounter with Jack at the theater. "He wouldn't look me in the eye, and he took off before we could talk. I don't know how to fix this. Should I write to him?"

Polly sprawled in the armchair. "You might be reading this wrong. Bringing that delivery was no accident; he knew you worked there. But you seeing his circumstances up close flustered him. Like Michael. Men put up a front."

Mabel puckered her eyebrows. "I don't know what he expects me to do."

"Don't you see what he's going through? He wants to be close to you, but he's uncertain about himself. He has to find his own way."

Millie's knock on the door interrupted them. Betsy padded in and grabbed Polly's leg, asking for a story before bed. Mabel left them and went into her room, Polly's words echoing in her mind.

Polly could read men, and she had a point. Jack's decision to leave the priesthood had made him a stranger in his own life. He was stumbling through the early days of starting over. At the theater, Jack had looked away from Mabel's pity, just as she had looked away from his, two years ago. She had been stewing over whether *his* love could survive Peggy's angry rant. But *her* love had to be steadfast as he forged an uncharted path. He had done that for her.

Later, when the house had quieted, Mabel sat at her desk in the library, chewing on the top of her pen, a blank piece of notepaper on the blotter. Then she wrote,

> *Jack,*
> *The Macready family thanks you for delivering the Red Cross box. They will stay in my house while they get back on their feet. Please join us here for Christmas. I hope you will.*
> *Mabel*

She sealed the note in an envelope addressed to Jack Finn, in care of the rooming house. Mabel was tucking it into her handbag when headlights in the driveway announced Michael's return from the theater. She greeted him at the door.

He shrugged off his coat. "All is well at the Lafayette." For a moment, he stood holding his hat and coat, then remembered which door in the foyer was the closet.

If Polly was correct about Michael's discomfort, Mabel wished to put him at ease. "Iris's routine is to leave a dinner plate for me on the stove. Tonight, it's for you. Come on." She moved toward the kitchen, and he followed.

Mabel sat with him as Iris's stew worked its magic. When he had eaten his fill, he sat back and fiddled with his napkin. It wasn't like him to hesitate over what he wanted to say, and Mabel stayed quiet while he figured it out.

"I kick myself for leaving them." He snapped the napkin taut between his hands.

Mabel nodded. "But they're okay."

He looked around the kitchen. "I know Polly, and she's talked to you, hasn't she?"

Mabel smiled. "Yes."

"Polly and Betsy need time. Shall we work it out, then, for my family to stay here while they mend?"

Calling on her business voice, Mabel said, "Let's make a deal, Mr. Macready."

Half an hour later, with numbers on a pad, they had a cost-sharing arrangement, Michael taking more than his fair portion of the expenses. Relieved that she hadn't had to persuade him to stay, Mabel went along. But she made one point.

"I will keep to my routine, going in early on the bus. At the office, nothing changes."

"Agreed. I'll drive us home." He thought for a moment. "Mabel, I can't say enough …"

She held up her hands. "Our ledger balances, Mr. Macready." He smiled and offered his hand, and they shook on the deal.

Before leaving the next morning, Mabel sat with Iris to gauge her opinion about the added cleaning, cooking, and laundry.

"Millie minds Betsy, and she pitches in. She's on her own, like me. Tell ya the truth, it's kinda' nice with her. We can manage."

"Polly's going back to work today. You and Millie work out a routine. On Sunday, we'll sit together, all of us, and settle the holiday plans. Patsy's coming, and I'm inviting my friend, Jack."

Iris raised her brow, and a smile played on her lips. "The more, the merrier."

On the way to the bus stop, Mabel dropped the letter to Jack into the mailbox. Riding along Woodward Avenue, she admired the city storefronts dressed in red and green garlands, ribbons, and sparkling lights. Christmas trees decorated the corners at the major intersections. Above J.L. Hudson's holiday windows, a huge greeting card fixed on the façade proclaimed *Merry Christmas and Happy New Year.* She would be merry and happy if Jack would accept her invitation. Mabel hummed *Jingle Bells* as she walked the blocks to the Lafayette.

Michael arrived at the office after lunch, having spent the Saturday morning in shops with Polly. His gracious and heartfelt speech thanking the girls for Betsy's basket had them dabbing their eyes. Mabel followed him up to his office with a mug of fresh coffee and his messages. He sipped the coffee and shook his head at those from the fire chief and his landlord.

"No matter the cause of the fire, we'll get nothing from the landlord. But I hope to assure Millie it wasn't her fault."

Jimmy had called several times about the contracts for the January and February shows. The high tide of earnings from *Annie* would end with the final performance on December twenty-third. But the Lafayette hoped to salvage some revenue in the slowest months by bringing in the same Gilbert and Sullivan operettas Jimmy had run in his New York house. Michael hung up his suit jacket and rolled his shirt cuffs for the long afternoon of telephone calls.

Mabel found Polly in her dressing room, examining her face in the mirror, surrounded by dress boxes and shopping bags. "I've aged ten years in two days." She spun around. "Thank goodness for stage makeup."

Mabel peeked into a bag. "Looks like you bought a wardrobe."

Polly scoffed. "Maternity clothes are *not* a wardrobe. But better than nothing."

"How are you feeling?"

She shrugged. "The show must go on. I have sixteen performances left, and I'll go out singing." She put a hand on her middle. "If I need to, I'll hold back a bit on the dancing."

By the time they closed the theater that night, exhaustion had overtaken Polly. When the three of them headed to the sedan, Mabel asked Michael, "Can Polly stretch out in the backseat?" Before he could answer, Polly crawled in. Michael looked weary enough to fall asleep at the wheel. Mabel knew better than to offer to drive. Sitting in front, she kept him alert with talk and the cold air seeping from the window. They made it home.

On Sunday morning, Mabel came into the kitchen while Iris and Millie were feeding Betsy her breakfast. Millie advised them about the Macready's habits on their day off. "I keep an ear out for Betsy waking around seven. Polly sleeps most of the day. The mister likes his coffee at eleven while he reads the paper. He has breakfast for lunch. They eat a regular dinner after Betsy's down." Millie shrugged. "I learned to work around their willy-nilly ways."

Mabel and Iris exchanged a glance. Running the kitchen like a diner went against the grain for Iris, but she had a soft spot for Betsy and Millie. She also respected Michael as Mabel's boss.

"We'll work it out," Iris said. "We got holidays to plan, too. I ordered a tree from the farm man who comes around."

With that, Mabel and the two girls talked through the pre-Christmas tasks. While they lingered in the kitchen, Michael came in, shaved, and dressed. When Iris jumped up to get his coffee, he stopped her.

"Please, allow me. I'm learning where you keep things, but I'll do for myself." After pouring his cup, he went into the dining room. With a *told-you* glance, Millie gathered the newspaper and went after him.

As the December days went on, a routine fell into place. While her parents were at the theater, Betsy had taken to hiding in closets, huddling with her dolls. To keep her in view, Millie set up a play area for her in the spare bedroom. Iris did the laundry, and Millie ironed. Six nights a week, three dinner plates waited on the stove, Iris and Millie already abed, the little girl sound asleep. Before going to her room, Mabel flipped through the day's mail left on the desk, her eyes peeled for Jack's handwriting. But no reply.

On Sundays, while Polly rested, Michael took Betsy out in the afternoon. The household ate dinner together in the dining room. Mabel insisted Iris and Millie take their places at the table. When she asked Michael to sit at the head, Polly winked.

On the Sunday of Christmas week, when the dessert had been passed around, Iris excused herself to the kitchen. She came back carrying a stack of paper-wrapped bundles and set one before each of them. Betsy began tearing at hers, and Polly reached to stop her.

Iris said, "Let her open it. All of yous, please, go ahead."

Ripping the paper away, Mabel gazed at a Christmas stocking made from green felt trimmed with red and white stars, with her name appliqued at the top. She traced the letters with her finger. The last time she had had a Christmas stocking was during high school, at Peggy's mother's house. And that was the "extra" stocking, with no name. Her heart swelled with affection for Iris, who was always there, steady, with the right touch.

Giggling, Polly held up her stocking. "Look at this! A snow cowgirl. Iris, you silly girl. This is wonderful."

Betsy's had a Santa face, Michael's a candy cane, and Millie's a Christmas tree. Iris looked on with a smile as they shared them around.

Mabel stood up to hug Iris. "Oh, Iris, this is perfect. Thank you."

Iris whispered in her ear, "I made a stocking for Jack, too."

Giving Iris a squeeze, Mabel excused herself from the table and ducked into the kitchen. Snowflakes pinged on the window above the sink. They were in for a blustery holiday. Mabel had hidden alone with dark thoughts on past Christmases. Jack could be in a similar mood, and she dreaded that for him. *Please let him come.*

CHAPTER 22

In her finale performance, Polly stole the show from the moment she took the stage. Her rich alto voice sang out; in the dance numbers, the ensemble followed her spirited lead, energizing the scenes. She mesmerized with a mix of grace and sass, edging stage-front to draw eyes to her. The star's miffed glance at Polly's calculated persona was obvious as the curtain lowered for the intermission.

Having sold out the theater, the girls had closed the ticket office in plenty of time to settle in to watch from the wings. When the orchestra began tuning, Mabel ran up the staircase to the first balcony, where the spotlight man had a chair for her.

Mabel had spent most of the afternoon backstage, supervising the caterers setting up the party tables in a cleared wardrobe room. The combined Christmas and closing cast celebration might go all night, and she had ordered extra champagne and a buffet spread to feed the cast, crew, and their guests. Michael had paced from Polly's dressing room and through the party room enough times that Mabel asked the stage manager to waylay him. But his stress would not ease until Polly took her curtain calls. They all needed the holiday break.

During the intermission, Mabel tapped her foot, eager for the evening to move on. Her jitters had also ramped up as the days ticked toward Christmas. At home, Iris had implemented a regimen of preparations. She and Patsy had menus and food shopping lists for the holiday meals that rivaled Mabel's ticket procedure book. A fir tree stood eight feet tall in the living room, decorated with light strings and the paper chains Millie had taught Betsy to make. Betsy had gulped the stories about Santa coming down the chimney, and, judging by the glut of toys hidden in the sewing room, her dreams would come true.

But Mabel's nerves hinged on Jack. He had sent no word about her invitation. When Mabel confided to Polly that she had written to him, Polly had no doubt he would show up. "Michael will enjoy the company of another man. And I look forward to chatting with your Jack."

"Easy, Polly. He might not come." Mabel tried to temper her butterflies by reminding herself of this. It wasn't working.

"No one wants to spend Christmas alone. He'll be with us."

Laughter from the audience at the start of the second act brought Mabel's attention back to the stage. During the last number, she left her seat to stand at the back of the balcony. The audience reacted with wild applause and whistles when Polly took her bows.

Mabel hurried down to the lobby where the ushers, eager for the party, coaxed patrons through the exits. When they assured her no one remained in the theater, she locked the doors. By the time she got backstage, the champagne corks were popping. Musicians from the orchestra jammed, and Cora and the typists relished their chance to dance with the handsome actors. The swarm at the buffet told her the food was a hit. With a Shirley Temple in hand, Mabel made the rounds, wishing the staff a Merry Christmas.

Cheers went up when Michael escorted Polly into the room. Michael reclaimed his former elegance in a dinner jacket, skinny bow tie, and satin-trimmed trousers Hudson's touted as the latest fashion. On his arm, Polly, a red wrap-over cocktail dress trimmed with sparkly beads clinging to her ample figure, sashayed in to whistles and hoots. Mabel caught her eye and raised her glass to Polly's grin. The star did not appear, and the crew chief said she'd left in a hired car. It was Polly's night again.

Michael had tossed the keys to Mabel and climbed into the backseat with Polly when they made their way home in the wee hours. She had driven through the empty streets with flashes from the wonderful evening swirling in her head. Jimmy always said theater people were their own family, and she understood that now. As an adopted member, she held dear the handshakes and cheery wishes the staff had sent her way.

Mabel dozed for a few hours, not deeply asleep. She had promised her day to Iris for last-minute Christmas errands and chores. Reporting to the kitchen, she found Betsy sitting alone at the table, kicking her chair and eating a bowl of cornflakes. Mabel expected the little girl to ignore her, as she usually did.

"I don't bite people anymore. I'm not a baby," Betsy said, slurping.

Mabel raised her brows in surprise. "I know." Then she asked, "Do you need anything?"

"More cereal, please." She pushed her bowl across the table.

Mabel shook flakes from the cereal box into the milk left in the bowl. "Good?" Betsy nodded and dug in with her spoon. The little girl was learning Polly's straight-up ways.

Mabel poured a mug of coffee and watched Betsy chomping. She was about to ask her about Iris and Millie when she heard steps bounding up the basement stairs. Iris came in, peeling off her work gloves. "Morning, Mabel. Millie's hanging the last laundry to dry. I stowed the extra firewood in the garage."

"I'm ready for my assignments. Michael left the keys to the sedan with me."

Iris gave Mabel the list of last-minute items to pick up at different shops. Holiday traffic made the city streets frantic. By the time Mabel pulled the car to the curb at her last stop, the diner, her stomach growled with hunger. The *Closed* sign hung in the window. Mabel tapped on the glass, and Patsy came to open the door.

"You timed this right, Mabel. I got grilled cheese for you before we pack up the stuff I'm taking to your house."

As they munched the sandwiches, Patsy pointed to the pie boxes sitting at the end of the counter. "I don't know what kinds of pie your people like, so I'm bringing apple, pumpkin, cranberry, and banana cream."

Mabel laughed. "They will love all of those."

"You sure you got room for me?" Having Patsy sleep over had been Iris's idea, and Mabel had kicked herself for not thinking of it first.

Mabel patted her arm. "Always."

"Iris says you got a young man coming." That Iris.

"I invited Peggy's brother, Jack. Have you met him?"

"Nah, heard about him. The priest, right?"

"He's quit being a priest. Decided it wasn't right for him."

Patsy shrugged. "Never cared much for priests. Go my own way."

Mabel shifted the conversation by sniffing the air. "What smells so good in the kitchen?"

"That's my special *kompot*." Patsy chuckled. "It's the one thing I taught Ma how to make. I've been cooking the prunes and apples with spices all morning. We'll chill it to serve cold for Christmas Eve dinner." She shook her head. "Better than any beer or spirit, and the little one can drink it, too." In the kitchen, Mabel tasted a sample while Patsy poured the liquid into jars.

After they loaded the sedan with the pies and what seemed like half the stock from the diner's larder, Mabel headed for home. The afternoon sun was waning when she pulled into the driveway; the girls came outside to unload the car. Then Iris and Patsy got to work preparing a traditional Polish Christmas Eve dinner. Millie set the table and helped in the kitchen while Betsy napped with Polly, who had yet to emerge from her room.

Mabel found Michael lolling by the fire in the living room. He wore the trousers from the night before with a freshly starched shirt and a sweater. When he smiled, it looked as if the lines that had creased his forehead since the house fire had softened. Mabel couldn't help but tease him. "Lounging suits you."

He chuckled and sank into the armchair. "I plan to have a fireside chair as cozy as this one in my new house."

"Enjoy a well-deserved rest. Until Betsy comes looking for you."

"You were right about her coming around, Mabel. When she climbs into my lap and whispers in my ear … there is nothing better." He looked into the fire with a smile turning up his lips. "Jimmy telephoned while you were out, with holiday greetings to all and reminders of the work ahead to keep our revenue up."

"Will you be going to New York soon?"

"Not right away. But let's not discuss business today."

Polly was coming down the stairs with Betsy in tow, both dressed in red skirts and white sweaters. Betsy ran across the foyer and straight onto Michael's lap. He glanced at Mabel as the little girl nestled him. Oh, Polly, Mabel thought, you won the prize with this man.

Millie tinkled a little crystal bell to call them to dinner.

As they gathered in the dining room, they toasted with glasses of the fruity kompot. Patsy nodded with satisfaction at the table laden with serving platters and bowls. "We set out all twelve courses. This way, yous can taste everything, have more of the ones you like." She explained each dish as she passed it. Betsy turned her nose up at the whitefish; the pierogi was her favorite. Patsy's stories about her mother and grandmother cooking for holidays, and the sweet dumplings made with poppy seeds, honey, and raisins, won everyone over.

After dinner, they all made a show for Betsy of hanging their stockings on the mantel. When Mabel wasn't looking, Iris hung the stocking she had made for Jack next to Mabel's. "We don't want him to feel left out." Polly gave Iris a thumbs-up.

Polly and Michael helped Betsy write a note to Santa and leave it by the tree on a plate of cookies. When they were sure she was sound asleep, Michael and Mabel carted the hidden stash of toys and games down to the living room. From the rocking chair, Polly munched on Santa's cookies while directing her husband in staging the haul around the tree.

Mabel sat on the davenport by the front window with her coffee, listening to the parents giggling and Iris and Millie chatting on the rug near the fire. Next to her, Patsy was quiet. They exchanged a glance, and Mabel nodded. *Merry Christmas, Ma.*

The radio station chimed midnight and signed off. Polly gazed at the group and said, "Fair warning, everyone. Betsy will wake early, and we won't be able to keep her upstairs. Don't feel you must come down with us. Sleep in."

Chuckles all around. Patsy said, "I wouldn't miss the main event." Everyone agreed.

Polly yawned. "I must get some sleep before the show." Saying good night, she and Michael trudged upstairs. Iris tended the fireplace, spreading the ashes, sprinkling baking soda to snuff out the embers, and setting the screen. They had become quite careful since Polly's house fire. After Iris and Millie had gone to bed, Mabel walked upstairs with Patsy, who settled into the spare bedroom.

Mabel snuggled under her bedcovers, not bothering to close her eyes. The coffee had intensified her jitters. Yet she slept because she woke to Polly's voice in the hallway shushing Betsy. The first streaks of daylight streaked the sky outside the window. Christmas was starting early. Mabel bundled in her robe and slippers, made a stop in the bathroom, then hurried down the stairs to put on fresh coffee.

She was pleased she beat Iris to it, but not by much. Betsy's happy squeals, and their own anticipation of the day, awakened everyone. Patsy, in her hairnet and flannels, took a mug into the front room, sipping and chuckling at the little girl's delight over her toys. Michael, dressed in sports trousers and an open-collar wool shirt, hovered over his daughter's frenzy, taking snapshots with a Brownie camera. Polly, wrapped in a pink floor-length quilted robe, her dark hair pulled up and tied with a green ribbon, posed Betsy for the camera with each toy. Millie built up the fire, then sat on the rug and cooed as Betsy showed her the wonderful things Santa brought. Iris brought mugs of coffee in for the parents and smiled from the sidelines.

Mabel looked on from the rocking chair. As a girl, she had never had such a Christmas morning, not even a stocking after her mother died. Her father said they should be grateful he kept a roof over their heads. He and her brothers drank their Christmases. The love and care Polly and Michael lavished on their child, and the loving looks between them, pulled at her emotions. Aching with longing for that kind of love, she rocked the chair to keep from crying.

Iris came next to her. "Santa left something in the stockings."

Mabel took a breath before answering. "We all agreed not to spend on gifts, except for Betsy."

With a shrug, Iris said, "Santa has his own ways."

Santa had indeed stuffed the stockings. Fishing inside hers, Mabel found hard candies and handkerchiefs embroidered with an *M*. Patsy oohed over her dusting powder. Millie and Iris froze with fifty-dollar bills in their hands. Mabel caught Polly's eye, and she pointed at Michael. He lifted a shoulder with a wry smile.

Iris went to him and stuck out her hand. "Thank you." Millie, crying, came next. Michael nodded and said, "Santa thanks both of you," and squeezed their hands. Patsy lightened the moment by saying, "Let's fix a big breakfast for Santa." The girls chuckled and went with her to the kitchen.

Mabel turned to Michael. "That was kind of you, and generous. Thank you."

"I hope they'll have some fun with the money. Maybe see a show." He winked. Betsy, astride her new pedal tricycle, bumped his leg with the front wheel. He leaned down and turned it aside. "Later, we can take this outside to ride in the driveway." Picking her up in his arms, he kissed her forehead. Polly came next to him.

"Mabel, this is a perfect Christmas morning. We are so grateful to you." She threw her arms around Mabel's neck and pulled her close, whispering, "Your Christmas present will come. I know he will."

As if Polly had a crystal ball, while they lingered around the breakfast table, Betsy feeding toast to her new doll, the girls debating how they would spend their money, Patsy keeping the coffee cups full, Michael and Polly holding hands, the doorbell rang. Mabel locked eyes with Polly, who said, "Are you getting that?"

Mabel hurried across the foyer, aware of the whispering at the table. Taking a breath, she pulled the vestibule door closed behind her. No need for everyone to watch her let him in. When she opened the outer door, Jack, a knit cap pulled low on his forehead, his face flushed from the cold, gave her a tight smile.

"If it's too early, I'll come back later."

She would not have sent him away, no matter what the hour. "You're in time for breakfast. And the entire day."

"Merry Christmas, Mabel." He held out a pot wrapped in florist paper, the red of a poinsettia leaf poking from the side.

"It's freezing. Come inside." She stood aside to let him step in, then closed the door. Facing him, the pot between them, she put her hand on his shoulder and drew his chilled lips to hers in a light kiss. Nose to nose, she whispered, "Merry Christmas, Jack." With that, she flung the inner door open and pulled him into the foyer.

Jack pulled off the cap and ran his hand over his hair. He was eyeing Mabel, but the others grouped around him. Iris was there to take his coat and Millie, the plant. Polly, with her hand on her hip, greeted him and introduced Michael. Betsy sat on her trike, and when she heard his name, she said, "I got jacks from Santa."

Polly said, "Looks like Mabel did, too." Mabel blinked at her, but Jack smiled.

Patsy guided him to the place set with a clean plate and urged him to warm up with coffee. Iris served, and Jack accepted every dish she offered, eating with gusto. Mabel reveled in his closeness and the quick kiss they had had. But she was also alert to Polly's smirk across the table.

Michael engaged Jack in manly small talk about the disappointing Detroit Lions season. Then Jack asked, "How have you been managing since the fire?"

Michael sighed. "We're getting our bearings, thanks to Mabel opening her home to us."

Polly added, "This is a grand house for a family."

Mabel extended her leg under the table to nudge Polly's ankle. Turning to Jack, who had finished eating, she said, "Would you like to see the Christmas tree?" As they rose from their chairs, Polly winked. Mabel shook her head behind Jack's back. Michael, observing, took the cue and asked Polly to go upstairs with him.

In the living room, Jack surveyed the tree and the toys displayed around it with a low whistle. "This is quite a haul for a little girl."

"Polly is making up for what they lost in the fire, and more." Mabel pointed to the mantel. "Santa brought you a stocking." He looked at her as though he thought she was teasing, then saw his name. She coaxed him. "Look inside."

He reached his hand inside the stocking and pulled out a small, dark green box. Glancing at her, he lifted the lid. His eyes lit up. "Is this …?" Taking a round gold case in hand, his thumb flicked the clasp on the side to open it. "A compass. Army surplus, right?"

Mabel nodded. "Do you like it?"

Cupping it in his palm, he moved his hand and watched the needle jiggle for direction. "It's a beauty. I lost my compass during that last tour with the corps up north."

"I didn't know that. But I wanted you to have this." One day, a newspaper left in the pantry, folded open to the ad for the compass, had given her the idea. When she called the shop, she discovered the owner was a Lafayette subscriber. The man delivered it in person. She had slipped it into Jack's stocking when the others weren't looking.

He gave her a playful look. "I thought Santa brought it."

She smiled. "Santa asked me to make sure you'll always be able to find your way."

They gazed at each other. He started to say something, but Betsy came running across the foyer into the living room, Millie behind her. Jack mouthed *Thank you* and put the compass in his pocket.

Millie said to Mabel, "Sorry. Mr. Macready will take her outside to ride the bike when he comes down."

Mabel nodded. "Can you keep Jack company while I get dressed?"

Jack said to Betsy, "Will you show me your toys?" Which was all Betsy needed to introduce the dolls. Mabel hurried upstairs.

In the upstairs hallway, she ran into Patsy leaving the bathroom. The older woman had toiled in factories before Ma gave her a diner job, and she was not one for fussy dresses. She wore wide, dark trousers with a plaid shirt, the sleeves rolled above her elbows, her short, graying hair combed straight back, in Ma's style. Patting Mabel's arm as they passed, Patsy said, "He's a fine young man. Not brash like his sister."

Mabel smiled, squeezed Patsy's hand, and went to her bedroom. Her household welcomed Jack, but what was he feeling today, estranged from his mother and sister? One of the many questions they must talk about. The kiss at the door, and the compass, had drawn him close, smoothing the way. Rifling in her closet, she pulled out a black corduroy skirt buttoning down the front. A short time later, she descended the stairs wearing the skirt with knee socks and a red-and-white pullover sweater, her hair brushed out, her face made up, hoping to light his eyes as much as the compass had. But she didn't find him in the living room.

Iris and Patsy were busy tidying and resetting the dining room table. Iris said, "Jack's gone outside with Michael and Betsy. Polly's still upstairs. Millie's having a bath."

Mabel peered out of the living room window, trying to spot the men, when Polly joined her. "You got your wish. Make the most of it. The man is clearly on the hook."

"I wish you wouldn't put it quite like that."

Polly shrugged. "Okay."

Mabel stared out the window. "I need to find out if he feels for me the way I do for him. Or if he has doubts."

"Oh, Mabel. My money is on both of you. Sorry, not to be glib. I'm happy for you."

"It's too soon to be happy for me."

"Happiness is never too soon."

"You know what I mean."

"I guess I do. I also know happiness doesn't have to be perfect. It grows with you." She patted her middle. "No pun there." Her eyes glinted with fun. She looked like an elf in a dark green velvet maternity dress over black stockings and patent leather flats.

"Help me by not teasing today."

Polly said in a Popeye voice, "I yam what I yam." Seeing Mabel roll her eyes, she nodded. "No more teasing. Promise."

Not long after, the front door opened, and Betsy, nose running, cheeks red, pushed her tricycle inside. Michael, behind her, wiped her nose with his handkerchief and untied her wool hat. When he saw Millie there, he said, "Can you take her to Polly? I want to show Jack something. We'll be back soon." When Millie nodded, he left.

They had planned dinner to be ready for the late afternoon hour as darkness fell. The kitchen hummed in the thick of preparations. Patsy, Iris, and Millie coordinated their movements as smoothly as a theater dance ensemble, and Mabel tried to help without getting in the way.

Polly sprawled on the living room rug, having a tea party with Betsy and her dolls, the radio blaring the Hollywood Christmas broadcast. "You hear that voice, Betsy? Mommy sang in a show with Doris Day." When the men returned, Michael joined them.

Jack poked his head into the kitchen. "Anything I can help with?"

Iris, at the stove, jerked her head in Mabel's direction. "Take her outta here. She's done all she knows how to do." Millie and Patsy exchanged amused glances.

Mabel feigned offense, but was happy to leave the kitchen with Jack. "I'll see to our guest. Thank you very much." She led him into the library. "Have a good walk?"

"Yes, Michael's an interesting guy. We got along fine." He chuckled. "He told me the story of your coming out of the rain into the Lafayette."

"I told you about that. Was his side different?"

"No, but he's protective of you. I took it as his wanting me to know he's watching."

Mabel smiled. "Does that worry you?"

Jack took her hand. "Not at all." He looked into her eyes. "We have a lot to talk about."

She nodded. "After dinner, stay a while." He smiled his agreement.

Iris tapped on the door. "We're ready in the dining room."

Mabel had never seen a dining room so inviting and festive, except in the movies. The chandelier shone on the intricate pattern of red and green embroidery Iris had worked around the crisp white tablecloth. The poinsettia plant, surrounded by pinecones and green boughs, adorned the center of the table. Candles in crystal holders flickered and caught the gleam of the silver settings. Iris pointed out the name cards at the seats. Michael at the head, Jack at the other end, Polly, Betsy, and Millie on one side, Patsy, Iris, and Mabel on the other. She met Patsy's eye and imagined Ma looking on with approval of her "found" family sharing this grand house.

Mabel clapped her hands. "Merry Christmas, everyone!" The serving dishes were on the table and on the sideboard. Betsy began pointing to the foods she wanted. Patsy tapped her plate with her fork. "Before yous dig in, I just want to say thank you and Merry Christmas." She raised her glass of kompot. "Bless us all."

Mabel stole a glance at Jack, wondering if he would say grace. With glass in hand, he said, "I second that." She raised her glass and declared, "All of you have made my first Christmas in this house the one I will always remember as the best."

Michael said, "Here, here. Happy Christmas to all." He clinked his glass against Polly's, starting a chain around the table. When Mabel and Jack clinked glasses, he picked up her other hand and kissed it. Mabel felt the blush rise in her cheeks and dared not look at Polly.

Patsy started passing the dishes, and with the first bites, the cooks basked in compliments. The group settled into eating. Polly began a lively conversation by telling the story of a terrible holiday meal on the road. The curious girls probed her and Michael and Mabel with questions about New York and other cities they had traveled to.

Millie sighed. "I'd love to travel someday. There's a big world out there."

Polly snickered. "Me, I've had enough of living out of a suitcase."

Mabel challenged her. "You wouldn't go back on tour?"

"Well, never say never." She looked at Michael. "But I'm a homebody for now. When we get our own house."

Michael exchanged a glance with Jack, who smiled and shrugged. Mabel looked from one to the other, wondering what passed between them. Michael took Polly's hand.

"Merry Christmas, honey. I bought the house next door."

CHAPTER 23

Polly cried out in shock, "What are you saying? A house, for us, next door to Mabel?" When Michael assured her he had bought the property, she jumped up and threw her arms around his neck. "I want to see our house!" She turned to Betsy. "C'mon, let's put on our coats."

The neighboring house had been unoccupied since Mabel came to live on Canterbury Road, but she had not noticed. Iris read an advertisement for the estate sale and left the newspaper, folded to that page, atop Michael's briefcase in the library. He had found her in the kitchen and asked, "Are you trying to tell me something?" to which she replied, "There's no harm in looking." During the hubbub at the dining table over his announcement, he gave her the credit.

Millie exchanged a glance with Iris, and Iris smiled at Mabel. Mabel gaped at Michael. "When did you have time to buy a house?"

He grinned and followed Polly into the foyer. Over his shoulder, he invited all of them to join the tour of the house. "The furnace is running, so we can look around." Millie and

Iris went to the back hall for their coats. Jack helped Patsy with her coat, and outside, he and Mabel took her arms to follow the snow prints Michael's family made across the driveway.

Jack said, "Michael told me about the house when we were outside with Betsy earlier. I saw the rooms on the first floor."

Mabel chuckled. "My houseguests will be my new neighbors."

Patsy said, "It will be a nice setup for both families." Mabel crossed her fingers in her pocket.

The homes on Canterbury Road were distinctive, designed to the specifications of the original owner. Michael had purchased a three-story Tudor with a decorative pattern of timbers laid over the brick and tall, narrow windows. The structure was as stately as the monogram on Michael's shirt cuffs. He whipped out the front door key with a flourish befitting the lord of the manor. Polly pushed inside ahead of him, Betsy in tow.

Iris and Millie hesitated in the foyer, but Patsy coaxed them. "Polly's going to be over the moon to see all the rooms, but yous better check out the kitchen and see what they got for laundry." She led the girls through the center hallway to the back of the house.

Mabel and Jack were left standing under the crystal chandelier. She would see Polly's house another time. Now, she relished being alone with him. Taking him by the hand, she wandered into the living room. The feel of his warm touch, his presence, tingled through her.

A worn carpet ran the length of the room, and the walls were covered in flocked silvery paper. There was no furniture, only a lamp standing in a corner, making a pool of light. The dark wood mantel encasing the fireplace was twice the size of the one in her house. She said, "This is a grand house. I can see why Michael bought it. But I don't think Polly will like this fussy wallpaper."

Jack stepped closer to her and put his other hand around her back. His eyes scanned the crown molding spanning the walls. "It would be years before I could afford a house half this size. In fact, I'll be living in a one-room apartment come January." He had accepted a job as an assistant athletic coach at Wayne University. The head coach needed a man to train the new baseball and track teams. Colleges in Michigan and Ohio had formed a conference to compete against each other, and titles were at stake.

"I jumped at the opportunity. Felt like I was selling myself too hard. But they worried I wouldn't like living in a tiny apartment in a student residence hall."

Mabel squeezed his hand. "Oh, Jack, that's wonderful news. Does this mean you ..."

"Yes. The bishop received the papal order. I signed, and it's done." He sighed.

"You took a big step, facing yourself." She looked into his eyes. "Ma used to say, trust yourself to take a leap of faith. She was not a churchgoing woman. But she'd tell me, you must believe in yourself enough to go forward. I've learned what she meant."

Jack nodded. "I wish I had known Ma."

"You would have liked each other." Mabel sighed. "I miss her. She had faith in me. Even when I didn't trust myself."

"I made peace with my mother." He had gone to her house, not to try to convince her he had made the right decision, only to let her know he loved her. The old woman broke down when he took her hand. "She says the rosary every night for me. That can't hurt, and it soothes her."

"It must be a relief for you, reconciling with your mother."

"We're on a different footing with each other, but at least we can talk."

"Your mother was always kind to me," said Mabel.

"She's fond of you."

"Still? The way Peggy talked about me …"

"Mabel, I didn't listen to Peggy. I know my sister. She lashed out at you because my decision blurred her high-and-mighty view of her place in the world. She's angry with me. I can't change her."

He hadn't wavered under the blow of Peggy's malice. But Mabel pressed on. "I haven't told you all of my story. I *was* a drunk, and I sank low, but not like Peggy said."

"You and I," Jack said, "we're starting from now." He put his forehead against hers, and she raised her face to meet his kiss, but he drew back with a smile at the sound of footsteps pounding down the staircase.

Polly bounded into the living room. "Can you believe this, Mabel? Three floors! Five bedrooms! Look at this fireplace! Next Christmas, we'll celebrate in *this* house."

Mabel moved to give Polly a hug. "Michael did well. You'll be happy here."

Polly held up fingers, ticking off a list. "Change all the wallpaper, clean the rugs, buy *everything* for the kitchen, and upstairs, a nursery, a playroom …"

Michael joined them, holding Betsy's hand. Mabel teased him. "Ready to renovate? Or should we call Thomas?"

Jack asked, "Who's Thomas?"

Mabel and Polly exchanged glances. Polly couldn't resist. "Oh, he's Mabel's architect from New York."

Mabel made a face at her. "He is *not my* architect. And I was making a joke."

Michael held up a hand. "I hired the home design service at Hudson's to take care of everything Polly asks for."

Patsy, Iris, and Millie came into the foyer. Betsy ran to Millie. "I have a new bedroom!"

Millie clutched the little girl's hand and spoke to Polly. "The laundry room in the basement has a washer *and* a clothes dryer! I never seen one before."

Michael put an arm around Polly. "I say we lock up and go sit by Mabel's fireplace to make our plans."

She kissed him. "I'd follow you anywhere, Mr. Macready."

When the celebrating finally ended and the others had gone to bed, Mabel and Jack stayed in her living room. In the light from the streetlamps, fluffy snow was falling outside the windows. The colorful bulbs strung on the Christmas tree cast a glow near the hearth. He stoked the fire, and with a shy smile, asked her to look inside her stocking.

"Are you playing Santa now?" Mabel teased, tucking her hand into the stocking, watching his face. When her fingers closed over a small box, she drew in her breath. Holding the black leather case in her palm, her mind flashed back to her and Peggy questioning the Ouija board about their future husbands. The pointer sliding as they asked, will he be handsome, will he be true?

Jack whispered, "I'll devote myself to you, Mabel. My heart has no doubt. I've loved you for years, and I always will." He had never looked more handsome. He got down on one knee. "Mabel Hunt, will you marry me?"

Once she opened the box, her future would unfold. She heard Ma's voice, *What ya waiting for, girly?* She thumbed the lid open. Mabel gasped at the diamond sparkling on a gold band. She gazed into his eyes. He would be true.

"Yes, Jack Finn, I will."

His hand trembled as he slid the ring onto her finger. When he stood to embrace her, they fell together onto the davenport. Kissing him felt as natural as breathing. They giggled as she posed her hand to catch colors from the tree lights in the diamond. Snuggling under a blanket, they began to talk about when.

"We have no need to hurry," Jack said. "Of course, I want to be with you—but I'm just starting the job and need to get my feet under me." He looked at her. "If you agree."

Mabel remembered Polly's remarks about men saving face. But she was content to wait for her own reasons. "I *do* agree. The Macready family will live here until their house is ready, however long that takes. And we have a full schedule at the theater. I have to back Michael up."

"Then let's not set a date yet."

She began exploring the territory of Jack, the man she had agreed to marry, by tracing his lips with her fingertip. He waited while she discovered the contour of his chin and its slight bristle of whiskers, then kissed her with a tender passion that jittered through her. Her hand worked its way under the back of his shirt and clutched his taut muscles. He lifted it up and off. Under the blanket, she pulled her arms out of her sweater and jerked it over her head. Jack pulled her against his warm chest. It was as if they had been together before, yet astonishing to both of them.

The fire had snuffed itself out, and the day had broken when Mabel woke lying against his shoulder. She gently roused him and leaned over to find her sweater. Jack ran his hand over her back as she pulled it over her head.

"Careful there, Mr. Finn. The household will be waking up."

He chuckled. "I've got to clean up to report for my last week of working for the Salvation Army."

Mabel offered to make coffee. But Jack wanted to leave before the others awoke. Her knees buckled kissing him goodbye. She watched from the library window as he bounded through snowdrifts toward the bus stop.

Mabel was in the kitchen drinking coffee when Polly came in. She knew what Mabel was going to say before she got the word "engaged" out. "Jack and Michael hit it off and told each other their secrets. He saw my house before I did." She admired the diamond Mabel was wearing. "It's a beauty. Michael said Jack's landed a good job."

"It's the perfect job for him." Mabel explained what Jack would do at the college. "He might have been a baseball player if things had been different."

"I'm glad for things as they are. We'll be neighbors."

"Michael certainly surprised me."

"That's my husband. Don't worry—Millie and I will work on the house. Michael has a full plate at the theater."

"Jimmy will call first thing today." Mabel looked at the kitchen clock. "Time for me to get ready for work."

Polly poured a cup of coffee. "For once, I am happy to stay home."

At the theater, Mabel entered the ticket office with trepidation about telling everyone about her engagement. Since the Macready fire, she had eased up on what Polly called her "bossiness." But to blurt out, "I'm engaged," would invite questions. Cora had met Jack when he delivered the box, so Mabel would have to explain.

It turned out to be simple enough. Cora spotted the ring when Mabel removed her gloves. "Mabel, is that what I think it is?"

Mabel held up her hand with a nod. When Mabel said his name and that he had been there to deliver the box, Cora gave a satisfied nod. "I knew there was something between you." The girls were as gleeful as if they were wearing the ring. When asked about the wedding date, Mabel hedged. "Sometime after the baseball season. Jack will work as many hours in his job as I do here."

The office chatter settled down when the New York call came through. Michael hadn't yet arrived. Mabel tried to calm Jimmy by saying, "It's the day after Christmas and the downtown traffic is a mess. We'll telephone you as soon as he gets in."

Jimmy's rise among Broadway theater owners was paying off for the Lafayette. Not yet at the scale Jimmy pushed for, but he had made waves that their chief competition, the Cass, couldn't ignore. For the 1949 season, the Cass beat him for the road company of *Brigadoon,* but he booked *Kiss Me Kate* for the same time the other theater was to run *Death of a Salesman.* "That play is depressing. People are going to choose the laughs, trust me."

In addition to the subscription sales, individual ticket sales were steady. When he had conferred with Jimmy, Michael bumped up the advertising. "Jimmy has an instinct. *Kate* did great business in New York." With a smug smile, Mabel imagined Miss Barnes pursing her lips at the Lafayette's success.

●◆●

CHAPTER 24

April 1949

Greta pushed her baby's carriage into the Lafayette office. The tiny hand poking from under the blanket gave Mabel a shiver, yet she cooed over the baby with the others. Greta chatted with Mabel about the sales for the upcoming shows, saying with a sigh, "I miss the theater. When this one is older, I might come back."

Mabel couldn't imagine *not* working at the theater. Michael seemed to read her mind, because he said, "I don't expect you to leave when you're married. Even if you were expecting. Seems like we could work something out." He had learned from Polly not to ask Mabel about a date for her wedding, yet such comments hinted at his hope she would continue working at the theater.

Did she *want* a baby? Mabel lay awake at night imagining her head on Polly's pregnant body. She had never questioned motherhood in her old life, accepting it as a woman's fate. But her stomach knotted, remembering the pain after the miscarriage.

She was having Sunday morning coffee in Polly's dining room, with a window view of the back garden where Millie played tag with Betsy. The little girl had begged to go outside, despite the nip in the air that was more like winter than early spring, and weary Polly had given in. Betsy had thrown off her bonnet, and Millie chased her with it.

The Macready family had moved from Mabel's house in phases as the rooms in their home underwent renovation. As Polly adored costuming and Hollywood stars, magazine photographs from homes she admired guided her décor choices. A small army of wall paperers, painters, cleaners, and furniture delivery crews received Michael's checks and followed Polly's orders. Each room had been crafted as if it were a stage set. The neutral color of the living room walls and draperies drew attention to the bright colors of the garden-patterned upholstery on an abundance of chairs and settees. Betsy named the tufted, curved, made-to-order bench placed before the fireplace "the worm," and Mabel agreed it resembled a caterpillar. The dining room window was bare waiting for the drapery, letting the weak sun fall on the maple table with ten chairs.

"This baby isn't coming today," said Polly, rubbing her hand over her maternity blouse, taut across her bulging middle.

"How can you be sure?" Mabel asked.

Polly shrugged. "It should be two more weeks. Tomorrow the doctor will tell me what's what."

Mabel hoped Polly was right. Michael was out of town. She poured more coffee into her cup and twisted the ring on her left hand. "I talked with Jack."

Polly looked at her. "Are you leaving it up to him?"

"No, he's in my corner on this."

"Then you'll see my doctor?"

Mabel sighed. "I made the appointment."

Her physical longing for Jack matched his for her. Most Sunday afternoons, they found themselves entwined on the small bed in his apartment. He led her into the dormitory from the side entrance. His room was at the far end of a hall; the seclusion allowed them to keep their trysts private. Jack teased her about having her own house yet sneaking around with him like a college girl. Mabel admitted that the secrecy added some spark to the encounters. But her sense of propriety insisted that Iris not see her take him into her bedroom before the marriage.

They had come closer and closer to giving in to their desire. After one of those heady afternoons, she asked him, "Why do we stop?"

Jack ran a hand through his hair. "I don't know." He fondled her leg. "Or maybe I do. We haven't talked about …"

She plunged in. "I'm scared. The miscarriage wrecked me." She took his hand. "Do you want to have children?"

"That was not in the cards for me before. Now, yeah, I think about being a father. But am I ready to have children? Probably not." He squeezed her hand. "There's no hurry. We can get married and figure this out as we go. There are ways to …"

Mabel blushed. "I'm embarrassed to say I don't know the ways." When he described what he knew, she sighed. "Would it bother you if I talked to Polly about this?"

He shrugged. "If you want to."

They had agreed to follow Polly's advice. "Go to my doctor for a diaphragm. I'll be using mine after this baby. Not using it brought us this bundle."

So, Mabel lay on an examination table, a sheet covering her naked bottom half, her feet in metal stirrups keeping her legs splayed apart, the doctor's fingers probing inside her. He was a short, almost tiny man, and careful. He apologized when she flinched as he inserted an instrument.

She dressed and met him in his office. "I see no obvious problems with your organs. Irregular cycles can make conceiving difficult, but you've had one pregnancy. Miscarriage is impossible to predict. The nurse will show you how to use the diaphragm."

The nurse's matter-of-fact manner guided Mabel's fumbling with the rubber cap. She carried home a paper bag holding her diaphragm and a tube of white "spermicide." In her bathroom, she practiced following the instructions. Her fingers slipped, and she had to dry her hands and start again. How would she do this quickly if Jack waited?

Polly had another thought. "You know, he can use condoms, too. Do his part."

Mabel bit her lip. "I'll bring that up." She wasn't sure how.

"Men have no idea what we go through. They have to learn."

"Doesn't all this ...*preparation* kill the romance?"

"Believe me, he won't give up." Polly was right about that.

Michael returned from the final trip to New York he made before Polly's due date, but his mind was not fully present in the office. Each time a telephone rang, Mabel's nerves jangled, wondering if Polly was summoning him for the hospital. She had grown so large she would not leave the house. Millie and Iris surprised her with a stork shower at home. Patsy came, as did Cora and Polly's wardrobe mistress from the Lafayette, bringing gifts for the baby's layette. The women teased Polly about never getting her figure back. Betsy spoiled her dinner by eating cookies and pie.

Patsy offered to babysit. "I ain't missed having a man, but I sure wish I'd had the blessing of a little one." Mabel wondered about that regret, but she didn't pry.

Michael and Polly's son, Patrick, was born a week later, on Mother's Day.

When Michael pulled into his garage late that night, Mabel came through the gate separating the two properties to meet him in the driveway. "Iris has supper waiting for you." He had been at the hospital since before dawn. Baby Patrick was the first birth that day, and he showed Mabel a copy of a photo taken for the newspaper. Polly beamed at the infant in her arms, and Michael stood tall, grinning, his arm around his wife and son. He looked younger and lighter than he had in a long time. Polly had been good for him after all.

Mabel delayed meeting little Patrick until Polly brought him home. She tiptoed into the nursery, where the window shades blocked off the sunlight and the thick carpet cushioned footsteps. Polly didn't ask if Mabel wanted to hold the baby; she handed him over. Mabel stiffened, and she was afraid to breathe on him. Polly guided her arms to cradle his head. "He's asleep, Mabel. Relax. I have to use the bathroom. I'll be right back." Mabel opened her mouth to protest, but Polly slipped out of the room.

Only the baby's face peeked from the swaddled blanket. Soft breaths moved through the little nose, and his lips twitched. The wisps of hair over his forehead were dark like Polly's, but Mabel could see his resemblance to Michael. Her arm tensed under him, though he was almost weightless. She held still until Polly returned.

"See, Mabel, the earth kept spinning while you held a baby." She reached to take Patrick, and Mabel eased him into her arms.

"I know what you're up to," Mabel said.

"Let's call it a rehearsal for the understudy. Doesn't mean you'll go on, but you'll know what to do." Polly settled the baby into the crib. "He wakes every two hours to nurse. Don't worry, I do that part."

Iris cooked for both houses while the Macready family adapted to the demands of caring for Patrick. Betsy caused upset when the attention turned to her brother. Millie reported, "She's not back to biting, thank goodness, but her pouting and throwing toys are testing Polly's patience."

Michael recalled how his daughter behaved when he first met her, and he began bringing her to the theater one day a week. He told Mabel, "The girls make Betsy feel special, and she's calmer when we go home." He shrugged. "We're both getting used to Polly being wrapped up in the baby." Michael had not been part of caring for infant Betsy. But patient Mr. Macready had developed a closeness with his daughter, and the sight of Betsy on his knee while he took telephone calls warmed Mabel's heart.

One night, when Mabel came into the house after work, Iris was still up, waiting for her with supper. Mabel dug into her plate, aware of the girl fidgeting with the edge of the tablecloth. "What's on your mind, Iris?"

"You'll be getting married. Patsy will take me back at the diner. When will you be wanting me to move out?"

Mabel dropped her fork onto the plate. "You're leaving?"

"When you marry Mr. Jack, you don't want me here."

"Iris, you live here. I'm not asking you to leave."

"What about him?"

Mabel thought for a moment. "It never crossed my mind to ask him. You're part of the family. And what would Millie do without you?"

Iris shrugged. "She don't want me to move, that's true. But we figure it's not up to us."

Mabel shook her head. "If it makes you feel better, I will talk with Jack. But I want you to stay."

Iris nodded. "That big bedroom upstairs needs some fixing up for the two of you. You thought about that?"

Make a home. Ma's words came back to her. After Polly and Michael had moved out of the suite, Iris pointed out the worn carpet and dreary look of the older furniture. Decorating baffled Mabel, and she had let it go.

She and Jack had agreed to live in her house after their marriage. Mabel believed keeping her place, rather than selling to buy another property, was the practical choice, but she had asked Jack to meet Mrs. Nelson and come to his own conclusion. He knew, too, that Ma's legacy was the heart of Mabel's love for the house, and he honored that.

But Iris had a point. What did Jack expect as comforts of home? Mabel waved a hand at Iris. "I will talk with Jack about the room."

The next morning, she telephoned Jack. "Can you meet me at Hudson's this afternoon?"

"Today? What are we doing at Hudson's?"

"If you can get away for an hour, I'll explain."

Jack met Mabel on the ninth floor of J.L. Hudson's department store, next to a poster reading *Bride's Week - a Tradition at Hudson's, Home Comes the Bride.* She took his hand and led him into a model bedroom. Lamps cast a soft light on gingham-print wallpaper. The same gingham print on a quilt covered a hand-crafted maple four-poster bed. Arranged around the bed were a matching dressing table, a chest of drawers, and side tables. Two pretend windows styled with red draperies framed images of trees.

Jack looked around as if he didn't know what to say. Mabel stood next to the bed. "Imagine this as our bedroom. The salesman tells me they could make ours look exactly like this."

He sat on the edge of the bed and patted the spot next to him. When she sat, he said. "Mabel, is this what you want for our room?"

"It's the style now."

"But is this what you want for us? We'll be spending years in our room."

She looked at him. "I don't know. I don't know how a wife is supposed to make a home. If we bought all of this … it would be a start."

Jack put his arm around her. "I don't know about furniture, but you and I will make a home."

She leaned on his shoulder. "This wallpaper makes me dizzy."

He laughed. "Let's get out of here."

Riding in the elevator to the street level, Mabel remembered Iris. Outside, she said, "Do you wish for Iris to leave after we are married?"

He jerked his head in surprise. "Does she want to leave?"

"She wonders if she has a place with us. If we'd rather be on our own." Mabel blew out her breath. "Jack, I can't cook; the house takes a lot of care; and Iris has been a lifesaver. If you want to let her go, I will. But I have depended on her."

Jack put his arms around Mabel and drew her close. He spoke into her ear. "Mabel, I never imagined I would be this lucky. Iris is welcome to stay. Let's start our life together. We'll figure out the rest as we go."

$$\bullet \blacklozenge \bullet$$

CHAPTER 25

"I have an idea for our wedding."

Jack's eyes lit up. "Tell me."

Mabel had opened Ma's footlocker. Each time she took clothes from her closet, her foot bumped the trunk. It had waited for her long enough.

She fanned away the musty smell that wafted from the long-closed box. On top were packets of old photographs. Shots of Ma and her cronies at the lake where for years she had camped in the summer. Ma had taken Mabel to the lake one summer. She had loved sleeping in the army surplus tent on the iron bedstead where she and Ma cuddled on a feather mattress. Mabel smiled, thumbing through the fading prints—Ma laughing, cooking over a fire, fishing, wading in the water. And then she stared at a snapshot of Ma in her bathing suit, holding the hand of a small girl with curly hair, knee-deep in water. Mabel touched her little girl's face. She held the photo to her chest, then placed it on her dresser; she would keep it in a frame.

Shaking away watery eyes, Mabel next took out a bundle of newspaper clippings. Ma had saved the ads from when she began selling her signature pies at stores around the city. Beneath those were the framed photos that once hung on the diner wall, and Mabel braced at seeing Miss Front End among them. That girl was a stranger she didn't recognize. She pushed it under the others and set them aside.

Mabel lifted a cardboard box out from the bottom of the case. Inside, official-looking documents told her more of Ma's story. Her birth certificate and a baptismal certificate, bearing her christened name, Anna. Mabel had always known her as "Ma" and had heard no one use her real name. Clipped together were their marriage certificate and the death paper issued when her old man died. It was difficult to picture Ma as an eighteen-year-old bride. Mabel looked for a wedding photograph but didn't find one.

She came to a parchment folder printed with the address of a graveyard in the Upper Peninsula town where Al had taken Ma for burial. Mabel's hand shook as she read Ma's death certificate. With it, someone had written instructions for the engraving of three headstones at her burial site. Al's signature was on the receipt. Why would he order three headstones?

Mabel read the note and gasped. Ma's grave was between those of her two children.

Reading the old-style cursive of some doctor on the faded papers strained Mabel's teary eyes. One daughter, Margaret, died of influenza; the other, Helen, of scarlet fever. When Ma buried her second child, she had taken a plot between them for herself. Al had replaced their broken stones when Ma was laid to rest with them.

Oh, Ma. Mabel's heart wrenched with sorrow for the grief Ma must have felt. Ma had said nothing about children, and

Mabel had assumed she'd had none. But she had given birth to two girls. And lost them before they were a year old.

Ma was always strong-willed, telling Mabel, "Don't get mushy on me." She defended against grief by pushing feelings away and moving on. But she knew she would go back to her babies.

Mabel wanted to be with Ma when she married Jack.

"We need to go Up North." When he heard where she wanted to have the ceremony, he repeated her words.

"You want us to be married in a graveyard."

"She chose to rest there with her children. Ma meant the world to me, and I want her near."

"You haven't been up there, have you? The northern forests are another world." He saw the pleading look in her eyes, but he was already there in his mind. "When I stayed with Dan, some nights, millions of stars blanketed the sky as if heaven touched the earth. It's paradise for a honeymoon."

An outdoor ceremony in Upper Michigan was workable only in the summer. The college's baseball team had fallen short of the playoffs, freeing Jack for the month of June. When they settled the timing, Jack telegraphed Father Dan. "He knows the town we're going to, and he'll help us with a local judge."

Michael accepted Mabel's short notice about her honeymoon trip with a smile. "Forget about the office. Make the most of your time with Jack." Iris had the house in order, as usual, and Cora would oversee the office.

Michael and Polly, with their son in a pram, saw them off at the station. Polly teased Jack about the lingerie Mabel had received from the girls.

The honeymoon began on the train. After the porter left them, Mabel locked the compartment door and unbuttoned her blouse. Jack reached for her. Mabel had never felt as true to herself as she did with Jack. A few awkward moments dissolved into tenderness and laughter.

At Mackinaw City, a ferry carried the train cars the five miles across the strait to the Upper Peninsula. Jack had done the crossing several times, but it was Mabel's first sailing on such open water. They climbed to the top deck of the ferry for the view. The day was sunny and warm, but the stories Mabel had heard about ships going down in the lakes because of a quick turn in the weather worried her. The wind blowing a chop on the water caused her moments of queasiness.

When the wind picked up, they took seats inside the cabin, and Mabel held tight to the handrail. Reaching the midpoint of the strait, the ferry lifted up and over the waves like a roller-coaster. Jack anchored her within his arm, and Mabel breathed through the rough waters. When the ferry neared the rocky shoreline, the water calmed, and the dense forest came into view. Jack's description of the wildness of the north country had understated its rugged beauty. The Great Lakes had been crashing on these shores, and the forest growing, for eons and always would.

Father Dan was waiting when they disembarked. First taking Mabel in a bear hug, then shaking Jack's hand, before he led them to his car. "We'll head to the inn where you'll be staying. The judge and his wife will meet us there." He opened the front passenger door for Mabel, but she shook her head.

"Jack, why don't you ride up front with Dan? I'll take in the view from the back." While the men chatted, Mabel watched out the window. The houses they passed on the road were log frames with massive chimneys, sloping roofs, and thick walls.

Ma had been a young woman and mother in this place. Her harsh manner was forged from enduring bleak conditions city people never faced. Mabel had known her to be as hardy as the pine forest. But her generosity to her neighbors around the diner was also a legacy of her years in this isolated village of people who had only each other to rely on. Especially when she lost her babies.

Dan pulled the car toward a three-story Victorian-style house sitting in a cleared field, facing the harbor. In the old days, the inn was the grand home built for a logging company owner. As they got out of the car and approached the wrap-around porch, a portly man and woman seated at a table rose to greet them. Dan introduced Jack and Mabel to the judge who would marry them, and to the judge's wife, who offered Mabel a seat.

The judge shook Jack's hand. "I must say, I never had a request like yours. Folks up here go to their churches or don't wed on the record."

Mabel spoke up. "It was my wish that brought us here. We're grateful for your help."

The judge nodded. "May I see the license?" Jack handed over the paper issued in Detroit. Perching spectacles on his nose, the judge perused the document. Mabel fidgeted in her chair. Dan had assured them that this judge would perform the marriage. She worried they had missed some detail.

The wife leaned over to Mabel. "Nervous, honey?"

Mabel gave her a weak smile. "It's been a long journey."

"Come inside for a cool drink while his honor talks to your man." She stood and waited for Mabel to rise. Mabel didn't want to go, but she took the cue from Dan's nod and stood. Polly's voice in her head said, *Men.*

Inside, the large front room was cozy with armchairs before the fireplace. A wide staircase led to the upper levels. Ahead was a formal dining room. They walked through to the kitchen, where the judge's wife greeted Mrs. Booth, the innkeeper, and introduced her to Mabel. Mrs. Booth set a glass of iced tea in front of Mabel and the two local women began gossiping as though she wasn't there. They resembled each other in rotundness and their cropped hairstyles. Their talk was a shorthand that eluded Mabel as an outsider. She sipped the tea and pretended to listen.

She had sipped half of the tea when Dan tapped on the kitchen doorframe. His nod told Mabel that all was well with the license. "Mrs. Booth, may Mabel use her room?"

The judge's wife winked. "She's got to put on her wedding duds."

Mrs. Booth led Mabel to a third-floor suite. "Your suitcase is inside. Your man is changing in the bunkhouse."

A tremulous feeling in her limbs as she bathed excited Mabel. *I am marrying Jack today.* Mabel unfurled the tissue-paper-wrapped wedding dress, thanking Mrs. Miller at Winkelman's. The simple lines of the white crepe hugged her curves with an unfussy elegance. Wearing the demure hat and the pumps she had worn to Jimmy's wedding, she anticipated Jack's reaction as she took a last glance in the mirror.

He waited at the foot of the staircase as she came down. Grinning, he said, "Mabel Hunt, you do know how to make my heart race." She blushed and took his arm, and they joined Dan on the porch. He held out a bouquet of purple and yellow wildflowers bundled with a strip of white lace.

"Mrs. Booth made this for you."

"Oh, how nice of her. I forgot a bouquet." The scent of the blooms filled her nose, and she sneezed. They all laughed.

Dan gestured to his sedan. "The judge has gone ahead in his car. Ready?"

Mabel and Jack sat together in the back seat. He squeezed her hand and let go, then again, and it occurred to her he might be nervous. She glanced at him, taking in the set of his clean-shaven jaw, a slight twitch of his cheek, and the sweat on his brow. He caught her looking and smiled.

The gravel road to the graveyard swept along the lakeshore, the sun glinting off the water. Everywhere was a profusion of pine, birch, and maple trees. After they drove through the cemetery entrance gate, the car climbed the gradual elevation of a hill to an open area overlooking the water. Dan stopped the car and said, "We walk from here." The judge was there, standing outside his sedan, having a smoke of his pipe, his wife in the front seat.

Stepping out of the car, Mabel blinked at the brightness of the sunlight shining on the water. The sky seemed to have expanded and blended with the lake. The judge tamped his pipe on a rock and helped his wife out of his car. Taking Jack's arm, Mabel stepped gingerly along the rocky path in her pumps, noting the judge's wife's sturdier Oxfords. Dan took in the view for a moment longer, then turned to catch up to them and lead the way.

The path meandered amidst stands of pine trees, birds flitting among the branches, the lake breeze bringing down a few cones. Other than the birds, there was a quietness. Headstones nestled in open spaces here and there beneath the trees, as if the towering woods guarded the graves. Dan knew the place and soon motioned for them to turn off the path.

Ma's headstone seemed to grow from the pine needles and twigs clumped around it. A smaller stone on each side identified her girls. Dan crossed himself. The judge and his wife stood to the side with heads bowed.

Mabel rested her hand on Ma's stone. Jack placed his hand over hers.

He whispered, "You worried this was a crazy idea. I can't imagine a more perfect spot for us to marry. The rocks, the forest, the water—everything around us the native people hold as sacred. Do you feel the peace here?"

Mabel had made her way to this moment. She breathed in the pine scent and nodded. "I had to come here, and now I know why." She stooped to place her bouquet against Ma's headstone. *Thank you for believing in me. For everything. Do you see this wonderful man? I made it, Ma. You were right.*

Mabel grasped Jack's hand, and together they faced the judge. Chittering birds rustled through the boughs as if they were excited to witness Jack placing the wedding band on Mabel's finger. Mabel kissed Jack. When she opened her eyes, she was startled to see an owl perched on a pine branch with two tiny owlets nestled at its side. The wind ruffled their brown-gray feathers as all three looked on with their enormous eyes. Mabel believed in signs. She whispered, "Ma," and the mother owl blinked.

Jack grinned and offered Mabel the crook of his arm. She smiled and slipped her hand through. He held it close against his side, and they began.

Acknowledgements

Life in post-war Detroit continues to fascinate me. My understanding of the city's fabric and its people has grown through research for my books. Hardy Michiganders recalled from my youthful orbit loaned aspects of their personalities to characters in *The Ticket Girl.* The character of Ma closely resembles impressions of my paternal grandmother.

The Lafayette and the Cass represent the many venues that established Detroit's rich tradition of live performance theater. A synopsis of theater histories can be found in the performing arts archive of the Detroit Historical Society. In Detroit today, you can experience the aesthetic of classic theaters inside the Fisher Theater and the Opera House.

Photographs and artifacts on the site of *Historic Detroit* (https://historicdetroit.org/), and the digital collections of the Detroit Historical Society and the Michigan History Center, and the Burton Historical Collection at the Detroit Public Library, were invaluable for realistically setting the story. Special thanks to Helmut Ziewers of Historic Detroit for the use of his sumptuous photograph of the Opera House interior.

Editor Carlene Cobb and cover designer Roy Marshall graciously agreed to collaborate with me on this book. I thank them for their patience, enthusiasm for the story, and expertise.

The manuscript was close to the finish line when my personal story required the extraordinary skills of Dr. Richard Byrne and Dr. Joseph Breen of Mayo Clinic Florida. They, with the team at Mayo, particularly the nurses who cared for me, made it possible for me to continue my life. I sing their praises as healers and as humans.

My dear friend Argene Carswell stayed next to me, no matter what my mood, and listened. If I can give even part of that lifeline back to you, I will.

My gratitude to my sisters, Dana Dumas, Debra Kade, and Jill Robinson for the calm you brought to help me cope through surgery and rehab. It wasn't pretty, but you steadied me.

Endless thanks to my son, Jasper Walton Klein, who stands by me every day and rises to every challenge thrown his way. Jasper's strength and character saw me through the dark days, and he made me laugh. My love for him is immeasurable.

Thank you, readers, for supporting an independent author, for your encouraging comments, and for sharing my books with others.